VEIL OF FIRE

Book One in The Shadow Brides Series

SARA MCCLAFLIN

First Edition

ASIN: B0DYB8XNJ3

ISBN (trade): 979-8-9914135-7-2

Book Cover: Pia

Editing: Brandy Gibson

Social Media: Tawny Gratto

PA: Ashley Sullivan

Marketing & PR: Wildfire Marketing Solutions

Contents

Content Warning		1
The Society		3
The Brides		5
The I Do		6
1.	Talia	9
2.	Talia	17
3.	Talia	23
4.	Stellan	39
5.	Talia	55
6.	Talia	65
7.	Stellan	73
8.	Talia	81
9.	Talia	91
10.	Stellan	103

11.	Talia	117
12.	Talia	131
13.	Talia	145
14.	Stellan	159
15.	Talia	173
16.	Talia	185
17.	Stellan	193
18.	Stellan	203
19.	Stellan	213
20.	Talia	222
21.	Talia	233
22.	Stellan	245
23.	Talia	257
24.	Stellan	265
25.	Talia	278
26.	Stellan	287
Epilogue		295
Chapter		301
Bonus Scene		303
Intake File: Cerny, Talia		307
Candidate File: Rothwell, Stellan		311
Acknowledgments		315
Up Next		317
About The Author		319

Content Warning

T his book contains themes that may be triggering or dis-
tressing to some readers. Reader discretion is strongly
advised.

Content Warning:

This book contains depictions and references to emotional abuse,
psychological manipulation, pregnancy loss, grief, betrayal, parental
neglect, controlling family dynamics, toxic relationship patterns,
power imbalances (professional, emotional, and financial), gaslight-
ing, coercive legal threats, wrongful arrest, stalking, kidnapping, physical violence, assault, abduction, firearm violence, murder investigations, corruption, blackmail, and criminal conspiracy.

Sexual content includes high-heat consensual intimacy, power play
dynamics, and verbal discussions of past sexual assault, rape, and sex
crimes (including on-page recollections of non-consensual encoun-
ters).

Additional themes include law enforcement trauma, homicide and
sex crime investigations, corporate espionage, cybercrime, class power

structures, alcohol use, gambling, and emotionally intense conflict tied to both personal and professional relationships.

Please take care of yourself while reading. Your wellbeing matters. If you need help, reach out.

Support Resources

International:

findahelpline.com

United States:

988 Suicide & Crisis Lifeline | 988lifeline.org

Crisis Text Line: Text HELLO to 741741

thehotline.org | loveisrespect.org

United Kingdom:

Samaritans: 116 123 | samaritans.org

Canada:

Talk Suicide Canada: 1-833-456-4566 | talksuicide.ca

Australia:

Lifeline: 13 11 14 | lifeline.org.au

The Society

T he Society was never born out of love. It was born out of necessity. When power became too dangerous to leave unguarded, the wealthiest families in the world did what they've always done — they found a way to protect themselves.

Mireille Noirel saw what others didn't. She watched men destroy legacies over ego, scandal, and greed. She understood that power wasn't about fortune. It was about control. And control required precision.

So she built the Arrangement.

Behind the polished facade of La Fondation Noirel — a discreet philanthropic body with no public board and sealed records — Mireille designed a system to secure empires through carefully calculated marriages. Powerful men are matched to brides hand-selected for their intelligence, adaptability, and ability to survive inside the most dangerous rooms in the world.

Mireille doesn't choose at random. She studies. She tests. She finds the women who can carry the weight of these contracts — and the risks that come with them. Women who can thrive where others would break.

These marriages are not built on romance. They are built on legacy, loyalty, and long-term control. The Arrangement binds empires together one bride at a time, ensuring that the wrong people never gain too much power.

And when the stakes are highest, when failure isn't an option, The Society sends in its most highly trained operatives.

The Shadow Brides.

The Brides

The Shadow Brides were never meant to be ordinary. They are The Society's most valuable investment. The final layer of insurance when the stakes are too high for mistakes.

Each bride is chosen with care. Beauty matters. So does skill. But it's never random. Every man within the Arrangement has a problem to solve and every bride is selected for her ability to solve it.

Whether the issue is public image, corporate stability, political access, financial control, or personal weakness, the bride assigned to each husband carries a skill set designed to protect his position, his legacy, and ultimately, The Society's interests.

Once selected, the training begins. Negotiation. Behavioral profiling. Psychological strategy. Crisis management. They learn to read people, manipulate outcomes, and manage risk before anyone realizes there's danger. Their job is to steady the empire from behind the scenes and make sure it never falls apart.

Their loyalty belongs to the Arrangement. Their safety depends on their skill. Every bride knows one truth from the beginning.

This life was never designed to protect their hearts.

The I Do

By: Weddings Royale

As professional wedding officiants of over a thousand ceremonies, we have the unique privilege of celebrating and showcasing the stories that attract two strangers and compel them to commit to share their forever with each other.

Indeed, no two stories are ever exactly alike and revisiting the highlights of a couple's real life journey together is endlessly satisfying both personally and professionally. We see ourselves as their ultimate cheerleaders as we stand with them on their big day and guide them through the sacred rites of passage to make it official. Our aim is to stir up a sense of celebration for them and their guests complete with laughter, happy tears, and a renewed sense of admiration for the two souls fortunate enough to find each other in this space and time.

We met Sara and her fiancé five years ago in the usual manner we meet most engaged couples when an email inquiry for availability on her wedding day appeared in our inbox. However, the circumstances in the year 2020 were anything but usual as my wife and I became well acquainted with the unique challenges the pandemic presented them with.

Our initial conversations with Sara began with the logistics of performing her wedding ceremony, but quickly developed into a natural friendship that continues to this day. Over the next several months, we bonded through the challenges of social distancing, changing venues, and complex family drama. It's easy to become closely acquainted with a couple so raw and honest with the details of their blossoming relationship. Along with the beauty of their deep commitment and connection to each other also came the complications of their own share of real life villains and unfavorable circumstances. Despite it all, they overcame with a rare wisdom and maturity that has only enhanced the subsequent chapters of their married lives they continue to write together.

At the time of her wedding, we knew Sara as a book lover who enjoyed writing reviews of the stories she immersed herself in. And now just four years later, her status today as an accomplished author is both inspiring and impressive. While we esteem her published literary contributions to the world, what we find most admirable is her ability to channel her real life experience of true love, adversity and triumph into intimate works of art.

As you progress through the pages of fantasy and fiction, know that they come from an authentic place of vulnerability, passion and belief that love blossoms even in the most unlikely circumstances.

It is truly our honor to know the authentic person behind the pen.

May her words, art and imagination immerse you in yet another love story that is unlike any other.

And may you be inspired that, even in the darkest and dangerous of circumstances, love can win.

Always Celebrating Love,

    Officiants Ryan & Valerie Kingsman

CHAPTER ONE

Talia

I think about my life as I stand in front of La Fondation Noirel. The building is sleek, tucked into downtown Las Vegas like it's daring someone to notice. Mirelle Noirel. People either love her or fear her, but no one ignores her. Founder. Executive Director. The kind of woman who signs checks big enough to erase mistakes. Usually, she sends someone else to handle introductions. Not today.

I look down at the invitation still in my hand.

Talia Cerny,

You are hereby invited to a preliminary consultation at La Fondation Noirel.

Date: Thursday, June 12

Time: 9:00 AM

Location: 23rd Floor, La Fondation Noirel, Las Vegas

Further details will be provided upon arrival. Discretion is required.

Consent is assumed.

No confirmation is necessary. We look forward to your presence.

Mirelle Noirel

Mirelle Noirel has done more for victims of crime than anyone I've ever met. No cameras. No interviews. Just results. Working freelance with the police, I see it all up close.

I didn't mean to end up there. It started simple—stolen cars, missing persons, the kind of cases nobody brags about. I sorted through witness statements, picked out the cracks. A glance too fast. A date that shifted. A story that sounded too smooth.

It didn't stay that simple, things never do, it wasn't long before they pulled me into bigger cases, deeper ones.

Sex crimes. Murders. Vegas isn't just neon and champagne, nothing that happens here, stays here. It's promises broken in locked rooms. It's silence bought cheap and guilt traded like currency. It's blood soaked into floors that no one even pretends to scrub away anymore.

You learn fast here. How to hear the apology hiding inside a lie. How to tell when a survivor reshapes their own story just to make it easier for someone else to believe. How to recognize when a case is meant to disappear quietly, filed under "unfortunate," forgotten before the ink dries.

The villains aren't always obvious. They can wear badges. Sometimes they wear wedding rings. They wear smiles so perfect you don't realize you're bleeding until after you shake their hand.

I don't scare easily. I never have. But I learned early that fear isn't the thing that'll break you. It's what you notice, the things you can't unsee.

I sit in interrogation rooms and just listen. I read case files until the words stop being words and start being people — breathing, hurting, still hoping someone will care enough to remember them right. I trace patterns until they stop feeling theoretical and start feeling personal.

Vegas wears its sins out loud. But the real heartbreak—the kind that crawls under your skin and stays there. It happens where no one is looking. In the spaces between the noise.

Working these cases didn't harden me. It didn't build walls. It built a deeper kind of listening.

It taught me that some things can only be survived if someone, somewhere, is willing to see what everyone else chooses to look away from.

And if I have to be that someone, even if it costs me, then so be it.

I sigh and walk into the building. It's beautiful, but not in the way most people would expect.

The lobby is expansive, wrapped in polished marble that looks almost soft under the overhead lights. No garish colors. No logos shouting for attention. The floors are a pale stone, the kind you have to hand-polish every day to keep the shine. The walls are lined with minimalist artwork—pieces so expensive and abstract they barely register unless you know what you're looking at.

It's quiet in here, too quiet for Vegas. A city that hums and buzzes even in its sleep shouldn't have spaces like this—still, polished, almost sterile. Here, the silence is intentional, part of the architecture.

Everything about the space feels curated to say they have nothing to prove. Just a single, understated reception desk placed at the exact center of the room like a sculpture.

Even the air smells expensive—clean, cool, and faintly floral, like a hotel.

"Hello, Ms. Cerny. Ms. Noirelle will see you soon. Please have a seat," the receptionist says as I walk up to the desk.

She knows my face. My file, I'm sure, whatever's in there, anyway. I wonder if she rehearsed the greeting or if she just sounds that way.

I offer her a smile, the easy, genuine one I try to give to everyone. You never know what someone's going through, it's best to lead with kindness. "Good morning."

She blinks just once, like she wasn't expecting my courtesy.

I move to sit down directly across from her. Just to stay connected.

People show you things when they think you're not paying attention. But they show you even more when they realize you actually care.

I clock the cameras immediately. There's six of them, all pointed at me.

This isn't a normal interview. Not only because I have no idea what I'm actually interviewing for, but because it's a study.

Curiosity is a luxury not many people have here. When fear tries to close your eyes, I keep mine open.

The minutes stretch. Five. Ten. There's no receptionist chatter, no keyboard clicks. Just silence, humming low between us like a second skin.

She moves once, just barely, her right arm shifting under the desk.

I clock the faint sound of a button being pushed, and the elevator to my left dings open.

A woman steps out.

She doesn't glance at the desk. Her attention is locked onto me immediately, she didn't have to search the room for me. She moves with the kind of purpose you can't fake. It's efficient, like someone who expects the room to rearrange itself around her without asking.

She's maybe five-seven in the heels she's wearing under her tailored black slacks. A white blouse with clean lines drapes over her lean, strong shoulders. There's no jewelry except a thin watch that glints once under the lobby lights. I can't stop the thought that she's the personification of the room.

Her hair is dark, pulled back into a low, perfect knot at the nape of her neck, it reminds me of the military hair styles I've seen. Whoever she is, she's not here to ask if I'm ready. She's here to see if I deserve the next step.

I stand slowly, smoothing my hands down the sides of my coat.

Before I go to the woman, I catch the receptionist's eye and give her a small wave.

For a second, her mouth almost lifts into a smile.

"Ms. Cerny," the woman who walked out of the elevator says, extending her hand. "My name is Brenna Kerrigan. Ms. Noirelle will see you in her office."

"You can call me Talia," I say, smiling wider than before.

Her posture loosens by a fraction. It's not much—but it's there.

She gestures toward the elevators, and we fall into step beside each other. The air between us feels... normal. Light. Not heavy with the kind of formality I half-expected.

We step inside the elevator. The doors glide shut with a soft click. Silence envelopes us, the kind that usually begs for small talk. But Brenna doesn't seem like someone who talks to fill space. Neither am I.

Still, I offer it. Because it feels right. "You're good at this," I say, offering the faintest smile.

She huffs a soft laugh, almost surprised by the compliment. "I've had practice."

"I believe it," I say warmly.

She leans her shoulder lightly against the elevator wall, relaxed now.

"You know," she says, voice dropping into something almost conspiratorial, "most people try to fish for information before they even sit down."

I chuckle and shrug my shoulders. "I figured if they wanted me to know more up front, they would have told me."

She watches me, something almost like approval sparking in her expression.

"And if they just wanted someone to show up for a charity gala," I add, "the invitation would have said 'celebration' or 'benefit' somewhere in the text. It didn't."

Brenna's mouth tips into a real smile now. "You're quick," she says.

The elevator dings softly as we reach the 23rd floor.

Brenna straightens, smoothing the front of her jacket, but when she glances at me again, there's something different in her eyes — a cautious kind of trust. "You're going to do just fine here," she says quietly, almost to herself.

And somehow, without fully knowing why... I believe her.

We walk into an office built for precision. The walls are a muted gray, textured like stone, the kind that eats sound. A massive walnut desk anchors the room, dark and polished, its clean surface interrupted only by a single folder and a heavy glass pen. Two chairs sit across from it—lower than they need to be, by design. Behind the desk, a wide window frames the city in a hard line of morning light. No clutter. No photographs. It makes me wonder who exactly this person is.

There's a painting behind the desk, too—an abstract sweep of deep red and silver, messy at first glance but ordered underneath if you know where to look. Like the room itself, it hides its meaning unless you know how to see it. And waiting in the center of it all, perfectly still, perfectly aligned with her environment, is Mirelle Noirel. She doesn't rise or smile. She simply watches as I cross the threshold, like she already knows which version of me will walk out.

"Ms. Cerny," Mirelle announces. "Please have a seat. We have a lot to discuss."

Brenna closes the door behind me with a soft click as I cross the room and take the chair across from her.

I sit quietly, hands resting lightly in my lap. I know a test when I feel one, and the smartest move right now is to keep my mouth shut.

"I see you received our invitation," Mirelle continues, her voice smooth and unhurried.

"I did," I respond simply.

She watches me for a long moment, as if weighing how much I understand already.

"And yet," she says, tilting her head slightly, "you came despite having no further information. Why?"

I meet her gaze evenly. "Sometimes the invitation tells you more than the details ever could."

Her mouth curves—almost a smile, but not quite.

"You're right," she says. "It was designed for us to see who is willing to step through a door without knowing what's on the other side," she says. "Who trusts their instincts over their fears."

I nod slightly, letting that sit between us.

"Now that I'm here, what exactly have I stepped into?" I ask, keeping my voice steady.

Mirelle's fingers fold neatly on the desk.

"The Society of the Shadow Brides," she says.

Chapter Two

Talia

"We are an intervention. A correction. A stabilizing force for systems that are too important to fail," Mirelle declares.

"Systems," I repeat slowly, tasting the word. "You mean corporations. Political families. Legacy wealth."

"Among others," she agrees, her tone inflectionless. "When fractures appear—when weakness threatens to rot the structure from the inside—we do what must be done to preserve it."

"How?" I ask. No sharpness. Just curiosity.

Mirelle leans back slightly, the sunlight from the window cutting a clean line across her face. "Sometimes it's influence," she says. "Sometimes guidance. Sometimes... proximity."

"Proximity?" I ask.

"A wife," she clarifies, voice soft but final. "A trusted partner. A stabilizing presence placed precisely where she is most needed."

I let the words settle before asking, "So you're matchmakers?"

"No," she says. "We are architects."

I sit back, absorbing that. "You build marriages for strategy."

"We build safeguards," she corrects gently. "Marriages are merely the structure."

"And the brides?" I ask quietly.

Her gaze sharpens. "The brides are the foundation."

"And me?" I ask. "Why me?"

Mirelle's smile is almost imperceptible—less amusement, more approval.

"You are rare, Ms. Cerny," she says, voice even. "Most people in your position — those with your talent for observation — fall into one of two camps. Either they distance themselves from emotion entirely, relying only on logic, or they drown in what they see and lose their edge."

She pauses, watching me carefully, as if gauging whether I already know this about myself.

"You," she continues, "balance the emotions, they've strengthened you."

I don't respond, waiting to see what else she'll say.

She taps a single finger lightly against the desk — a soft sound that still cuts through the quiet. "We've been watching you for some time," she adds. "Through your work with the police, through your freelance cases. You don't just map behavior. You understand it. You don't flinch from ugliness, but you don't become it either. You adapt without losing your empathy."

Her voice softens just slightly—not sympathy, but something near it. I absorb that. She isn't flattering me. She's stating facts.

"And you don't break," Mirelle finishes, folding her hands neatly again. "That is the rarest quality of all."

"So you don't want someone invisible," I say slowly. "You want someone unforgettable."

"Exactly," Mirelle replies, her eyes gleaming faintly. "Not a ghost, nor a spy. A presence." She smiles, this time real but razor-thin.

"Who would be my husband?" I ask.

"A go-getter," she laughs, while picking up the phone on her desk. "I like that. Can you page Hallie please? I'm ready for her."

"Hallie?" I ask.

"Before we continue, I need you to sign some things. Nothing bad. Just a formality," she says.

A woman walks into the office, there's no doubt in the knowledge that she's an attorney.

She's tall, built like someone who knows exactly how to use posture as armor. Her dark gray suit is cut so precisely it could double as a scalpel. She moves to the desk without hesitation, her steps clipped but controlled, a slim black folder tucked neatly under one arm.

I stand as she approaches, offering my hand before she can even introduce herself. "Hallie, I'm Talia," I say.

Her mouth pulls into a small, assessing smile—not approval, not yet, but close. "You're perfect," she says, gripping my hand briefly before releasing it.

"I have some paperwork for you to sign," Hallie says, opening the folder and flipping it neatly to the first page. "Standard confidentiality agreement," she explains. "Non-disclosure. Non-retaliation. Standard behavioral clauses. After you sign, we'll be able to explain your assignment in full."

She slides a pen across the desk — glass-bodied, heavy, and expensive.

I take the papers without hesitation but don't immediately sign. Instead, I start reading. Line by line. Clause by clause.

Hallie doesn't rush me. She just watches, arms folded lightly across her body.

The language is tight. There's no hidden clauses buried in legalese. Confidentiality. Intellectual property. Behavior protocols. Standard protections — nothing surprising.

Once I'm sure the contract is exactly what it appears to be, I pick up the pen and sign.

I push the folder back across the desk. Hallie glances at the signature, then nods once. "You're very thorough," she says.

"Seemed like the smart thing to do," I say simply.

Mirelle leans forward slightly, folding her hands on the desk. "Now that the paperwork is complete," she says smoothly, "we can speak openly. "You've been selected for a specialized placement," Mirelle continues. "The client is high-profile. Insulated. Vulnerable, though he does not yet realize how much."

"And who is the client?" I ask, voice steady.

Mirelle slides another folder toward me.

The name hits me like a soft impact I was bracing for without realizing. Stellan Rothwell. CEO, Rothwell Strategic Holdings. I don't need the rest of the page to know who he is. Everyone knows his name.

This man isn't just wealthy — he's legacy. Empire money. Political ties stitched into every major deal on the West Coast. His public reputation swings between ruthless businessman and tabloid headline. A bachelor in every sense of the word. He's charming, polished, and only ever been photographed with the same two woman.

Genevieve Redgrave — the biggest event planner in Las Vegas, the kind of woman whose name appears in every glossy society column worth reading. Perfect on paper. Perfect in photographs.

And before her was Maris Greer. His college sweetheart. They were together before the world cared who he loved. Before cameras followed his mistakes like they were stock prices.

Maris isn't part of the public record. She's part of the story he left behind when he became the man everyone else thinks they know.

I close the folder carefully, feeling the shift under my hands — not heavy, but undeniable.

"He has a leak," I say quietly.

Mirelle's expression doesn't flicker. She holds still like a judge who already knows the verdict. Hallie just lifts an eyebrow slightly, the barest invitation to continue.

I don't wait for permission. It's clear why I'm here now. "The police department's been buzzing for weeks," I say. "Not officially. Just locker room talk. The kind of rumors that move faster when no one wants to write them down."

Mirelle tips her head, giving me space to keep going.

"Whispers about Rothwell cleaning up messes for the people no one touches. Politicians. Casino owners with bloody hands. Even foreign royals slinking through the city under fake names."

Hallie's mouth tightens, a flicker of recognition passing through her posture.

"Backroom payouts," I add. "Nightclubs tied to syndicates. PR miracles that erase scandals so cleanly it's like the damage was never real."

Mirelle taps a single manicured nail against the desk. A quiet, deliberate tick.

"And now," I finish, "the leaks are giving the rumors teeth."

"And once belief takes root, it doesn't matter how well the empire was built. It rots from the inside first," Mirelle responds.

"It's already rotting," Hallie adds dryly. The words hang there. Like a clock ticking down to something no one can stop.

I stay silent for a moment, turning it over in my mind. Maybe the rumors are true. Maybe Stellan Rothwell really does bury scandals for the highest bidder. Maybe he's just another part of the machine that keeps this city breathing in the dark.Stellan doesn't clean with bleach. He cleans with influence, perception, the right phone calls made at the right hour to the right terrified man. He doesn't erase people. He erases the stories that could ruin them.

And I'm good at seeing stories, too — not the ones people tell, but the ones they live through without realizing.

They aren't asking me to fix the system. They're asking me to manage the fracture before it reaches the surface.

Because right now, he doesn't need a savior. He needs a mirror that sees the cracks before anyone else does. And I can be that.

I lift my chin slightly, looking at Mirelle. "I'll do it," I say quietly.

"When you're done there will be freedom, no commitments, nothing to tie you to him," she promises. Mirelle rises smoothly from her chair, extending her hand.

I stand and take it.

"Welcome to the Society of the Shadow Brides," she says.

CHAPTER THREE

Talia

We drive for a long time — longer than I expect. Vegas falls away fast. The neon fades into low power lines, and the last gas station looks like a toy left in the sun too long.

The desert opens up, raw and blinding. No signs. No markers. Just flat land and heat distortion twisting the horizon.

The tires hum over the cracked asphalt. Finally, a break in the endless flat. The mountain rises in the distance, rough and sun-bleached, and at its base is something that glints in the sunlight.

A set of doors — massive, gray industrial, are pressed straight into the rock face. They're big enough to fit a semi-truck through them. It's a bunker.

We pull up slowly.

"There's no one out here," I murmur, eyes flicking to the entrance. "No guards. No cameras."

"Doesn't mean no one's watching," Brenna says, calmly.

I sit up a little straighter, instinct sharpening. "It feels exposed."

"It's supposed to," she replies. "Gives the illusion of trust. Makes you think you're being welcomed in."

The heavy doors open without a sound, and we drive through. The road dips underground, smooth and seamless, the tunnel is lined with rows of white lights that flash past like vertebrae.

Neither of us speaks for a while.

We pull into a massive open bay to see a warehouse tucked beneath the earth. Brenna puts the car in park and opens her door. She glances at me over the roof.

"Okay," she says simply. "We're here."

I step out of the car. The air in here is cooler than I expected, filtered and still. Every sound feels louder in the quiet—our doors closing, the soft click of Brenna locking the car.

Walking around the hood, I see Brenna talking to another woman.

The woman moves like someone who's used to being obeyed. Her suit is muted gray, sharp enough to catch the light without trying. Her hair's pulled into a sleek twist, not a strand out of place. When she turns to glance at me, her expression is even, unreadable, the kind of calm that feels more practiced than natural.

"Talia," Brenna says. "This is Renata Charbonneau. She's the Site Director here."

"Nice to meet you," I say, offering my hand, and forcing a smile that I know doesn't look genuine.

Renata takes it in a firm grip and holds my gaze just long enough to make her point. "Welcome," she says, completely monotone.

Brenna smiles slightly, like she knows something I don't yet.

"Let's get inside," Renata says, already turning toward the building. I follow without hesitation.

The building looks different on the inside than I expected. Just smooth walls, blank doors, and corridors wide enough to make you think you're not trapped — until you realize you don't know the way out.

No maps. No arrows. No sign you're supposed to find your way without permission.

"You'll be staying on the east wing," Renata says as we walk. "Private quarters. Limited access."

I nod, keeping pace beside her. "Just me?"

A faint smile crosses her mouth. "You're not the only one training here," she says. "But you won't meet the others. Everyone remains anonymous. By design."

I glance at her. "Why?"

Renata looks straight ahead, her tone even. "Clean boundaries. No entanglements. No alliances. This isn't a sisterhood. It's a system."

I absorb that quietly. It makes sense. Still... it stings, a little.

As we turn another corridor, I ask, "Will my name change?"

She glances at me, the faintest arch of an eyebrow. "No. Your background stays intact. Your name. Your education. Your family history."

"Why?" I ask again, curious, not challenging.

"Because authenticity is harder to fake than invention," Renata says simply. "We want you to feel real because you are real."

I'm not sure how that makes sense, but there's no room for argument, and she offers no further elaborations, so I accept it.

We stop in front of a door that looks like every other one we've passed — blank, seamless, anonymous. Renata scans her badge. The lock clicks open with a soft sound, almost like a sigh.

"This is your home for the time being. Here is your binder," Renata says, handing me a huge leather-bound folder. "Your schedule is in there. And you'll need to study everything."

It's heavier than I expect. Dense.

The first page is simple. A schedule, broken into tight blocks from morning to evening. Every hour accounted for. Every day mapped out.

0800 — Physical Conditioning & Movement Training (Brenna)

0930 — Styling, Wardrobe, and Personal Branding (Lorelle)

1100 — Relationship Immersion & Social History (Anselma)

1230 — Meal & Processing Period (Solo)

1330 — Public Behavior, Gala Protocol, & Upper-Class Dynamics (Renata)

1500 — Technical Communications, Research Protocols, and Encryption Training (Juno)

1630 — Communication Flow & Field Interaction (Iris)

1800 — Dinner with Assigned Team Member (Rotating)

Eight to six. It's not the longest day I've ever worked, that's for sure, but I wonder if we get any time off.

But that's just the surface. Behind it is a wall of tabs, thick, laminated, and color coded.

Anything and everything is in this binder. Hundreds of pages, color-coded like some deranged version of a wedding planner. They have it all mapped out — how we meet, how we fight, how we make up. What to say, what not to say. His triggers, his tells, the exact tilt of his head when he's calculating. They even know how he takes his coffee. Black, no sugar, always poured on the right side of his desk. Every suit arranged in perfect symmetry, like control bleeds into every inch of his life.

The galas are scripted too. Where I stand for the cameras. How long to let him hold my hand. How far to lean in when the photographers catch us mid-conversation. Every charity event, every board meeting, every single public moment designed to look natural—without ever being real.

They're not just teaching me how to belong beside him. They're teaching me how to hold the walls up when they start to crack.

I wake up at the crack of dawn. I've never been one to sleep in. Probably because of my mother.

Sleep didn't feel safe. It felt like leaving the door unlocked.

She had me up before sunrise most days — lessons, drills, posture checks, weigh-ins disguised as "wellness." Late was lazy. Lazy was failure.

By the time I was old enough to know better, my body already moved on instinct. No need for alarms when the fear does the work for you.

I sit up. Stretch once. And get ready.

The shower is cold, fast, efficient — exactly what I need. Scrub the stiffness out of my muscles, the leftover dreams out of my skin.

Each hanger is tagged to match my schedule.

I dress quickly in black leggings, a slate-gray fitted top, and sneakers that barely make a sound on the floor. A small smile spreads across my face when I notice they got my sizes perfect. I tie my hair back, grab a water bottle from the small fridge, and follow the map to the training corridor.

When I reach the doors at the end of a hallway, they slide open without a sound.

Brenna is already waiting for me, dressed in same set I'm wearing.

Her posture is relaxed, but there's a precision to it. Like she's been standing there for exactly the right amount of time, and not a second longer.

She tosses a padded sparring helmet onto a bench and a black resistance band toward my feet.

"Warm up," Brenna says, voice clipped. "You'll need it."

I move through the stretches like they showed me. Slow. Focused. My heart stays steady. My mind sharper.

Brenna watches for barely three minutes before stepping forward. She taps two mats together with her foot and nods for me to come closer.

"Defense positioning," she says. "You ever trained?"

"Only in theory," I admit.

"Good." She smirks. "Theory doesn't bleed bad habits into your reflexes."

She shifts into stance. No warning, no buildup — feet planted, body low, hands up.

"Mirror me."

I do.

I know why they're doing this. Insurance. Preparation. They're making sure I can survive if things go wrong. And God knows, things always go wrong. But the part I didn't expect? I like it. There's a control to it. A focus that belongs only to me. No one else can take it. No one else gets to own it.

Week two comes faster than I expect.

My arms are still bruised from Brenna's last takedown, but Lorelle doesn't notice. Or maybe she does, and just doesn't say anything.

She's dressed like someone who doesn't have time for second drafts — wide-leg black trousers and a sculpted blouse so crisp it probably came with a warning label. Her deep brown eyes sweep over me like measuring tape. Not a wrinkle. Not a smile.

"The jacket's fine," she says, tugging gently at the seam near my shoulder. "But you're standing like someone who doesn't know what it costs."

I offer a small smile. "In my defense, it still has the tag on it."

That earns me exactly nothing.

She circles me once, eyeing every inch like it owes her something.

"Power isn't loud," she says. "It's tailored. It enters the room three seconds before you do."

"I'll try to catch up," I say lightly.

Still nothing. Not even a flicker.

The next two hours are fabric, pins, and judgment. Silk blouses, crisp collars, wide-leg trousers, and sleeveless dresses. Everything sharp and clean, intentional.

She calls for a rack to be brought in—tagged pieces, all in bone, slate, black, ivory, and muted steel blues. No prints, whimsy, or softness, a contrast to my typical bright clothes.

"These aren't supposed to change you. They're meant to match what people expect when they hear your name."

She nods toward the rack, not watching for my reaction.

"Pick what feels like yours," she adds. "Just make sure it's the version of you that can stand in any room."

I skim my fingers across the fabrics. All expensive. All perfect. None of it an accident.

They're not asking me to become someone else. They just want the version of me that fits what they've already sold.

Something clean. Uncomplicated. Controlled.

Not too bold. Not too soft. Just enough to make people look—and never quite see everything.

The version of me who can stand next to him and belong.

I pick the perfect dress.

Two hours later, I'm in Anselma's office.

The lights are dim. The windows don't open. It smells like old paper and lavender.

Her silver hair is twisted into a loose knot at the nape of her neck and she has on a soft linen blouse. Pale eyes see through everything without having to move.

"Memory isn't what happened," she says, flipping a page. "It's what survives the retelling."

My file is full of memories I've never lived. Photos I've never posed for. Restaurants I've never eaten in.

"This is your story," she says. "One version of it. The one that counts."

She doesn't blink as she hands me a notecard with my engagement date.

"Rome," she says, her voice even, almost soft. "You said yes under the terrace lights of a rooftop restaurant in Trastevere. There were white candles on the table. A street violinist passed by just as he asked. He didn't kneel—he knows better than to stage sentimentality. You were wearing navy. Your hair was up. You hesitated for three seconds. Then you smiled. That's what he remembers. So now, it's what you do, too."

"Was I surprised?" I ask.

"You weren't dramatic," Anselma says, her voice calm and exact. "You were present. Focused. That's what made the moment feel real."

I nod once. I can play that version.

By the end of the week, I can list every meal we've shared, every argument we've survived, every city we've fallen in love in.

All of it fiction. All of it is mine now.

Week three is when I finally feel at home.

Or close enough. I know the rhythm now. I know which elevator buttons work without a badge and how long it takes to get from the residence wing to the main building if I don't stop for anyone.

Renata waits for me outside the mock ballroom they've built somewhere in the compound. She's leaning against the wall, arms crossed, pretending not to watch the door.

I raise a brow. "Were you looking for me, or just enjoying the architecture?"

She smiles. "Both. But mostly you."

There's a pause. And in that pause, I can tell. She's checking on me.

"Three weeks," she says. "You doing okay?"

"I'm fine," I say, which is true in the way coffee is filling.

She doesn't push, but her eyes don't leave mine. It's enough to make me add, "It's a weird kind of home. But I think I'm getting there."

She nods. "That's all we can ask."

We walk a few more steps in silence before she glances sideways.

"I keep checking the mailroom," she says. "No letters. No packages."

I smile softly. "That's because I'm starting over."

Not bitter or broken. Just true.

She gives a small hum of understanding, then nudges open the door to the mock ballroom.

"All right then," she says, stepping onto the polished floor. "Let's make sure you can waltz like you've belonged here your whole life."

Renata leads me to the center of the ballroom.

She cues the music — something soft, sweeping, the kind of song that's supposed to carry you.

We take our positions. Palm to palm. A hand at my waist.

We begin to move.

One-two-three. One-two-three.

My body doesn't hesitate. The rhythm lives in my spine.

My mother made sure of that.

Dance was never about joy. It was about control, a perfect posture, a painted smile. I was in my first pageant before I could spell my name. By six, I was walking in heels. By eight, I'd been told I was "difficult" more times than I'd been hugged.

"Still with me?" Renata's voice pulls me back, gentle and low.

The music is still playing. Our feet are still moving. I've kept the rhythm, somehow — even while my mind slipped under.

I glance up at her. "Yeah. Sorry."

"No need to be," she says, not missing a beat. Her hand is steady in mine. "You just went somewhere for a second."

I nod once. Just enough to acknowledge it. "Somewhere I don't go often."

She doesn't press. Just keeps us moving.

The room blurs around the edges. I find the count again. One-two-three. One-two-three.

I know how to keep going. Even when I want to stop.

The table is already set when we walk in — which feels impossibly normal considering the day I've had. Three steaming bowls, mismatched mugs, and the smell of something warm and homemade. Like this room isn't part of a secret society in a compound at all.

Iris sits tucked near the window, cardigan loose around her shoulders, her hair half-up in the way that looks like it stayed that way all day by accident and somehow still works. She glances up, eyes soft.

"I was wondering if you'd come," she says, voice even.

"You made soup," I reply, sliding into the seat across from her. "I'd walk through fire for soup."

Juno's already grabbed the seat next to her and is digging in.

"It's not just soup," Juno says. "It's Iris Soup. Capital letters. It cures headaches and heartbreak and whatever that weird leg cramp I got during combat drills was."

"I did add ginger," Iris says, like that explains everything.

I grin and take my first bite. It's melt your heart delicious, citrusy, a little spicy. Way too good for training compound cuisine. "Okay, this might actually be magic."

"It is," Juno mutters through a mouthful. "You get one bowl. Iris has rules."

"Boundaries," Iris corrects. "Boundaries are healthy."

I laugh softly, and the sound surprises me. It's been a long time since anything came out of me that easily.

I glance between them — Iris with her patience, Juno with her clumsy brilliance — and I feel something small and painful shift in my chest. I'm not used to this. Not the food. Not people who choose you without needing something first.

"Can I ask you something?" I say, setting my spoon down.

"Is it about how I once tried to build a microwave that could talk?" Juno asks, deadpan, like she's daring me to flinch.

I blink, caught off guard. "That's now my second question."

Iris smiles into her tea. "Ask."

"Why are you here? I mean—not just physically. But why this? Why stay?"

"Someone asked me to help once," Juno says, twirling her spoon. "And I liked being the one who could."

"Someone once gave me a choice," Iris says, lifting her mug. "I try to be the kind of person who remembers that."

It's not a lot. But it's enough. Enough to tell me that they have stories too, and probably scars, and that they don't owe me the details to be real.

I nod. "That makes sense."

"You ever think about going back?" Juno asks, tipping her chin toward me.

"To where?" I ask, though I know exactly what she means.

"Family. Church. That world."

I shake my head. Not bitter — just honest. "That version of me doesn't exist anymore. I think she tried. I just don't think she survived."

Iris's gaze softens. Juno doesn't speak.

I pick up my spoon again, breathing in the steam. "It's strange. I keep expecting the people I care about to walk away. But you two keep showing up."

"Maybe we're just stubborn," Iris says.

"Maybe we like you," Juno adds. "Against our better judgment."

I smile, slow and full this time. "That's very poor judgment."

"Maybe," Iris says, raising her mug again. "But we're still here."

And for the first time in longer than I want to admit, I feel it.

Not safety. Not comfort.

Connection.

I'm ready. Not perfectly trained. Not fearless. Just ready enough to mean it.

Everything they gave me, I took in like it mattered. Not just to pass. Because it helped me understand the role. The man. The world I'm about to walk into. And somehow, I don't feel like I've lost myself.

I feel more like me than I did four weeks ago.

Six women wait in a crescent arc. Brenna. Lorelle. Anselma. Renata. Juno. Iris. They shaped this version of me — the one who walks in with calm shoulders, finds the center chair, and means it.

I smooth my hands over my lap and meet each of their eyes. Not rehearsed. Just true.

The door clicks open behind me.

Mirelle enters without announcement. No greetings. No delay. She moves like she owns gravity. Every step says what words don't.

She takes the final seat and folds her hands.

"Begin," she says.

"I met him at a fundraiser in March. He was late. I was leaving. We were introduced at the bar by a mutual contact."

Anselma doesn't move her pen yet. "What were you wearing?"

"Navy wrap dress. Hair up. No jewelry," I say, keeping my voice clear but easy.

"And him?" Anselma asks, her pen hovering.

"Charcoal suit. Shoes scuffed. He forgot to polish them," I reply, a small smile tugging at the corner of my mouth.

A flick of interest crosses her features. "What did he say that made you stay?"

"He told me I looked like someone who'd seen too much to pretend to be impressed," I say, meeting her gaze. "I told him he wasn't wrong."

"And the proposal?" she asks, folding her hands.

"Rome," I say, and the memory settles easily in my voice. "Rooftop in Trastevere. Too many candles, too much noise from the street below. He didn't kneel. He doesn't perform. He waited until after dessert and said, 'I'm exposed in this life. But I'd rather be exposed with you.'"

Anselma leans forward. "And you said?"

"I smiled. That's what he remembers. Then I said yes," I finish, letting the silence carry just long enough to land.

"Why?" Anselma asks, her tone even.

"It didn't feel staged. It felt honest," I say.

She closes her folder, satisfied.

"Monaco benefit. Describe the look," Lorelle says, picking up without pause.

"Bone-colored gown. Clean neckline. Hair down, tucked back. Diamond studs. No necklace," I answer, voice calm but unforced.

"And shoes?" she asks, arching a brow.

"Silver slingbacks. Broke them in three days early. I wanted to walk like I wasn't trying," I say.

A slight exhale escapes her — her version of impressed.

"If a donor comments on your appearance?" she asks.

"I smile. 'Luckily, I wasn't dressing for them,'" I reply.

"You arrive at a gala with your husband. What's your move?" Renata asks, her voice thoughtful.

"Right hand in his arm. No immediate greetings. Three-count pause. Let them look first," I say.

"And if someone lingers?" she prompts.

"I shift closer to Stellan. Let proximity speak. No escalation," I reply, keeping my tone steady.

"Good," she says quietly.

Juno cuts in. "Three anomalies in week-three travel logs?"

"Zurich flight was delayed by four hours. Timestamp wipe didn't finish," I say.

"Badge clone fails. Now what?" Juno asks without looking up.

"Scrub the attempt. No second scan. Re-enter from a different device," I reply.

"You're quicker now," she says, clicking her pen once.

"You taught me well," I say, smiling.

She doesn't reply, but I see the corner of her mouth curve slightly.

"Distress phrase?" Iris asks, lifting her gaze to mine.

"'I'm thinking of switching wines,'" I say.

"If he veers off-script?" she says next.

"I return us to something we share. A real memory. I don't lie. I reframe," I say.

"Why'd you say yes to this assignment?" she asks, studying me without rushing the moment.

I pause. Not because I don't know the answer — because I want to say it right.

"Because I've spent a lot of time feeling like I had to shrink to survive. And here, I get to take up space. Not just to observe, but to care. That's what I'm best at," I say.

I glance around the room.

"I'm good at seeing what people miss. But more than that, I want to make people feel seen. That includes him."

The quiet that follows isn't tense. It settles like breath after a held note.

Mirelle stands.

Her gaze meets mine and holds. No smile. But something in her eyes I haven't seen before — not distance. Not disapproval. Something like acknowledgement.

"Congratulations, Talia," she says. "You're ready."

CHAPTER FOUR

Stellan

This isn't where I thought I'd be. A jewelry showroom, gleaming like a museum of curated lies. Glass cases, velvet trays, and silence that costs six figures—minimum. But here I am—choosing a ring I don't care about for a woman I've never met.

I don't care about the cut or the clarity. Not really. This isn't a love story. It's logistics. A ring is just a symbol, and symbols are only as valuable as the people who believe in them.

The only reason I'm doing this in person is because of Francine De Luca—my cousin, and the force behind this entire operation. She found the Society, made the calls, signed the nondisclosures before I even saw the paperwork.

Of course, if she ever heard me call her *Francine*, she'd probably break my jaw and leave me somewhere off I-15 for the coyotes.

So, Frankie it is.

She insisted I get something perfect. "She needs to belong in your world," she told me. "Start with her hand."

She's not wrong. I hate that she's not wrong.

This place only takes appointments from people whose names echo through cities. Custom work? Almost never. Unless you're me. Or, more accurately, unless you're Frankie—dragging me through this like she's planning the opening scene of a film.

"This one," Frankie says, tapping the glass with a red-painted nail, "emerald cut, platinum band, oval halo. Clean, sharp, serious. Like her."

"You've never met her," I say, barely glancing up.

"Neither have you," she replies, like she's been waiting to say it.

"I've read her file," I say.

"Right," she mutters, tilting her head, "because love is so easy to bullet-point."

"This isn't about love," I mutter, this place is known for their discretion, but I'm not taking any chances.

"No shit, Sherlock," she says, turning to face me fully. "But it is about perception. And if this woman walks in wearing something that looks like it came out of a vending machine, they'll eat her alive."

"She won't care," I say.

"She will if she's smart," Frankie says, her voice softening just slightly. "And if she's not, she'll still need something that makes people hesitate before they speak. That's what a ring like this does. It makes the world second-guess itself."

I don't respond, because she's right. Again.

"We'll take that one. And the matching band," she says, flicking her fingers toward the associate. "Size five and a quarter."

"How do you know her ring size?" I ask.

"I read the file too," she says, not even bothering to look up. "I figured someone should actually prepare for this marriage."

I stare at her.

She hums, pleased with herself.

Of course she does.

After I hand my credit card to the client associate and pay for the rings, we head out of the back door of the store.

My entire goal is to not get photographed leaving a jewelry store. The last thing I need is the press to go crazy thinking I'm getting married and speculating to who.

I've never been in love. I've had relationships—if that's what you want to call them. Temporary arrangements, convenience with a time limit. But never marriage. Never intimacy. Every woman knew what it was, and more importantly, what it wasn't. My heart was never on the table.

That came from home. My parents lived in a marriage built on spectacle and silence. My father cheated constantly. My mother drank like it would solve something. She never left him. She just slowly faded out until the bottom of a bottle finished the job. And when she died, my father needed someone to blame. He chose me.

I was eighteen. Alone. Disowned. I haven't seen or spoken to him in over twenty years. I probably never will.

Everything I have, I built myself. The money. The control. The name. Rothwell wasn't mine by birth—it belonged to the woman who took me in when I had nothing. She didn't ask questions. She didn't offer advice. She just made space. Fed me. Let me be quiet. The name felt clean, so I took it. And I never looked back.

I always assumed that if I ever got married, it would be a contract. A business decision. Something cold and mutually beneficial. Not emotion. Not sentiment.

But needing to get married to save my company? That pisses me off.

Everyone I've been with knew the rules. They understood what it was — temporary, surface-level, never headed toward anything resembling permanence. No one got close. No one tried to. Until Genevieve Redgrave.

She thought she could change me. That she'd be the exception. She wasn't the first to try, but she was the most persistent. I ended it, cleanly and quietly. I don't owe her more than that.

But I still work with her. I see no reason not to.

Genevieve runs Redgrave Events — one of the most ruthless event architecture firms on the planet. She doesn't plan parties. She builds power. Legacy fundraisers, private gatherings, galas so exclusive they don't even make the society pages. When she's managing the guest list, you're either about to be crowned... or quietly erased.

She's damn good at her job. I've never let personal history interfere with performance—and neither has she.

"Okay, I need to get back to work before the boss's son crawls up my ass again," Frankie mutters, grabbing her bag like it personally offended her.

"Beckett's not that bad," I say, because someone has to.

She whirls around, eyes narrowed. "He dresses like you and manages to be smug about it," she says, one hand on her hip.

"It's a suit, Frankie. Not a threat," I reply, keeping my tone even.

"It is when it's custom-tailored to your ego," she fires back.

"You're still mad about the wine list comment, aren't you?" I ask.

"He was *serious*, Stellan. He asked if a merlot had 'emotional integrity,'" she says, her voice full of disbelief.

"He's detail-oriented," I say, trying not to smile.

"He's pretentious," she mutters, folding her arms like she's putting the topic in time-out.

"You spent most of your twenty-first birthday with him," I remind her, watching her carefully.

"That was logistics," she snaps. "Cal disappeared, the DJ flaked, and Beckett had the only working bottle opener. I was trapped." She gestures like that should be obvious.

"You laughed at his jokes," I say.

"I was drunk," she replies, too fast.

"You high-fived him," I add, watching her try to backpedal through memory.

"I was *very* drunk," she hisses, like the memory personally betrayed her.

"You took a selfie," I say, flatly.

She lets out a frustrated noise—somewhere between a groan and a growl—and spins on her heel.

I don't follow. I'm not suicidal.

Frankie's been newly promoted to bar manager at The Dutch Wall, the Onyx Hotel's crown jewel. It's not just a bar—it's a velvet-wrapped pressure point. Politicians, CEOs, media magnates. You don't stumble into the Dutch. You're allowed in. And if Frankie doesn't like you, you don't get past the lighting.

The hotel is owned by Beckett's father.

And Beckett? He's back. Officially.

He's supposed to be taking over as CEO of the Onyx Hotel chain. Which means he's working on-site again—walking the halls like he never left. Like he was always meant to be there.

He wears luxury like armor. Black suits, matte textures, silk-cashmere blends. Dress shirts fitted like they were built for him—because they were. His sleeves are always rolled with surgical precision, like every movement has been calculated three moves in advance. His watch costs more than most condos on the Strip, but he wears it like it's just functional. He doesn't wear cologne that lingers. He doesn't need to.

His casual is other people's formal. And it's all intentional.

We're not best friends. That's Cal. Always has been. But Beckett and I go way back. Same prep schools. Same circles. Same expectations that we'd inherit empires before we could legally drink. He's louder than me. More dramatic. But underneath the show, he's surgical. Strategic. Ruthless when it counts.

He's one of the few people I trust.

Even when I don't like what he's doing.

Frankie says she hates him. I think she's still trying to convince herself.

The Rothwell Strategic building cuts through downtown Vegas like a blade of black glass. No signage. No welcome. It doesn't need it. The right people already know what happens here.

The lower floors are the face. Legacy finance, generational wealth management, family office consulting for names you'd recognize but never hear in headlines. Estate transitions. Quiet dynasty shifts. Soft-gloved empire handling.

But the top floors—they don't *officially* exist.

That's where the real work happens.

Restructuring power. Removing threats. Restoring order before damage becomes public. If I'm in the room, someone has already failed. I don't save people. I stop the bleeding before it stains.

My assistant, Kate Loe, meets me the moment the elevator opens—tall, sleek, and dressed in slate gray, her clipboard is in hand. Voice clipped and calm.

"You have Clarke at eleven, the board call at one, Erin flagged the prenup language again," she says, then pauses. "Genevieve called. Again."

"What did she want?" I ask, already knowing.

"She said it's urgent. She didn't elaborate."

"Call her back," I say, stepping past her. "Tell her to stop bothering me."

Kate doesn't blink. "Done."

When I walk into my office, Hallie is waiting—posture crisp, legs crossed, a folder resting neatly on her lap. Erin, my general counsel, stands beside her, holding another file with a silver seal.

"She's ready," Hallie says, sliding it across my desk.

I open it.

I already know the story. Talia Cerny. The timeline we crafted. The fake weekend in Florence. The rooftop kiss in Monaco. The private-label wine. The art auction that never happened.

I know every word.

But this is the first time I see her face.

She doesn't look how I expected.

That's not a bad thing.

"She cleared every milestone faster than projected," Hallie says. "Behavioral calibration. Language conditioning. Embedded backstory. Internalized, not memorized."

"She'll enter through the secondary division," Erin adds. "The IPO breach needs public framing, and a stabilizer. She's the narrative now. Publicly, it's romance. Privately, she's plugging the hole before the board starts bleeding."

"She thinks she's playing a role," Hallie says, tilting her head. "But she's walking into a controlled fire."

She's real now. And every second is glass cracking under pressure.

The door opens suddenly.

Kate steps in, sharp and tight. "I tried to stop her."

Genevieve walks in like she already knows the answer. Smile radiant. Lipstick perfect. Eyes full of certainty.

"I saw the press," she says breathlessly. "You could've told me sooner. But I get it—you wanted it quiet until the deal closed."

Before I can say anything, she steps in and kisses me.

I don't kiss her back.

She doesn't notice. Yet.

Pulling away, she smiles wider. "Do you have it? The ring? I don't need a reveal, I just want to see it."

I glance at Kate.

She crosses the room and holds out her tablet, screen glowing.

"It dropped about ten minutes ago," she says. "Multiple outlets. This one's going viral."

I take it. The photo is unmistakable.

Me and Frankie, walking out of Benedetti & Co. She's holding the bag. I'm holding the door.

ROTHWELL ENGAGED?

The Power Broker, the Red Dress, and the Ring That Broke the Internet

Stellan Rothwell, Las Vegas' most private power broker—and arguably its most eligible bachelor—was seen exiting Benedetti & Co., the city's most exclusive luxury jeweler known for its confidential, invitation-only clientele and multi-million-dollar commissions.

Rothwell was accompanied by Francine De Luca, his cousin and closest friend, sparking immediate speculation over the purpose of their visit. While no official statement has been released, insiders suggest Rothwell's long-rumored companion,

elite event architect Genevieve Redgrave, may be the intended recipient of what appeared to be a custom ring selection.

Redgrave has been a recurring presence at Rothwell's side for years, both personally and professionally. If the engagement is confirmed, it would mark one of the most high-profile unions in Las Vegas high society this decade.

I exhale once and hand the tablet back to Kate.

Genevieve's still smiling. "They always move fast," she says, laughing softly. "I suppose we should issue a proper announcement soon. I already have a statement drafted, by the way. Just in case."

"It's not you," I say.

Her head tilts in confusion. "What?"

"The article got it wrong," I say, slower this time. "It's not you, Genevieve."

Her smile fades. "Stellan. Come on."

"I met someone," I say. "Her name is Talia Cerny. We've been together for months. Quietly."

She shakes her head once. "That's not—no. That's not possible."

"She's the one," I say. "It's done."

Genevieve stiffens like her spine's holding her together. "So you're just going to let them publish that and not correct it?"

"We will. When it's time."

"And you weren't even going to tell me?" Her voice cracks, barely masked. "You let me walk in here thinking—"

"I didn't let you do anything," I say, calm. "You assumed."

"I've stood next to you for years."

"You've stood *near* me," I correct. "This is different."

Silence hits like static.

Then, softly, she whispers, "This was supposed to be mine."

Kate steps forward. "Ms. Redgrave—"

Genevieve holds up a hand, but it's shaking now.

She walks out without another word. Kate follows her and shuts the door behind them, soft as a warning.

For a moment, the silence holds. Still. Tight. Then the door opens again.

Clarke steps in—silent, square-shouldered, always watching everything before you know he's in the room.

"Do you want me to tail her?" he asks, voice low and flat.

"No," I say. "Not yet."

He nods once, then disappears just as quietly.

"Now that she's gone..." Erin pulls out a folder, thick and neat, and lays it on the desk between us. "Let's sign the prenup."

She places a pen next to it. I trust my team implicitly—but Erin knows me. She got the file to me days ago. I've already read every clause, every phrase, every loophole.

She's just handing me the final moment.

I flip to the signature page and slide my pen across the line.

"Clarke will keep tabs regardless," Hallie says as I sign. "But if she tries to move against the narrative, we'll be ahead of it."

"She already is," Erin adds, flipping a second document into the folder. "She just hasn't realized she lost."

I work late. Emails. Redlines. Silent confirmations. Pieces shift beneath my signature with the quiet confidence of a machine. Three meetings, two finalized contracts, and a staff that doesn't breathe unless I tell them the air is safe. When I finally leave, Vegas is alive in its usual roar of lights and alcohol and illusions. But I'm already above it.

The Onyx Hotel is Beckett's family's empire—quiet luxury veiled in black glass, where money doesn't make noise and power doesn't ask for permission. But the top floor belongs to me. My penthouse is accessed by a private elevator with no keycard, no staff, and no welcome mat. It opens into silence. Everything in the space is black, concrete, or steel. The windows stretch wall to wall, glass so clean it almost erases the city outside. The art is rare, cold, and selected by someone who understands I don't hang sentiment. The entire place is curated to keep the world out.

Cal is already on the couch, watching soccer on mute, drink in hand, and feet on the coffee table like he lives here. I walk past him without comment and head for the bar. Scotch, single cube, no words.

"You break in again?" I ask, pouring.

"You gave me the code," he says without looking away from the screen.

"I gave it to you once."

"And I remembered it. That's on you."

I drop into the chair across from him. "How was the trip?"

Cal shrugs. "Hot girl. Talked too much about her star chart. Told me we were karmically aligned and then asked if I could hold emotional space for her trauma. I ghosted her before dessert."

"You're a romantic."

"She cried in the Uber. Still texting me."

Before I can reply, the front door opens without a knock. Frankie walks in like a war crime—heels sharp, sunglasses still on, fury in every step.

"I swear to God, if that man breathes near the Dutch Wall again—"

"Beckett?" I ask, already sipping the scotch.

She points at me like I invited him. "He sent me a mood board labeled 'Emotional Architecture' and told me the bar lacked aesthetic vision. Then had the nerve to suggest a floating light installation and a Scandinavian decanter shaped like a deconstructed iceberg!"

Cal's wheezing with laughter. "You're kidding."

"I wish I was," she growls. "He said we needed to 'elevate the spiritual experience of bourbon.'"

There's a knock.

We all pause, then look at the door.

Of course.

Beckett Harrington walks in like the penthouse was made for him—which, it kind of was. He's wearing a black silk shirt, fitted pants, and a coat that cost someone's yearly rent.

"Evening," he says smoothly. "I felt a disturbance in the vibe."

"You are the disturbance," Frankie mutters.

"You're glowing, Francine," Beckett says, lounging back on the couch.

"Don't," Frankie snaps without looking at him.

"Didn't say it was from joy," he adds, raising his glass in a toast to her.

"She missed you," Cal deadpans. "Painfully."

Beckett leans back, arms stretched across the couch. "So, are we unpacking the Redgrave situation or just pretending it didn't happen?"

I blink. "What Redgrave situation?"

Cal whips his head towards me. "You haven't seen it?"

"Seen what?" I sigh and rub the bridge of my nose.

Beckett's already pulling his phone from his pocket. "She's not just riding the press wave. She's steering it. Wait for it," he mutters, turning the screen so I can see.

It's a clip from a morning interview. Bright set. Cozy lighting. Genevieve's perfectly lit, perfectly framed, smiling like she's just been voted most elegant woman alive.

"I think," she says, her voice soft and warm, "when you build something slowly, away from the noise, it becomes... real. Strong. Stellan and I have always believed in privacy. In protecting what we've built. When it's right, you don't have to rush. You just know."

She laughs gently. The host leans in, wide-eyed.

"So... are you confirming it?"

Genevieve smiles again. Coy. Strategic. "I'm saying... it's been a long time coming."

The clip ends.

I stare at the black screen for a beat longer than necessary before I hand the phone back.

God help me, I start laughing. I can't quite believe how bold she is. But I should've known.

Beckett blinks at me. "You're laughing?"

"She's playing checkers," I say, the words dry against the edge of the laugh, "on a chessboard."

"She's faking a relationship she doesn't have," Frankie growls. "And the worst part? Everyone *wants* to believe her."

"She's betting on your silence," Cal adds.

> Erin, we need to get ahead of this.

I attach a link to the interview, but I shouldn't worry.

> Already done. Press release is out. Kate sent it to everyone. Hallie approved it too.

I take a look at the release and bust out laughing as I show everyone else what it says.

OFFICIAL STATEMENT — ROTHWELL STRATEGIC HOLDINGS

Recent interviews and social commentary have attempted to misrepresent Mr. Stellan Rothwell's personal life, implying romantic involvement where none has ever existed.

To clarify, Mr. Rothwell is not engaged to Ms. Genevieve Redgrave. He never has been. No proposal occurred. No relationship exists between the two outside of the times they've worked together.

Any insinuation to the contrary is a fabrication. Ms. Redgrave's attempt to attach herself to Mr. Rothwell's name is unfortunate, inappropriate, and speaks volumes about her professionalism — or lack thereof. We remind the public that proximity is not intimacy, and repetition is not truth.

Mr. Rothwell is currently in a committed, private relationship with someone who does not require publicity to feel valued. Out of respect for that individual, no further comment will be made.

– Rothwell Strategic Communications Office

I knew Genevieve wouldn't be able to resist reaching out. She was just faster than I gave her credit for.

> What the fuck, Stellan? Did you have to be so harsh?

> You went on national television and lied. I corrected the narrative. If you find the truth harsh, that's not my problem.

"Hey!" Cal grunts, setting his drink down with a frown, "How come you never told me you were seeing someone?"

"She has a hard time with being in the limelight," I reply, cryptically as I sip the scotch.

Beckett tilts his head, narrowing his eyes like he's trying to catch a lie midair, "Wait... you're not denying it."

"I'm not denying anything," I say, keeping my tone deliberately flat.

"So the mystery woman?" he presses, voice sharp with interest, "That's real?"

"She's not a mystery," I say, casually.

Beckett blinks. "So you *are* seeing someone," he says, pointing at me like he's cracked a code.

"I married her," I say calmly, not even looking up from my glass.

The silence hits like a slap.

"You *what?*" Beckett coughs, nearly spilling his drink as he leans forward.

Cal turns toward me slowly, eyes wide, "Seriously?"

Frankie smirks, sipping her drink like it's champagne at a victory party, "Told you—he's not dramatic. Just efficient."

"When?" Beckett asks, voice high with disbelief.

"A few days ago," I say, watching him carefully.

"You're just telling us now?" he asks, half-laughing, half-offended.

"You were out of town," I say with a shrug, "Frankie was there."

"I *knew* something was going on," he mutters, glaring over at her, "You've been too quiet."

"She asked me not to say anything," Frankie replies sweetly, then adds with a wicked grin, "Also, you would've made it weird."

Beckett stares at me like I've betrayed him, "You eloped?"

"Yes," I say simply.

"You bought a ring?" he asks, tone incredulous.

"Custom," I nod.

"Do I even get to know her name?" he asks, clearly annoyed.

"No," I say without blinking.

"Of course not," Beckett mutters, falling back into the couch with a scoff.

Frankie raises her glass toward mine, her smile smug and sharp, "To secrets."

Beckett leans back with a dramatic sigh, "I feel like I just walked into Act II of a play I didn't know I was in."

"At least now we know why Genevieve got nuked," Cal adds, amused as he tips his glass toward mine.

The city flickers behind the glass like it's watching me back.

Let the games begin.

CHAPTER FIVE

Talia

By the time we pull up, Rothwell is already humming. It's just after ten, and everything is in motion — people on phones rushing by, the kind of professional buzz that doesn't pause for anyone.

The building itself gleams in the light, tall and exact. I knew it would be big, but something about seeing it now makes my chest tighten.

Renata puts the car in park. "Here we are."

Neither of us move right away. Anxiety is making its way through the car.

I look out the window, watching the constant rhythm just beyond the doors.

I don't know if I can actually do this," I say, my voice small.

Renata looks over at me, surprised. Not wide-eyed or dramatic, but still like she wasn't expecting me to say that. "You don't have to feel ready," she says gently. "You just have to go in."

Brenna twists to face me from the front seat. "You don't need to impress them, Talia. You just have to be who you are. That's more than enough."

"Okay," I blow out a big breath, hoping it sounds more certain than it feels.

I open the door, and the sound hits immediately — city noise, low and layered, folding around me like I've stepped into a current. I don't move right away.

Renata and Brenna stay parked, engine idling, doors closed. They don't wave. Don't nod. Just wait. Not to make sure I get inside. Just to let me know I'm not walking in alone.

That's enough.

I take a breath, tuck my hair behind my ear, and slide in the earpiece they gave me. Day one, it feels like more than protocol. It feels like backup.

There's a pause before a static sound.

"Hey," Juno's voice crackles in. "Can you hear me?"

I smile, just a little. "Yeah, Juno. I can."

"We're here if you need us," Iris adds, calm and steady.

And I believe her.

Pulling the door open feels like a vacuum — like the building sucks me in the second I break the seal. The bustling sounds just outside are muted, the temperature's dipped.

The lobby stretches in every direction. All glass and stone and careful lighting. It's beautiful.

People pass by in practiced lines, phones at their ears, eyes ahead. Not one of them looks at me.

It's not personal — it's policy. Still, there's something isolating about moving through a space that's already decided you don't matter.

Like I'm walking through someone else's rhythm, and no one thinks I know the steps.

There's a security guard and receptionist near the elevators, telling people where they need to be going and letting them through. Their rhythm is practiced and smooth, it isn't quite welcoming, but at least someone knows what's going on here.

The receptionist notices me first. I shoot her a smile, hoping that she can't tell how nervous I am. But no, I'm ready, I've trained for this, I've prepared, this is natural.

"Good morning, Mrs. Rothwell," she says. "I'm Stacy."

"Hi, Stacy. It's really nice to meet you." I stick my hand out to shake hers, reminding myself that I shouldn't be too eager.

"I heard you'd be coming in today," she says, after a brief pause, looking at me like she was caught off guard. "Everything's been cleared. You should be all set."

She reaches beneath the desk and pulls out a slim, glossy badge — clipped to a silver lanyard, my name already printed beneath the Rothwell insignia. "Here you go," she says, smiling wide now. "This gets you where you need to go."

"Thank you," I say as she hands me the badge. I glance down at it, then back at her with a soft smile. "This looks great."

Her shoulders ease. Just a little.

The security guard steps forward then, posture straight but not tense. "I'm Aaron," he says. "We were told you'd be arriving this morning."

I offer my hand. "It's good to meet you, Aaron."

He shakes it. Stacy glances over at him, then back at me, amusement flickering behind her eyes. "I have to admit... when Mr. Rothwell told us his wife would be coming in, we were expecting someone..."

"A little different." Aaron finishes for her.

"Someone scarier," Stacy adds, grinning.

I laugh — light, real, unbothered. "That's fair, he can be a bit intense."

The tension in both of them breaks like steam off glass.

Aaron nods. "Good to meet you, Mrs. Rothwell."

"Just Talia's fine," I say, and I mean it. "Really."

The aggressive sound of heels clicking on tile snatches my attention from the conversation and I turn to see Genevieve Redgrave storming into the lobby. She's dressed in a deep charcoal coat cinched tight at the waist, sleek and expensive. Underneath, a cream silk blouse with sharp cuffs and high-waisted black trousers that fit like they were tailored just for this confrontation. Lastly, a silver watch and a perfect red lip, like time and power are her only accessories.

Stacy instinctively moves from behind the counter. "Excuse me—"

Genevieve shoves past her without a word. A hard, flat push to the shoulder. Disrespect, fully formed.

Aaron steps in fast, blocking her path before she can reach the elevator.

"Ms. Redgrave, you need to wait," he says, firm but still professional. "Mr. Rothwell made it clear yesterday—"

"I have clearance," she snaps, eyes locked on the elevator. "You know that. And this is about the gala."

Aaron doesn't move. His jaw tightens. "He said no direct contact."

Genevieve tosses her hair like that ends the conversation. "Then he can tell me that to my face."

I watch Stacy carefully. Her shoulders are rigid, eyes down, jaw clenched like she's trying not to be seen. No one deserves to be made small like that. Especially not for doing their job.

"That's enough," I say quietly, but clearly.

Genevieve turns her head slowly, like she's only now registering that I'm here. Her gaze lands on me, sharp and assessing.

"You don't get to treat them like that," I continue. "You're frustrated. Fine. But don't drag other people through it."

"Don't you know who I am?" she says, like the answer should clear a path.

"I do," I say, calm and measured.

Before I can say more, Aaron steps in, his voice firmer now. "Do you know who *she* is?"

He nods toward me.

I shake my head slightly. "It doesn't matter, Aaron. Just check if she's actually here about the gala."

I'm not looking for a fight. But I'm not stepping aside, either.

Stacy is already picking up the phone. Her hands move quickly, but her shoulders are tight. This isn't new for her — just unpleasant.

Genevieve stands with her arms folded, silent. Waiting.

After a brief exchange, Stacy lowers the phone. "It's confirmed. She's approved to go up." She hesitates, then adds, "They said it's about the guest list."

Genevieve turns her head, just enough to smile in my direction.

"See?" she says, smug now. "About the guest list."

She steps forward, brushing past Stacy again, enough to make her stumble back a half step. A second shove. And no apology.

I move forward, instinct before intention. Stacy still hasn't moved. Her face is pale, eyes down.

"You want to see Stellan?" I say, voice even but edged. "Fine. But do things the right way. Don't throw people out of your way to get there."

Genevieve stares at me, but I don't return the challenge. I'm not here to fight her. I'm here to draw a line.

She walks away without a second glance.

I watch her head toward the elevators. But she doesn't go to the main bank — the one that leads to the thirty-sixth floor. She taps into a different set. Lower access range.

She's not going to him. At least, not yet.

Aaron follows my gaze. "That's not Stellan's elevator."

"No," I say softly. "It's not."

The elevator doors close behind her. Stacy finally sits back down, her hands resting flat against the desk like she needs to feel something solid.

"You okay?" I ask gently.

She nods, a little too fast. "That was just... a lot."

"Not your fault."

She looks up at me. "Thanks for saying something."

"You don't deserve to be treated like that," I say simply. "No one does."

Aaron gestures toward the main elevators. "You heading up?"

I nod, adjusting the badge at my hip. "Yeah. Might as well make an entrance."

He gives me a quick smile — something real this time. "Good luck up there."

I smile back. "Thanks."

The elevator doors open with a soft chime, and I step inside alone.

As they close, the lobby fades behind me — the tension, the noise, the aftershock of someone else's anger. For a second, it's just me and the low hum of motion.

A soft beep chimes out when I tap my lanyard to the panel. The screen blinks once. Access granted.

I watch the numbers blink upward. And then the chime sounds again. Floor thirty-six.

The doors open to the executive floor.

The space is wide — long corridors, high ceilings, smooth stone floors that reflect soft, amber light. The walls are paneled in dark wood, sleek and polished, broken only by minimal brass signage and recessed lighting strips that run clean across the ceiling.

A long stretch of glass lines one side of the hallway, floor-to-ceiling, revealing the skyline in sharp detail. No blinds. Nothing to soften the view.

Every surface looks like it's been wiped twice. The air smells faintly of cedar. There's no art. No color. Just black, silver, and soft gold accents. A space meant to impress quietly.

I step out of the elevator and turn left.

The hallway stretches wide, the same dark wood and stone from before, but now it opens into a corner of activity.

Near the end of the corridor, a small group stands gathered around a sleek, modern desk.

Four of them.

I know their names before they look up. I've memorized their files, studied their patterns, watched grainy footage of their expressions from across conference tables and security footage. I know how they speak when they think no one's listening.

But it's different standing here—in front of them, their real presence, the quiet strangeness of knowing people deeply, when they know nothing about you at all.

The woman behind the desk is calm and composed, her posture is straight as a blade. Kate. Efficient, respected. Not easily rattled.

To her left, a man leans against the counter, arms crossed, eyes narrowed. Guarded. Already assessing. Cal. Protective by instinct, suspicious by training.

Just behind them, two men are in mid-conversation. One tall and curious, voice warm even in quiet tones. The other quieter still—sharp eyes, hands in his pockets like he's more comfortable watching than speaking. Beckett. Dawson.

They haven't noticed me yet.

But I see all of them. And I know what each of them is about to learn — that I'm not just a name they've never heard. I'm here.

I can't wait to meet them, but I know I can't seem too eager.

I walk like someone who already belongs. Measured, intentional, open-hearted. Not performing, not pretending.

Just showing up exactly as I am.

"Hi," I say with a small, easy smile. "I'm Talia."

Kate straightens. "Of course. We were told to expect—"

But she doesn't finish.

The door opens and I hear him before I see him.

Stellan.

I've seen photos of him. I thought I understood the shape of him — the sharp suits, the stillness, the way everyone around him seems to hold their breath a little.

But the photos didn't do him justice.

He's... striking. In a way that doesn't try to be. Like everything about him was chosen with purpose and none of it was meant to be noticed — but somehow, you can't look away.

His charcoal suit is crisp, effortless. His dark chocolate hair is smoothed back, beautiful silver-grey eyes that land on me without hesitation.

Not cold, nor kind. Just precise, like he sees exactly what he's looking at.

I knew his presence would be strong. I just didn't expect it to feel like this—like it has a gravitational force of it's own.

I've seen pictures. I've read the files. But that's not the same as standing in front of someone who knows how to change the air in a room just by entering it.

His gaze lands on me and he smiles.

"Hi, darling," he says, voice low and perfectly measured.

The shift is immediate.

Kate freezes. Beckett blinks hard. Cal's jaw sets like something just rearranged the ground beneath him.

Only Dawson stays as he was — like he's been waiting for this.

His hand slides to my waist. He leans in, and kisses me. It's not hurried. Not soft, either.

There's precision in it. A practiced stillness. Like he knows exactly how this will be seen, and exactly what it will mean.

I kiss him back — not out of obligation, but control of my own. My hand rises to his chest, just enough pressure to be felt.

When he pulls away, he doesn't look at anyone else. Just me.

He turns to the group again, his tone as even as ever.

"This is my wife. Talia Rothwell."

CHAPTER SIX

Talia

"Finch," Stellan says, calm as anything. "How about we go into my office before the announcement."

The word hits before I'm ready for it. It flickers through me — sharp and unexpected. I flinch. Not visibly. Just a pause, a breath caught in the wrong part of my chest.

"Of course." I turn to the group, offering a soft smile. "It was nice to meet you all."

They nod, still processing. Dawson gives the slightest tilt of his head — like he saw the flicker, and won't mention it.

I fall into step beside Stellan as he leads me toward his office. His pace is steady. Mine is quieter. But that word follows me like it's caught in the fabric of my jacket.

Finch.

My mother used to say it when I was too soft, too slow, too much. *"You're like a finch,"* she'd mutter. *"Pretty and small. You don't belong in a world like this."*

I spent years trying not to be that girl — soft-voiced, open-hearted, easy to bruise.

But hearing it here, from *him*, unsettles something I thought I'd left behind. It doesn't feel like the slap to the face they way it did when it came from her mouth. He means it as something good, treasured.

Stellan closes the door behind me and takes a seat behind his desk, he gestures to the office chair on the other side, across from him.

It's just the two of us in a room neither of us chose, trying to figure out what this is supposed to be.

It's weird, sitting across from someone that I know every detail about, but don't know at all. We don't have to pretend that we're not strangers.

"So," I say, slipping into the seat. "Do I get a ring, or just the paperwork?"

He doesn't blink or smirk. Just reaches into the inner pocket of his suit and pulls out a small velvet box. He sets it on the desk between us. No flourish. No speech. I look down at it, then up at him.

"Our rings," he says simply.

I open the box to see a plain platinum wedding band. Solid. No engraving, no softness. The kind of band meant to be seen, not felt. The engagement ring is sharper. An emerald-cut diamond framed by a narrow halo, set in a platinum band that looks like it could cut glass. It refracts — all sharp lines and precision. Beautiful, but cold.

They don't look like me.

They look like what I'm supposed to be—a symbol, a signal. Something expensive and untouchable.

"They fit?" he asks, it's a logistics question, there's nothing personal about it.

I slide them on, one by one. "Perfectly."

He nods once, satisfied.

I close the box and set it aside and that's when I notice. He's already wearing his. He didn't wait for me.

"Are we doing the announcement today?" I ask, my voice quiet but even. "Or is this still in the rehearsal stage?"

"We're doing it," he says. "Lecture hall's being prepped now."

The door opens. Kate steps in, tablet in hand. She pauses when she sees us. "Apologies," she says. "Everyone's in the lecture hall."

I glance at Stellan as I cross my legs, tilting slightly toward him. Just enough to read as familiar.

He gets up and walks around the desk. He holds out his hand.

I rise and take it.

He leans in, his voice low. "Shall we go convince a few hundred people we're madly in love?" There's the faintest curve at the corner of his mouth. Not quite a smile, but more like the idea of one.

I lift a brow, a smile spreading across my face. "Lead the way."

To everyone watching, we're husband and wife.

The hallway narrows before opening into the hum of a room not built for quiet—voices overlapping, footsteps echoing, chairs shifting as people settle into their assumptions. It's loud in the way anticipation always is.

But the moment we step through, it starts to change. Like the air got caught mid-breath. Rows of seats curve in neat arcs, filled edge to edge—analysts, legal, operations. Every floor. Every title.

Stellan lets go of my hand and walks to the mic like he's done it a hundred times, and I'm sure he has. Nothing in his posture shifts. Nothing softens. He doesn't need to ask for the room's attention. It's already his.

"There's been a change to my personal status," he says, like he's delivering a quarterly report. "Not that it concerns anyone here, but I got married."

A shift moves through the room. It's just the sound of priorities rearranging.

"This is Talia Rothwell," he adds. "My wife."

He turns and hands me the mic.

There has to be about three hundred people, watching, waiting to learn anything and everything they can about me. I don't let my nerves get to me, instead, I smile.

"Hi," I say, with a small smile. "This is... easily the most dramatic welcome I've ever walked into. I heard this team was intimidating, and, yeah — not wrong. But I'm glad to be here."

A ripple moves through the room, soft laughter, the kind people don't know they're holding in until it escapes.

I glance at Stellan. He looks at me like he's seeing something he didn't expect to admire but does.

"I know this probably feels sudden," I say, my tone shifting with it. "But it mattered to him that you heard it from us. And it mattered to me to be here for it. He loves this team. He talks about the people here with the kind of genuine respect that's rare. And I wanted to be part of something like that."

The energy changes—subtle but certain. They're not just watching anymore. They're listening.

"I hope I'll get to know all of you," I say, smiling. "Over coffee. Hallway chats. Elevator rides where we all pretend not to look at each other."

A few grins. One soft chuckle.

"Unless you're the person leaving mugs in the sink," I add. "If so, congratulations—you're now my personal redemption project."

The laughter that follows this time isn't tentative. It's real.

I offer the mic back to Stellan. He doesn't take it. Instead, he steps forward. One hand at the small of my back. The other brushing a strand of hair from my face.

And he kisses me.

When he pulls back, his hand lingers a breath longer than it needs to. Just enough for every person in this room to understand something unspoken. Whatever this is, it's not temporary.

That's when I hear it. A scream—gut-wrenching and sharp. Not startled. Not scared. Something else entirely.

The kind of sound that doesn't belong in a place like this.

Heads turn. People shift in their seats, craning toward the upper tier.

It's Genevieve.

She's standing near the back of the lecture hall, high enough for everyone to see, but all she sees is me.

I know she recognizes me—from the lobby, from the moment she couldn't quite place me. She never expected this. Never expected *me*.

Her eyes aren't wide with heartbreak. They're locked on mine like a challenge.

Not grief or confusion. Just fury, tightly coiled around disbelief. She looks at me like I stole her most prized possession.

Dawson steps closer, his voice low, calm, and already moving. "We should leave."

Stellan doesn't speak. He just reaches for me and wraps his hand around mine. His grip is protective, not possessive. He's shielding me from whatever might happen next.

And I let him lead us out, even as the heat of Genevieve's gaze lingers between my shoulder blades.

Because no matter how dramatic that scream was—there was a whole lot more coming.

The doors are almost shut when I hear the sharp click of heels rounding the corner.

Genevieve.

"Wait—Stellan, please—just let me talk to you—"

She lunges. Dawson moves without hesitation, stepping into the gap. His arm lifts, palm pressing flat to the control panel.

"Move," she demands, voice rising. "This is a mistake. You don't even know her—"

"That's enough, Genevieve," Dawson says, his tone quiet but final—like a door closing before she ever had a chance to step through it.

I drop his hand gently and take a step to the side.

"Well," I say lightly, offering Dawson a small smile, "that was dramatic. Is it always like this, or do I just bring the weather with me?"

He huffs a breath—almost a laugh.

"Talia," I say, extending my hand. "Officially."

He takes it, no hesitation. "Dawson. And yeah, I know who you are."

"So you've been briefed on the whole 'whirlwind romance to wife' thing," I say, letting a small laugh of my own slip through.

His mouth pulls into a grin. "More than briefed."

"Great. That saves time."

The elevator opens and there she is.

Erin. Rothwell's attorney. The only person besides Dawson and Stellan who knows the truth.

She doesn't smile. She's dressed in sharp lines—black and white. Tablet in hand, posture perfect. But it's not performative. It's functional.

Everything about her says *I don't miss things. And I don't pretend.*

We've never spoken, but I know immediately she's not someone you bluff.

We step into the room and as soon as the door closes behind us, Erin moves to the table "Marriage license. NDA," she says. "Just signatures now."

I pick up the pen and sign.

I know what I'm in for. I already signed the prenup. The door opens behind me and Kate steps in, calm and composed, her tablet balanced neatly in one hand.

"Genevieve's upstairs," she says, with an exasperated sigh.She turns to Stellan. "Would you like me to stop her?"

"Yes," he says without a second thought.

"Let's talk about Genevieve," I say quietly. "She's upset — that much is obvious. But did she actually know about the marriage?"

"I told her yesterday," Stellan replies. "She knew I was getting married. That I'm in a serious relationship."

I nod, but something doesn't settle. "That scream... it wasn't heartbreak. It was something else."

Everyone in the room is watching me now. Not with expectation exactly, but like they're waiting for me to see what they've missed.

"Who is she, really?" I ask, quiet but clear.

"Gen?" Dawson says, brows lifting.

"Yes. There's definitely a reason she feels that betrayed."

"She thought we were getting married," Stellan says, his voice flat, like the outcome was obvious and the fallout irrelevant.

"Ahh, so that wasn't about losing love," I say. "So much as it was about losing control."

Dawson leans forward slightly. "Image-first. Curated."

"Transactional," Erin adds. "But... warm. At least on the surface."

"Lonely," Stellan says, voice low. "Attaches quickly. Hurts when she's ignored."

I take a breath, the threads starting to connect.

"She's not here for revenge," I say softly. "She's here for an edit. She built her identity around being close to you and you changed the story without telling her how it ends."

The room is quiet. No one says a word for what feels like forever.

"Holy shit," Erin murmurs.

"That's what we've been missing," Dawson says.

Stellan doesn't speak. He just watches me.

They weren't just waiting for answers. They were waiting for my input.

"She built an identity around being yours — publicly, privately, socially. You didn't just break it. You made it irrelevant."

"She thought there was a future," Erin says, softly.

"No," I say. "She thought there was a narrative. Something she was part of. And Stellan..."

I meet his eyes.

"You didn't just walk away. You stole the ending."

CHAPTER SEVEN

Stellan

Before I can even respond to Talia's bombshell observation, I hear yelling outside my office. Talia doesn't flinch. She tilts her head slightly, listening. Calm. Still tracking the pattern.

Erin glances toward the glass. Dawson steps back from the table, already moving into position like it's instinct.

"She has no right to be here!" Gen's voice cuts through the hall. "You don't even know who she is!"

Kate's response is quieter. I can't make out the words, but the tone is final. Professional. A wall.

"I need to speak to him now!" Gen demands.

I look at Talia. She meets my gaze, eyes clear. Not angry. Not insecure. Just... calculating.

The door flies open and it's loud enough to make every head turn.

Gen storms in, breathless, eyes glassy but focused. Kate follows a second later, hand pressed to her head, blood tracking down from a fresh cut at her hairline.

Before I can react, Talia's already there. She guides Kate toward a chair without a word, assessing the wound with quiet efficiency.

Gen doesn't stop. She moves straight toward me, heels hard on the floor, hands grabbing the front of my jacket like she owns the right.

"This is who you chose?" she spits, voice low and shaking. "You said it was serious. You didn't say it was done."

"I would've understood," Genevieve says, her gaze fixed on Stellan but her meaning pointed directly at me. "If you needed something political. Public-facing. I could've done that for you."

Talia doesn't say a word. But I notice her still. She is instantly alert. She heard something and she's figuring out what to do with it.

Genevieve turns now, eyes settling on Talia. "You don't know him. Not really."

"I know him enough to see what you're trying to do," she says it the way you'd speak to someone walking into the wrong room with the wrong assumptions.

"Oh?" Genevieve lets out a short, humorless laugh. "Let me help. I've been orbiting this man for over three years. Curating the rooms he walks into, smoothing over every sharp edge he didn't have time to care about. While you were wherever you were, I was here—building the version of him the world needed to see."

She takes a step forward, voice rising just enough to cut the quiet.

"I didn't just plan his events. I protected his image. I sold the illusion. I ran interference when his real life got too complicated to show. You think he did that on his own?" She glances at me. "*I* was the one standing next to him when the cameras weren't rolling. *I* built the stage he stood on. And now I'm supposed to smile while you act like you belong in the spotlight?"

"I'm not here for the spotlight," Talia doesn't raise her voice, she doesn't rush, there's no flush to indicate any emotions whatsoever. "I don't need his name. I don't need the money. And I definitely don't need to compete with you.

"I'm sorry you're hurting. Truly. That's not sarcasm. And you're allowed to feel it. You should. But I didn't come into this trying to take anything away from you," she says while drawing a slow breath.

"I don't need your pity," Genevieve snaps. "I deserve Stellan. He is mine. You will never have his heart."

I start to move, but Talia lifts a hand, gentle and sure.

Her voice is soft when she says, "That's not something you steal."

Genevieve stares at her, breathing hard, looking for a place to land the next blow. But Talia doesn't flinch.

"You're not his equal," Genevieve spits. "You're a placeholder. And deep down, you know it."

"He married me. Gave me a ring. He also made me a partner in his business," she starts. "That makes me a partner."

Gen starts sobbing when Dawson efficiently steps in. He takes her arm, and guides her toward the door. She doesn't resist. Doesn't even look back.

Kate and Erin follow, Erin already guiding Kate down the hall to get her checked out. No goodbyes. No commentary. Just the exit of people who know when the important part is over.

As soon as the door shuts behind them, Talia turns to me. She doesn't pace. Doesn't fidget. She just watches me like she already knows what I'm not saying.

"She won't be a problem," she says gently. "But she's going to hurt for a while."

I nod, but she's still reading me.

"You don't think she's the leak, do you?" I ask.

"Absolutely not," she says. "She's too in love with the idea of you to betray you like that. She wanted proximity, not destruction."

She lifts her chin a fraction. It's like she is trying to figure everything out.

"You know what doesn't make sense?" she asks, voice low. "You keeping her close for that long. Knowing how she felt. Letting her believe she had something she didn't."

There's no accusation in her tone. Just observation.

"You didn't sleep with a threat," she says. "But you made one. Whether you meant to or not."

I shift slightly, but she doesn't push. She doesn't have to.

"I'm not here to judge you," she says. "I'm here to help you carry what you've built and keep it from falling apart."

She steps forward but doesn't sit. Her arms are loose at her sides. And somehow, her gentle nature makes it worse. I've handled heads of state. Shadow accounts. Back-channel takeovers. But I have never in my life been managed like this.

"So this is bigger than a leak," she says. "What's being threatened isn't Rothwell Strategic. It's... the other thing."

I lean back in the chair, exhaling slowly. "Yes."

She doesn't rush me. Just watches, patient and clear. Like she's not waiting for the answer — just for me to be ready to say it.

"I built Rothwell Strategic to be clean," I start, my voice more measured than I mean it to be. "Public-facing. Polished. Elite asset management. Legacy preservation. Corporate control."

She nods once, but says nothing. So I keep going.

"But that was never the point," I say, my throat tighter now. "The real business lives underneath. Unrecorded."

I pause — not for effect. For air.

"I get called in when something breaks. When a dynasty starts to fracture. When a name is one headline away from collapse."

Talia's eyes stay on mine. Not hard, but unwavering. She's not blinking this away. She's taking it in.

"I restructure from the inside," I continue, slower now. "I cut what needs cutting. Replace what needs replacing. I don't fix mistakes. I erase them."

I see the shift. Her focus is tightening. She can carry it. This isn't going to be too much for her.

I look at her, really look at her. "You're not horrified."

It's not a question, but she answers anyway. "No," she says simply. "Because I see what it costs you."

I freeze. Just for a second.

"I'm not excusing it," she adds. "But I'm not blind, either. You built something that protects power and that kind of structure doesn't come clean. But I see what it does to you. I know what it looks like to carry things alone."

She takes a step closer. "And I'm not afraid of who you've had to be," she says, voice calm. "But I need to know who you are when you don't have to be him."

She doesn't say it like a test. Or a warning. She says it like she expects an answer.

And that's what throws me.

Because I don't explain myself. I act. I move. I clean up what needs cleaning, and I don't leave space for questions — especially not the kind that care about who I am underneath it.

But she's not asking for justification. She's asking for honesty.

"There's a part of me that isn't clean," I say. "Not because I want it that way. But because sometimes, that's what survival looks like. And if it ever came down to protecting the people I care about…" I meet her eyes. "I wouldn't hesitate. I wouldn't ask questions. I'd cross lines and never look back."

Her face doesn't shift. Not even a flicker of retreat.

The door swings open without warning, and Frankie bursts in like a storm in lipstick and high-alert curiosity, one hand still braced on the frame.

"Okay," she says, a little breathless. "I missed something. Clearly."

Her gaze sweeps the room like she's scanning for blood. "Kate's looks like she's literally seconds away from exploding, Gen's downstairs crying like someone shot her dog, and the Dutch Wall's got a goddamn betting pool on when she's finally gonna lose her shit over Rothwell's new wife."

She turns fully, eyes locking on Talia with the sharp curiosity of someone who's already halfway to deciding if she's a threat or an icon.

"So," she says, voice tipping into a grin. "Hi. I had to meet you."

Before Talia can respond, Frankie crosses the room in three strides and pulls her into a hug like they've known each other for years.

Talia lifts her arms and returns it. Frankie pulls back, hands still on her shoulders, beaming like she just adopted a puppy.

"Okay," Frankie says, eyes sparkling. "You're tiny. You smell expensive. And I can already tell you're smarter than me, which is deeply rude. But I've decided I love you anyway."

Talia chuckles a little dazed. "That's... a lot."

"I'm a lot," Frankie says proudly.

"That's one way to put it," I say, leaning against the doorframe.

Frankie spins around, grinning like she's just been caught mid-prank. "Oh good. The mannequin speaks."

I raise an eyebrow. "I see your restraint is still legendary."

"She laughed at my joke," she shoots back, nodding toward Talia like it's a badge of honor. "Which means she has taste. You should be grateful."

I am. But I don't say it. Not directly.

"She's my cousin," I tell her.

"Unfortunately," Frankie mutters under her breath.

"She's also the reason any of this happened," I say. "She saw the threat before I did. Tracked the leak before I believed it was real. Found the Society. Set everything in motion while I was still trying to contain the fallout."

Talia turns back to Frankie, and I can see it in her face — the shift. She gets it now.

"You called them for him," she says quietly.

Frankie shrugs, but there's weight behind it. "I knew he wouldn't ask for help until the floor gave out. So I asked for him."

I fold my arms loosely, watching them both. "She doesn't work for me. Never has. Never will."

"Damn right I don't," Frankie says, smug and sunlit.

"She works at ONYX," I explain to Talia. "New bar manager. Dutch Wall."

Frankie grins. "Got promoted last month. Title bump, paycheck bump, autonomy bump. Zero Beckett bump, thank God."

Talia tilts her head. "Isn't Beckett next in line to take over ONYX?"

Frankie's expression drops like a curtain. "Oh, yeah. Technically."

She says *technically* like it's an insult.

"If that over-groomed nepotism spawn sends me one more message asking why the citrus display is three inches off center, I swear I'll glue everything in the lounge to the floor and file a noise complaint against his personality."

Talia's brows lift. "So you don't get along."

Frankie snorts. "He doesn't get along with *reality*. He thinks just because his last name is stamped on the building, we all work for him. I don't. I work for the structure. The brand. The place. He's a title. I'm a spine."

Talia laughs, surprised. "You really hate him."

"She really *doesn't*," I say, deadpan.

Frankie whirls on me. "Excuse you?"

"You don't hate him," I repeat. "You enjoy hating him. Big difference."

"Wrong," she says. "I endure him."

I look at Talia. "Last week she told him if he sent one more 'feedback audit,' she'd set the espresso machine to leak directly into his shoes."

Talia bites back a smile. "Sounds like tension."

Frankie waves a hand. "It's not tension. It's survival instinct."

"She likes him," I murmur.

"I will throw something expensive at you," Frankie says sweetly.

I just smile.

Because she absolutely won't admit it. But I see it every time she rants like she's filing emotional HR reports.

"Okay," I change the subject. "I think it's time I take my wife home."

Frankie blinks. "It's only midday."

I usually work late into the night. But not today.

"I think we've all had a day," I say, arms crossing. "And I want Talia to get her bearings at home. Meet the staff there. The ones who don't ask questions."

Frankie watches us head for the door. "Adorable," she calls after us. "Marital bonding via household power structures. Love that for you."

I don't answer. I just open the door and lead Talia out.

CHAPTER EIGHT

Talia

I've been to the ONYX before, but always in the background. Always tracking someone else. Tonight, I'm walking in beside the man the building was probably built for.

The ONYX isn't loud. It doesn't need to be. Everything about it is smooth and intentional — from the soft amber lighting to the black marble floors that seem to swallow sound. The ceilings are mirrored, but not in a way that flatters. They distort. Stretch. Make you look twice at who you are.

The air smells like money dressed up as something more polite. Like sandalwood and velvet and a perfume no one admits to wearing.

I don't stop walking. I don't look impressed. But I notice everything.

The concierge doesn't blink. The jazz drifting from the casino isn't really jazz — it's curated movement. Just like the hotel. Just like the man beside me.

This place was built to keep secrets. It's good at it.

We approach the front desk, and the concierge straightens just slightly when he sees who's walking toward him. Stellan doesn't need to speak loudly. He doesn't even need to slow down.

"Do you have what I asked for?" he says.

The concierge nods once, quick and composed. He steps to the side, retrieves a slim black envelope from beneath the counter, and hands it over without a word. Stellan takes it without looking, like he's done this before. Then he turns, just slightly, to me.

"This is my wife," he says, voice even but unmistakable. "Talia Rothwell."

The concierge freezes for a half-second. Just enough to register surprise before he recovers.

I smile — soft, controlled, a little warmer than expected.

"Talia," I say, offering my hand. "It's nice to meet you."

The man takes it, just a beat behind. "Welcome, Mrs. Rothwell."

He doesn't ask anything else. Doesn't need to. But I can see it in his eyes — the recalibration. He's adding me to a list in his head. Deciding where I belong in it.

Stellan steps forward again, envelope now tucked inside his jacket. The moment's over. We keep walking to the private elevator in the corner.

The elevator opens straight into the penthouse. Stellan hands me the envelope from the front desk. It's slim and matte black, sealed neatly.

"Backup credentials," he says. "Untraceable cards. Emergency contacts. Access to the building and its systems — including ONYX."

I turn it in my hands. It's heavier than it looks.

"For if something goes wrong?" I ask.

"For if something goes very wrong," he replies.

I open the flap just enough to peek inside. On top, a platinum credit card catches the light. My name is printed across the front: *Talia Rothwell.*

I run my thumb over the raised letters. It's not about the money. I close the envelope, tuck it under my arm, and take in the room.

The space is stunning. Breathtaking in its own way.

Floor-to-ceiling windows spill morning light across steel and glass. The furniture is minimalist but expensive — all low, clean lines and impossible symmetry. A fireplace sits untouched along one wall, framed by built-in shelves filled with books that look selected, not read.

To the left, a kitchen. Sleek. Unused, probably. But beautiful. The kind of beautiful that makes you wonder who it's meant to impress.

Past it, the dining area. A long table, ten chairs, zero softness. It feels like a boardroom got dressed up and wandered into a design magazine.

And even though it's not my taste... I get it.

"I'm sure you're exhausted," he says. "I'll show you the bedroom."

I'm about to follow Stellan when something catches my eye.

A painting, near the far wall — just off-center, like someone wanted it visible but not obvious. It's grayscale, but not flat. Layered.

It reminds me of the piece I saw in the Rothwell lobby this morning. Same depth. The kind of work that can change a person with just a brushstroke.

I step closer.

The signature is small, almost hidden in the corner.

Ophelia Duvain

I say the name once in my head, just to remember it.

Whoever this is... has talent. No one else plays with grayscales like this. It's magnificent.

I don't linger long. But I do let myself admire it. Just for a second. Just enough to let the painting seep into my veins.

"This is the bedroom," Stellan says as we step inside. "The other two rooms down the hall are guest rooms. The last one's my office."

The room is what I expected. Big. Beautiful. Designed to impress. The kind of bed that looks like it's been styled for a catalog more than a person.

There's only one.

Of course there is, we're a married couple, after all.

"So we're pretending we share this?" I ask, half-smiling as I glance at the sheets.

"We're not pretending," he says. "As far as the staff is concerned, we're together in every way."

I nod, eyes still on the bed. "Mornings, nights, holidays, events — stay close. No emotional distance. No visible tension. They need to see a marriage."

"Yes," he says, softer now.

"And no sleeping separately?" I ask, though we both know the answer.

"No," he says, meeting my gaze. "That would break the story."

I look back to him. "Any other expectations?"

He pauses, just long enough to mean it. "Fidelity."

My brow lifts. "Actual fidelity? Not just for optics?"

"Actual," he says. No flinch, no shift.

"Big ask," I murmur. "Considering your history."

His jaw tenses, but there's no heat behind it. Just memory. "I've never cheated. I don't make promises I won't keep. I walk away before things get messy."

"So you're faithful," I say. "Just not abstinent."

His expression softens, just slightly. "That's accurate."

"And you think you can do that now?"

"I know I can."

I fold my arms, more thoughtful than guarded. "You're really not going to ask how I know all that?"

He steps a little closer, voice quieter. "I am. How do you know?"

"You're high-profile. High-profile leaves patterns." I shrug gently. "Four partners last year — all quiet. Three discreet, one... not so much. None of them stuck. But you kept things clean."

He tilts his head. "The press doesn't show that."

"I didn't use press. I used everything else. Travel schedules. Press releases. Interview footage. Facial reactions. Tabloid metadata. Internal chatter. I wasn't guessing."

He watches me like he's seeing something new — or maybe just accepting something he already suspected.

"You read me like a file," he says.

I give a small smile. "I read you like a pattern."

He doesn't push. Just holds my gaze a little longer.

Glancing back at the bed, I say, "For what it's worth, I'm not pretending abstinence either."

His brow lifts, curious. "No?"

"No," I say. "I'm not in the business of unnecessary suffering. Especially when there's a six-foot solution in the same bed."

He huffs a quiet breath. "So... you're saying you'll take other partners?"

I look at him, deadpan. "No. I'm saying if I want sex, I'll ask the person whose name is on the lease."

He studies me, more amused than surprised now.

"If either of us says no," I continue, "we drop it. No negotiating. No guilt. No weirdness the next morning."

"And if one of us says yes?"

"Then we handle it like functional adults," I say. "Preferably with a towel nearby."

That earns a real laugh — short, but honest.

"I don't need this to mean everything," I say softly, not shy, just real. "But I like sex. It gets the static out of my head."

"I can work with that," he says.

I nod. "Good. I hate passive-aggressive celibacy."

We don't shake on it. That would be weird. Instead, I walk to the dresser, open the top drawer, and find what we built.

Pajamas, folded with Lorelle's precision and my preferences. Black. Soft. Functional. Nothing I didn't sign off on. We'd gone through it all together. She made sure everything matched the space. The status. I made sure it still felt like something I could breathe in. Tactical elegance, we called it. It stuck.

I choose the plainest set, a black tank with matching drawstring pants.

He's already heading to the bathroom, peeling off his jacket like this has been our routine for years. We change without spectacle. Me behind the closet door. Him in the en suite. A quiet rhythm already settling into place.

When I return, the lights are low and Stellan's already in bed. He's just in joggers, nothing else, radiating the kind of casual confidence you can't fake.

He's broad across the chest — not gym-showy, just solid. Strong in the way that makes you think about leverage. Muscle wrapped in stillness. Defined, but not for display. Like he was built for impact, not attention.

He's lying back like this isn't strange. Like we've done this before. One arm tucked behind his head, the other stretched across the sheets.

It's not performative. He's not trying to be looked at.

Which, of course, makes it worse.

Attractive, I mean.

I climb in on my side, careful not to glance again. But I already saw enough to know the angles are annoying.

"Comfortable?" I ask, as neutrally as I can manage.

"I've had worse roommates," he says.

There's space between us. At least a foot. Maybe more. It feels like a boundary, and a dare.

"Night," I say.

"Night."

We don't speak again.

I stare at the ceiling, listening to his breathing slow. He falls asleep like he trusts the world to leave him alone.

I've never known how to do that.

Eventually, I close my eyes. This is fine. It's all fine.

I wake up early and turn to my left. Stellan is still asleep.

Of course he is. I've always been the first one up.

I check my phone. It's a little after six, still early, but I've never been able to stay in bed long.

I slip out of bed and make my way to the closet. The light's soft, barely touching the edges of the room.

Everything's in its place — organized by color, season, and purpose. Lorelle and her team spent hours putting all the clothes away.

I didn't think I'd care about wardrobe coordination until she started making it feel like it was special. And I'll admit it — I love it now.
Not the clothes, exactly. The feeling of pulling out the perfect outfit.
for any occasion without having to think about it.

I run my fingers across a few hangers before choosing a slate green
blouse and slim black pants. Married, but not unapproachable.

The bathroom's quiet. Still faintly scented from last night — his
cologne, something expensive with too much depth for this early. I
shower quickly, rinsing away the stiffness of sleeping somewhere new.

I pull my hair half up — clean, and a little romantic. When I'm
finally done, I feel... good. The woman looking back at me in the
mirror is someone I know.

And she's ready.

When I walk out of the en suite, I see Stellan standing by the
window, coffee in hand, still shirtless.

"You're up early," he says, matter-of-fact.

"I always am," I say. Not monotone, but not exactly thrilled about
small talk this early in the morning either.

He looks at me fully for the first time. Hair done, makeup light but
intentional, outfit clean and composed.

"You look..." His brow lifts slightly, like he's searching for the right
word. "Official."

I smile. "That's the point."

He takes a sip of coffee. "Where are you going?"

"Rothwell," I say, meeting his eyes. "I'm ready to start."

"You're not easing into it?" he asks.

"I don't ease into anything," I reply, smoothing the cuff of my
blouse. "You put me on the payroll. You gave me a title, it's time to
do my job."

He nods once, thoughtful. "Director of Employee Relations."

"I know," I say, a small smile tugging at the corner of my mouth. "I helped write the job description."

"You think the leak's coming from inside," he says, his voice low, more statement than question.

"I know it is," I reply, steady and sure. "And this role puts me exactly where I need to be to find it."

Stellan doesn't argue. He just watches me for a second longer than necessary, before turning toward the door.

"Come on," he says. "Let's get breakfast."

We head down to the kitchen. There's a chef already there, moving between the stove and the counter like she's been up for hours.

"Good morning, sir," she says, without turning. "Mrs. Rothwell."

Stellan reaches for a mug from the counter. "Jean."

I step forward, hands relaxed at my sides.

"Jean, this smells incredible," I say, voice warm. "Are you the one behind the breakfast magic?"

She pauses and turns, her brown eyes meeting mine. There's a flicker of surprise, quickly masked.

"I handle all household operations," she says, polite but clipped.

"All of them?" I ask, genuinely impressed. "So you're the one keeping this place from collapsing under its own perfection?"

There's the faintest pull at her mouth — not quite a smile, but maybe something that used to be one.

"Yes, ma'am. I run the house."

"Well, you're doing a beautiful job," I say. "And please, call me Talia. 'Mrs. Rothwell' sounds like someone with a pearls drawer and a country club problem."

"I'll try," she says after a beat.

I catch Stellan watching the exchange, but he doesn't say anything. Just sips his coffee.

"How long have you been with the household?" I ask.

"Seven years," she answers. "Since this property was acquired."

"That explains it," I say, pulling out a chair at the island. "It feels lived in, but not by accident. That's all you."

Jean finally lets a small smile through. "Most people don't notice that."

"I'm not most people," I say, lightly. "But you already knew that, didn't you?"

She glances at Stellan, before looking at me again. "I had a guess."

I smile and glance at the breakfast she's laid out. Perfect, of course.

"I should probably admit this now," I say, lowering my voice like it's a secret. "I can't cook. Not even a little."

Jean raises an eyebrow, curious.

"Like... I've burned oatmeal. Twice. I once set off a smoke alarm trying to boil pasta."

"Well," she says, amused, "we'll keep you away from the stove."

"Wise," I nod. "But if you ever want an enthusiastic assistant who can chop things badly, I'm your girl."

That earns a real laugh from Jean. Stellan, across the island, is smiling too — one of those quiet, barely-there expressions that says more than it should.

According to the file, he doesn't smile much.

But from what I've seen, that's not the entire truth.

CHAPTER NINE

Talia

I've never liked first days. Too much energy. Too much pretending. Everyone smiling a little too wide while calculating your worth like it's printed on your forehead.

It always felt like walking into a room full of mirrors and realizing you're the only one who sees the cracks.

When I was younger, I could never explain it — how I just *knew* things. When someone was lying. When someone was performing. When someone smiled with too many teeth. I thought everyone could feel that shift in the air.

Turns out, they couldn't. That kind of knowing makes people uncomfortable.

Stellan's hand settles gently on the small of my back and, without thinking, I lean into it just enough. A crowd waits near the elevators, their cameras ready and pens poised. They knew when we'd arrive.

"They weren't supposed to be here," he murmurs.

I don't miss a beat. "Then let's give them something worth talking about."

His hand grazes my back, but I step slightly ahead, already reading the posture shifts, the cameras angling for a clean shot.

"Mr. Rothwell!" one reporter calls. "Is this your wife's first official day at the company?"

"Yes," Stellan says tightly. "But this—"

I cut in smoothly, smiling before my voice hits the air.

"It is," I say. "And I appreciate the welcome — even the surprise kind."

A few chuckles. One photographer lowers his camera, thrown off by the lack of tension.

Another reporter chimes in. "Mrs. Rothwell, what's your official role at Rothwell Strategic?"

"Director of Employee Relations."

"Did that position come before the wedding—or was it something you were offered after?" the reporter asks, his voice light, too smooth to be innocent. While his tone is polite, the implication isn't.

"Who told you to ask that?" Stellan says, his gaze narrowing.

The reporter stiffens. "It's been circulating online. Gen Redgrave posted something this morning—implying you created a role to give your wife status."

"Genevieve Redgrave runs an event company," he says, his tone clipped. "She's never been employed by Rothwell Strategic in any capacity. And she's not qualified to comment on our internal structure."

I step in gently, my hand brushing his arm—a simple reminder to soften the edge. I offer the press a smile.

"We haven't been on social media," I say, my tone almost placating. I want to give them something that would make a statement. "We've been focused on our marriage. Learning the rhythm of something new. It's private, and we've kept it that way for a reason."

A few reporters ease forward, pens still but interest rising.

"But since we're being open," I say, holding their eyes, "yes, I was offered the position after we were married, but it wasn't a favor. My background is in high-pressure team management and behavioral strategy. I've worked with law enforcement, private consulting groups, and cultural transition firms. That kind of work doesn't come with a ring. It comes with experience."

A few pens start moving again. One of the cameras dip, replaced by a more curious gaze.

A woman near the back lowers her phone and nods slowly. Another smiles faintly, already shifting her impression.

"That's all the statements we'll be making on the matter," Stellan says, voice clipped and final. "Everything else will go through our attorney, Erin Harding."

He rests his hand lightly on my back and leads me toward the elevators. Aaron is already holding the press at bay.

As soon as we're safely inside the elevator, Stellan presses the button and leans back against the wall with a groan.

"I'm sorry about that," he says, glancing over at me. "I should've seen it coming. You were prepared though."

I smile faintly. "The Society drilled media protocol into us pretty hard. Especially when we're matched with someone... high-profile."

"You made it look easy," he mutters.

"It wasn't hard," I reply, smoothing my blazer. "They just weren't expecting me to sound like I meant it."

Stellan watches me for a second. Really watches.

"I can't tell if you're a phenomenal actress," he says, "or just like that."

He thinks I'm playing a part. That this whole thing—my posture, my calm, the way I speak to people like I want to know them, not impress them—is just another layer of the role.

"I'm not acting," I say gently. "This is me."

He tilts his head, still studying.

"The ring's the only thing I didn't come in with," I say, low and unforced.

We walk toward his office, and I spot a small group already gathered—Cal, Opal, and Kate.

I know who they are before he says a word.

Cal Ames, founder of Ames Advisory. He helps powerful families hold themselves together—at least on the outside. Transitions, inheritances, reputations. He doesn't just manage legacy, he softens the damage it leaves behind. He isn't Rothwell, but he's close. Trusted. Steady. He listens more than he speaks, and when he does speak, it's with intention. People don't interrupt him. They lean in.

Opal Greer, junior analyst. Sharp, perceptive, and already wary. Her sister's history with Stellan might be over, but she's still holding a piece of it like it belongs to her. She hasn't said a word, but I can feel the resistance. She's already decided I don't fit.

"Cal," Stellan says, stepping forward and pulling him into a quick hug. "This is my wife, Talia."

Cal steps forward first. Early forties, silver at the temples, eyes like they've seen too much and still come out kind. His reputation is built on discretion, charm, and a talent for steering chaos without ever raising his voice.

"Wife," he says, like he's letting it roll around in his mouth. "Well, damn. I thought you were bluffing."

Stellan's jaw tightens a little. Barely. "I don't bluff."

Cal's grin grows. "Guess not. And you—" he turns to me, offering a hand. "—are officially the most interesting thing to happen at Rothwell in years. Not to mention stunning."

Stellan gives him a look. Cal ignores it.

"You picked a good one," Cal adds, eyes still on me.

I take his hand, shake it with just enough pressure to suggest I don't need anyone to speak on my behalf.

"I'd say 'thank you,' but I'm pretty sure I did the picking," I reply, smiling just enough.

Cal laughs, clearly delighted. "Even better."

Stellan shifts beside me.

Cal catches the look and lifts both hands like he's surrendering. "Hey, I'm just giving credit where it's due."

"You're giving commentary where it wasn't requested," Stellan mutters.

I glance between them, amused. "Do you two always do this? Or am I just the occasion?"

"Little of both," Cal says. "But I'll behave. Mostly."

I arch a brow. "Define 'mostly.'"

Cal grins. "With charm. And plausible deniability."

That earns an actual breath of laughter from me.

"This is why you're only invited to half the dinners," Stellan says, dry as bone.

"And yet somehow still seated next to the host," Cal shoots back, smug.

"Because you bribe the kitchen staff," Stellan adds, without missing a beat.

"I bribe everyone," Cal says like it's gospel. "It's the cornerstone of diplomacy."

Stellan exhales like he's tired of him, but there's a pull at the corner of his mouth — faint, but real.

I watch the whole exchange, quiet and alert. The way they move together says a lot. There's history, and comfort, and just enough friction to keep it interesting.

But what catches me most is the shift in Stellan. He's standing closer now. Not performative. Just... aware.

Because Cal's charm is effortless.

Stellan glances toward Opal. "And this is Opal Greer," he says, tone even but less relaxed. "She'll be giving you the tour today."

Opal nods once, polite but not warm. "Nice to meet you." It's the kind of "nice" people say when they've already decided it isn't.

I smile anyway. "Looking forward to it."

She doesn't smile back.

"We have something to talk about," Cal says, the tone shift so sharp it cuts the air.

"She knows everything," Stellan says, eyes still on me. "You don't have to be discreet."

"Wait," Cal chokes out. "Everything? As in secondary business everything?

"Yes," I say, unbothered. "The restructuring. I've read the ledgers. I know how the machine works."

The silence after that is rich.

Cal stares at me like I've just grown wings. Kate's eyebrows lift. Even Opal's expression flickers for the first time all morning.

"What?" I ask, tilting my head. "You thought I married a man with this much influence and didn't bother to ask what he actually does?"

Stellan laughs. Actually laughs. A real, short, surprised laugh — the kind you don't expect from a man like him.

Cal spins toward him, mock-stunned. "Did you just... laugh?"

"I love that I get to be the one to shock you with it this time," Stellan says, still shaking his head.

Kate recovers first, smoothing her hands over her tablet. "Well. Okay then. Time to work."

Stellan leans in, one hand brushing my waist like it's second nature. He kisses me.

"I'll talk to you in a bit, Finch," he murmurs, like it's meant only for me.

"You ready for the grand tour?" Opal asks. "I've been told I'm slightly more helpful than the welcome packet." Her voice is dry, not unfriendly. Like she's reserving judgment, not passing it.

I smile. "Well, I do like a good underdog pitch."

That earns the ghost of a grin. "This way."

The hall is bright and designed to feel open. Opal moves with efficiency, but not rush. She knows this place, and I can tell she knows exactly how to read who doesn't.

"This is comms," she says as we pass a set of double glass doors. "Technically strategic messaging, but mostly controlled leaks and corporate spin. Don't quote me on that."

"I wouldn't dare," I say. "Though I'll probably steal the phrasing."

A pause.

"Kate's snack drawer is in that corner office," she adds, glancing sideways. "Touch it without asking and you'll be escorted out of the building."

"I brought my own," I say. "But I might offer a trade agreement." That gets a chuckle.

She points out different divisions—analytics, investor strategy, HR clusters. I clock each nameplate, each subtle shift in tone.

"You've been here a while," I say, not a question. Just observation.

"Six years," Opal replies. "Started in internal documentation. Basically paperwork hell. Got stuck for a while before moving departments. Now I'm with risk, operations, and strategy. For the legitimate *and* underground sides. Although more work is on one side than the other."

"Risk, ops, and strategy," I echo. "So basically the department where you fix things before they become problems... or before Stellan decides to go crazy."

Opal huffs a laugh. "You'd be surprised how often those overlap."

"I wouldn't," I say, grinning. "I read the files. And I've been married for more than five minutes — so I'm fully briefed on Rothwell drama control."

We continue walking, heels soft against the polished floors as we pass a row of glass offices — sleek, minimal, all show. One of them holds a conference table no one's using but someone's always resetting. For the illusion of productivity, maybe. Or paranoia.

Opal gestures down the next hallway. "East wing's mostly risk analysis and internal operations. Also where the printer jams three times a day, and no one wants to admit they caused it."

"Cowards," I say, with mock solemnity. "I'd confess under oath if it meant fewer passive aggressive signs about paper trays."

"So," she says, side-eying me. "What made you say yes?"

"I love him because he gives me space to grow. Because when I'm lost, he doesn't rescue me—he helps me find my own way. He doesn't treat me like a housewife or an accessory. He treats me like a partner. He meets me where I'm at, even when it's messy. He pushes me to be better, not because he needs more from me, but because he sees more in me. Honestly... sometimes he believes in me more than I believe in myself," I say, not shy. Like it's the most natural thing in the world to love someone that deeply.

"I get why he picked you," she says quietly. "It's not what I expected. But... I get it."

I nod once and we keep walking. Just two people who might be figuring each other out.

By the time the elevator opens, I know exactly where I'm going next. Back to Stellan.

Kate's at her desk, typing something fast, eyes flicking between her screen and the phone pressed to her shoulder. She still manages a smile when she sees me.

"He's in there," she says, nodding toward the office door. "Go ahead."

"Thanks," I say, and mean it.

She returns to her typing like she never paused.

I cross to the door, knock once out of habit, then ease it open.

He's the only one in the office. Cal's gone. Stellan's at his desk, sleeves rolled, phone to his ear, voice low. Fully engulfed in his work. He doesn't look up.

This is where he's most himself. He's in control and focused. I know how much is slipping through his fingers and he's still holding the world like it's nothing.

He finishes the call within seconds.

"Yeah," he says into the receiver, tone clipped but calm. "Flag it for legal and route it to Harding. I'll circle back by close."

He ends the call and finally looks up at me. "How was the tour?"

"Better than it started," I say, stepping farther in the room. "Opal's sharp. And surprisingly honest."

"She likes you," he says, leaning back slightly in his chair.

I arch a brow. "Is that based on anything other than wishful thinking?"

"She didn't text me halfway through asking to be reassigned," he replies. "So yes."

I smile as I take the seat across from him. "What now?"

He taps his fingers once against the desk before sliding a folder toward me.

"Your title is Director of Employee Relations," he says. "It's not just optics. You'll have access to every department, especially internal structures—hiring, retention, conflict resolution. Anyone who's uncomfortable with you in the room probably has something to hide."

"Nice," I murmur, flipping open the folder.

"Kate set up your office next to mine," he adds, casually. "She'll be your assistant when you need one."

I look up. "Your assistant is now my assistant?"

He shrugs. "She runs this floor anyway. Might as well have her watching both of us."

His jacket is draped over the back of my chair. I hesitate for half a second, then pull it on. The sleeves swallow my hands; the fabric is warm, smooth, still carrying his scent — expensive and clean, but edged with something darker I can't name.

It calms me in a way it shouldn't.

When Stellan glances up from his laptop, he stops for just a breath longer than usual.

His gaze skims over me — slow, calculating. There's heat there. And something else. Possessive. Unspoken.

"You're cold," he says, voice low.

"I'm fine," I reply, but I don't move to take it off.

He nods once. Sharp. Like something inside him just clicked. "You can keep it," he says. "It looks better on you anyway."

Before I can answer, there's a light knock on the door. Kate steps in with a small takeout bag in one hand.

"Lunch just arrived," she says, already moving toward the desk. "Grilled sea bass for you. And for Talia—grilled chicken bowl, extra chili oil, no almonds."

My brows lift. "You remembered?"

"You scanned the menu for six seconds yesterday and your eyes kept moving back to it," Kate replies, setting the bag down.

I laugh, surprised and delighted. "It sounded good."

Stellan glances between us, amused.

Kate turns to go, but I catch her with a soft smile. "Hey—do you want to stay? Eat with us?"

She blinks, like she didn't expect the offer. "I usually—don't."

"I know," I say, still smiling. "But maybe just this once?"

Kate pauses before nodding, pulls up a chair, and unwraps her sandwich like this isn't a big deal. But it is. You can feel it in the way the air shifts. She eats like someone who never slows down—but today, she lets herself.

We don't talk much. Just small comments, shared glances, soft reactions.

Stellan doesn't interrupt. He just listens, eats, watches.

And for a moment, it feels easy. Natural. Like we've been doing this for longer than a day.

I have to remind myself this is temporary.

But I like it anyway.

CHAPTER TEN

Stellan

O f course there's something wrong. There always is. Especially when you deal with the underbelly of Vegas. They come in young, loud, reckless—full of bad ideas and borrowed time. I clean up what's left.

I read the email again, it still pisses me off just as much as it did the first time I went through it.

Subject: Strategic Clarity — Lomier

From: g.lorimer@lorimerholdings.com

To: s.rothwell@rothwellstrategic.com

Stellan,

Initiating Strategic Clarity protocol. No board contact. No legal chain. Just you.

It's about Grayson.

And what Delphine Marlowe is accusing him of.

She's nineteen. Temporary admin out of the Vegas office — staffing agency placement, two weeks in. The usual clearance. No flags.

He took her out Friday night. Car service. Dinner. Club table. Hotel suite.

She says she said no.

She says he didn't stop.

She filed the report yesterday with HR. Included her statement, and part of a voicemail she left her roommate after. She's calling it assault. Says she froze. Says she told him to stop — once, clearly — and that he didn't care.

There's no security footage from inside. But there's hallway video. Her leaving alone, fast, shaken. His room key was used again two hours later. Not hers.

She hasn't gone to police. Yet. But the agency has flagged it to legal. And if this hits the press — if even the *word* rape attaches to Grayson — it's over. For him. For all of us.

I'm not debating what happened.

I'm telling you what needs to happen next.

- Make sure the video never surfaces

- Draft a narrative: regret, misunderstanding, confusion

- Reposition Grayson: not a predator, just privileged and immature

- Discredit her gently if we must — unstable, overly ambitious, fragile

- Buy silence. Or make it irrelevant.

I don't need it pretty. I need it over.

Tell me what it takes.

— Gregory Lorimer

Chairman, Lorimer Holdings

I shake my head. Grayson, again. This isn't the first time he's acted like an untouchable imbecile, and I know it won't be the last.

He's addicted to parties and hemorrhages money like it's printed in his name. Which, in a way, it is.

His father is billionaire elite. Grayson's just the footnote—thirty-five, still chasing anything under twenty with a pulse and a social media presence.

Before I clean up the mess, again, I do what I always do. Due diligence.

> Kate. Gregory emailed. Initiating Strategic Clarity. Grayson's up to his usual shit.

> Got it. Mattie's on it. She'll pull the report, get the evidence, and loop you in.

> Add Opal. I want it fully vetted. If the girl's telling the truth, we're not covering for him.

> Understood. I'm on it.

I move on. Documents that need signatures. Approvals. I leave the public-facing side alone—it runs itself. This side, the one in the background, never stops bleeding.

My mind flickers—Talia. We've been married two weeks. She's already settled into the role like she was born for it.

Her office is always full—people come in with problems, leave with peace. She never asks for help. Never complains. She's lifted a weight off my shoulders I didn't realize I was carrying.

A ping, it's an email from Mattie, efficient as always.

Subject: Request for Full Materials — Marlowe Report
From: m.ward@rothwellstrategic.com

To: g.lorimer@lorimerholdings.com
CC: s.rothwell@rothwellstrategic.com

Mr. Lorimer,

Per directive, I'm reaching out to collect all existing materials related to the matter referenced in your recent communication with Mr. Rothwell — specifically regarding Delphine Marlowe and the events.

For immediate review and protocol structuring, please forward:

- The original HR complaint

- All written or recorded statements submitted by Ms. Marlowe

- Any internal correspondence referencing the event

- Existing footage or digital records tied to the date in question

- Legal or settlement documents currently in draft or circulation

If additional parties have seen or handled the file, kindly include names, roles, and timestamps of access.

This is time-sensitive. The faster we have everything, the cleaner the result.

Please reply directly to this thread with attachments or access credentials.

Regards,

Mattie Jameson

Executive Liaison | Rothwell Strategic

m.jameson@rothwellstrategic.com

Now all we can do is wait for Gregory's response. I'm not thrilled with the idea of bailing them out again, but it's the nature of the business.

I want to get up and go see Talia. I don't know why, but I feel like she could help with all of this. Maybe she can see something that I missed.

One more ping as I look at my laptop once more. Opal.

Subject: Repeat Pattern — Grayson Lorimer

From: o.greer@rothwellstrategic.com

To: s.rothwell@rothwellstrategic.com

Stellan,

No new evidence from Lorimer Holdings yet. Mattie's still chasing it down. I'll hold formal assessments until we have the footage and the HR thread, but I've started the background trace.

This isn't incident number two or three.

This is number ten.

Different cities. Different women. Same architecture: temporary hires, minimal oversight, limited family support, short-term contracts. He targets soft spots — intentionally. The last nine were mostly settled, mostly silenced. Four required full Rothwell intervention. Two of those required us to restructure internal leadership to shield him.

Same phrases used every time: "misunderstood intent," "overreaction," "private encounter," "confidential context."

And the same outcome: she leaves, he stays.

This is escalation, not coincidence. And Gregory knows it. I pulled the edits to the fallback language his legal team embedded into the NDA templates last spring — they were preparing for this to happen again.

If you're asking whether we can still contain this, the answer is probably yes.

If you're asking whether we should — that's a different question.

Will follow up when Mattie sends the source file.

Opal Greer

Junior Analyst | Rothwell Strategic

o.greer@rothwellstrategic.com

Now I have a choice to make. And I think it's time to pull Talia in on this side of the operations.

I grab my laptop and head to her office. When I open the door to my own, Kate looks up from her screen.

"She in?" I ask.

"Alone. And seriously, make her VP already. She's the best."

"I know," I say and I mean it, the things she's done are more than impressive.

I step inside.

Talia's made the office hers. Subtle, but undeniable. Dual monitors hum—one tracking analytics, the other a color-coded calendar that would terrify anyone without her brain.

A stack of reports. A ceramic mug that reads *"Ask me if I care. (Spoiler: I do.)"*—probably a gift. Or maybe she picked it herself, just to make people blink. A plant on the corner. Low maintenance. Still alive. A framed skyline photo—not of Vegas. It's older, maybe Chicago.

Her navy blazer's tossed over the back of the chair. Shoes kicked under the desk. She's barefoot, legs crossed, leaning forward, focused on her screen and the call she's on.

"I understand the department's at capacity," she says, voice smooth. "But if three people are logging sixteen-hour days and no one's tracking burnout, that's not resilience. It's mismanagement." A pause. "No, I'm not asking for excuses. I'm asking for solutions."

She doesn't flinch. Fingers glide across the trackpad—pulling up real-time data. She doesn't even look up.

"Then escalate it," she says. "Because when a good employee collapses, your calendar won't be what gets audited. Your judgment will."

Another pause.

"I'm not coming down on you. I'm making sure we don't lose someone who still wants to be here."

She ends the call, pulls the headset off, and turns. Finally seeing me.

"Sorry," she says, casual. "Didn't realize you were watching me."

"I wasn't watching," I lie. "I was admiring the dual monitors."

She grins. "Power move, right?"

I nod toward the mug. "Threat or confession?"

"Depends," she says, lifting it. "You asking as my husband... or my boss?"

I don't answer, truthfully, I don't think I have an answer to give.

"Lomier Holdings emailed. It's about Grayson."

She raises an eyebrow. "Again?"

"How do you know it's not the first time?"

"I reviewed the secondary client list. Lomier's a frequent flyer," she says, like it's just common sense.

I sit beside her and hand over the laptop I carried in here. "Take a look."

She goes through the emails, while I look over her shoulder. Of course, I've already looked at everything, but there's something fascinating in the way her mind works, I want to know every detail she clocks, every thought.

Another email comes in while she's looking. It's from Opal, with the footage Gregory sent over attached, and her deep dive. It's bad. Patterned. Predictable.

"He's a little boy who never learned consequences," she says, calm. "Check if the woman's after money. If she is, shut it down. If not—don't protect a predator."

We fall into work, side by side. I stay mainly because I simply don't want to leave. I like the sound of her voice. I like... not being alone.

Hell. I think I'm starting to like my wife. I'm so distracted, I don't even see the next email until Talia clears her throat.

"You've got mail," she says, laughing. "Mattie and Opal."

She catches me staring again. Only at her.

Subject: RE: Strategic Clarity Protocol – Grayson Lorimer

From: m.jameson@rothwellstrategic.com

To: s.rothwell@rothwellstrategic.com

CC: o.greer@rothwellstrategic.com

Stellan,

It's not good.

Delphine Marlowe is leveraging the footage. We flagged activity on a private media bidding forum. She's not handing it to the police—yet. But she is fielding offers from two outlets with direct links to tabloid syndicates. One bid already includes partial payment for exclusive rights.

This isn't about justice. It's about money. That works in our favor—for now.

But she's not reckless. She's smart. The video is backed up, likely to multiple locations, and she hasn't sent it yet. She's testing the water, calculating value.

Gregory's already calling it extortion. He wants us to push a private settlement immediately and cut a PR line for "emotional instability."

I don't recommend we move that fast.

She's being strategic. If we corner her, she'll go public. And if that happens, we don't just lose the cleanup—we become the story.

Mattie Jameson

Executive Liaison | Rothwell Strategic

m.jameson@rothwellstrategic.com

Subject: RE: Strategic Clarity Protocol – Grayson Lorimer

From: o.greer@rothwellstrategic.com

To: s.rothwell@rothwellstrategic.com

CC: m.jameson@rothwellstrategic.com

Adding context:

Delphine's auction is quiet but real. She's masked her IP, but the forum activity confirms intent. She's tagging the file under anonymized metadata, likely a stall tactic while she evaluates leverage.

As for Grayson, his history is catching up.

I just finished a cross-reference of past settlements. One of the former NDAs was broken six months ago. No media took it then, but if Delphine's story surfaces, that one might resurface with it. And if more than one name appears on a timeline, this goes from damage control to systemic rot.

Gregory's furious, but this is the tenth time we've smoothed his son's trail. This one may not stay clean.

It's my recommendation that we stall Gregory's press statement. Push for a negotiation path—one that neutralizes her before the sale completes.

If this leaks, it won't stop with Grayson. It will stain the Lorimer name.

Opal Greer

Junior Analyst | Rothwell Strategic

o.greer@rothwellstrategic.com

"I think you have your answer now," Talia says.

"Actually, I don't," I reply. "Any insight?"

"Clean up his mess. Then make sure Gregory knows it won't happen again," she says, like it's the most obvious thing in the world.

"Okay. How about this?"

I start typing—looping in Mattie, blind-copying Opal. Gregory doesn't need to know who else is watching.

Subject: Strategic Clarity – Immediate Containment Required
From: s.rothwell@rothwellstrategic.com
  To: g.lorimer@lorimerholdings.com
  CC: m.jameson@rothwellstrategic.com
  BCC: o.greer@rothwellstrategic.com

Gregory,

We are pursuing full suppression protocol regarding the Delphine Marlowe situation. Early indicators suggest she is actively pursuing media outlets and weighing monetary offers. Her motivation appears transactional, but the damage could outpace the spin.

This is a direct consequence of Grayson's behavior. I understand you've prioritized discretion in the past, but his pattern is no longer deniable. He's not just a risk—he's a liability.

This will be contained to the extent that we can contain it.

But understand this, if he engages in one more incident of this nature—one more scandal, one more accusation, one more compromise—you will not just lose our firm, you will lose our discretion.

Put a muzzle on your son.

Stellan Rothwell
Chief Executive Officer | Rothwell Strategic
s.rothwell@rothwellstrategic.com

"Sounds good," Talia says.

I hit send and glance at the clock. It's just shy of five and I'm ready to call it a day.

"Ready to head out?" I ask.

She nods, already slipping her shoes back on.

Kate doesn't even flinch at me spending most of my days in Talia's office anymore.

The first time I told her no meetings after five—and that I'm actually leaving—she looked like I'd announced a corporate merger with a piñata company.

Now? She likes it. It means she can leave early too.

Outside my office, I catch them—Talia and Kate—mid-conversation.

Talia's leaning on the edge of Kate's desk, hands loose, eyes warm. Kate's smiling. Not the professional kind. The real kind.

For a second, I just watch. "You ready to go, Finch?"

She looks over, already smiling. "Yep. Ready when you are."

Kate throws me a look—half teasing, half knowing—then turns back to her screen.

By the time we reach the ONYX, dusk is creeping across the sky like a bruise fading slow.

The penthouse is warm when we step inside, the lights are low, and the smell of garlic and lemon drift through from the kitchen.

Jean's at the stove. Moving like it's hers, it might as well be, she runs this place better than I ever could.

Talia slips off her coat and heads for the island. "Need a hand?"

Jean looks over, smiling softly. This has become part of the routine after work, Talia shrugging her jacket off and waltzing right into the kitchen to help in basic ways.

Without hesitating Talia washes her hands, and starts chopping. She asks questions, laughs, and leans in like she's known Jean her entire life.

She laughs again—head back, light in her eyes. She takes the time to ask about Jean's brother, her nieces, and her husband.

Until Talia came, I didn't even know Jean had a brother.

The penthouse is... different now. Brighter.

On my way to the bedroom, I pass the corner chair—her corner. A throw blanket draped across it. The spot where she works, reads, sometimes even falls asleep.

The bed's changed too. There's new, matching decorative pillows, it's more than just black fabric.

She didn't ask. Didn't announce it. I just came home from work one day, and it was done. She turned my penthouse into a home, A true one.

She's a breath of fresh air. And my world is different now because she's in it.

I just don't know what to do with that. Not yet anyway.

Later that night, I find her.

She doesn't know I'm here.

I pause in the doorway, watching her move through the bedroom. The sleeves of my shirt are rolled halfway up her forearms. Her hair's damp—towel-dried and unruly. Barefoot, pacing, muttering under her breath as she scrolls through her phone.

I should say something. Make noise. Clear my throat. But I don't.

Because there's something about this—her in my space, in my clothes, angry at something that isn't me—that makes my lungs ache.

She looks real like this. Untouched by performance. It's a version of her I don't deserve to see. But I take it anyway.

She sighs, finally glancing up. Our eyes lock.

"You're staring," she says, voice dry.

"I am," I admit.

She doesn't look away. "Do I pass inspection?"

My jaw tightens. "You always do."

Her smile falters—not coy, not flirtatious. Just... off-balance.

I push off the doorframe. I don't touch her. Don't have to. My presence is enough. I pass her on the way to the bathroom, my voice low in her ear.

"Keep wearing my clothes, Talia. See what happens."

I feel her breath hitch, just barely. She doesn't answer.

But when I glance back, she's still watching me — eyes pulsing, mouth parted, pulse visible at her throat.

And I know exactly what will happen. Soon.

Chapter Eleven

Talia

We're too close. I know that.

But I don't move. Neither does he.

His hand is braced against the wall behind me. His eyes search mine like there's an answer in them he's not sure he wants to find. His breathing is shallow. Controlled—but barely.

"I don't understand you," I whisper.

Stellan's eyes flick to mine, cool and steady. "Yes, you do. You just don't want to admit what that understanding costs you."

My breath catches.

He steps closer—just enough that I feel the heat of him, the tension coiled tight beneath his calm.

"You see me," he says, voice low. "That makes this real. That makes it dangerous."

"Is that what you want?" I ask, softer than I mean to. "Something dangerous?"

He looks at me like the answer is obvious.

"I want you," he says. "Nothing about that is safe."

He leans in—almost. Close enough I can feel the heat of him, the quiet devastation of being wanted but not touched. His voice is a whisper when it comes.

"If I kiss you, I won't stop."

I inhale, sharp and aching. "But you want to," I say.

He pulls back. Just enough to shatter the moment.

I swallow, pulse still fluttering. My hands fist gently at my sides, grounding myself.

"I should—I need some air," I murmur.

He nods once, slow. Letting me go, but not letting me off the hook. I exhale, trying to pretend my legs aren't shaking.

That's when my phone buzzes. My mother's name lights up the screen.

I shouldn't answer.

The moment I hear her voice, syrupy and sharp, I know I've made a mistake. "Well," Maribelle Cerny, my mother, starts, "I suppose congratulations are in order. Though I do wonder—was the wedding held in an alley or just a courthouse?"

My stomach knots. "It was private."

"So was the Titanic before it sank," she says with a laugh. "Talia, really. Stellan goddamn Rothwell? Of all the men in the world—you picked him?"

She doesn't pretend to not know who he is. She doesn't have to. Everyone knows who he is. What he is.

"I married the man I wanted," I say evenly.

"Wanted," she repeats, voice dripping with disdain. "Sweetheart, women like us don't want. We secure. We build. And we marry men who elevate our image, not bury it under blood-soaked headlines and silent security teams."

I pace the edge of the rug, trying to stay calm. Trying to breathe.

"You could've had Hunter. You remember him, don't you? Educated. Wealthy. And from a family with class. Not one with bodies in the floorboards," she says, like she's reciting a wine label. Like her dream for me has always been perfectly chilled and utterly soulless.

"You mean the one who sexually assaulted me at twenty?" I ask, voice monotone only because I've practiced making it that way.

"Oh for God's sake, Talia. You were wearing lip gloss and that red halter. You flirted with him. Don't act like a victim now," she snaps, the disgust in her voice so high pitched it makes my ears bleed. As if my body, my boundaries, were an inconvenience she'd rather forget.

My throat closes.

"And now this," she sighs like I've ruined a centerpiece. "Marrying a man who runs Vegas like a mafia don and dresses like a bouncer. And that dress you wore? You looked like you'd eaten a full buffet. Twice."

I say nothing.

"You used to glow," she hisses. "Pageants, galas—you used to turn heads. Your thighs didn't touch. Your jawline could slice paper. Now you're soft. You're comfortable. Do you know what men do when they get bored of soft?"

I swallow hard. "Stellan isn't that kind of man."

"No, he's worse," she snaps. "He's cold. Dangerous. And not even photogenic. If you're going to ruin the family name, at least do it with someone who looks good in press releases."

"I didn't marry for you," I bite out.

"No," she says coldly. "You married like a girl with daddy issues and a self-esteem problem. You married like a disappointment."

She's always known where to hit. Right in the ribs. Where you'll feel it every time you breathe.

"Still there?" she asks sweetly. "Or are you too busy crying in satin sheets?"

I hang up. My hand is shaking. My chest feels full of concrete and static and rage.

I don't scream. I don't cry. I feel something deep inside me crack.

She's always been awful. But never this vile. Never this cruel.

My father has always been spineless, watching from the edge of the frame like a man waiting for permission to speak.

And no matter how much it hurts, or how deep it cuts, I don't know how to stop needing their approval.

Needing someone.

I turn on my heel, take a deep breath, and go find my husband.

When I walk into the bedroom, I slam the door.Hard.

It rattles in the pictures on the wall, but I don't care. My mother's voice still slithers through my head—cutting, cruel, sweet enough to rot teeth. I won't cry, I haven't cried over her in years.

But I need to burn something down.

Stellan's already in the room. Jacket off. Sleeves rolled. Watching me like I'm an incoming storm he has no intention of stopping. "Are you okay?" he asks hesitantly, his brow furrowed.

"No."

I close the distance between us like I own it.

My hands are in his shirt, fisting the fabric, dragging him into a kiss that's all teeth and fire. He grunts—surprised, maybe—but doesn't stop me. His hands land hard on my waist, fingers flexing. He's not taking over, he's letting me lead, letting me decide how far this goes.

I kiss him like I want to leave a mark. I grind down on his thigh—hard muscle against the soft, aching heat between my legs—just to feel something.

"Let me," I whisper, lips brushing his jaw.

He doesn't answer. But his hands slide into my hair. He lifts me without effort, backs me into the wall like it's instinct—like saying yes would've wasted time. His mouth finds mine, rougher now, breath catching like he's been holding back too long.

I pull back, strip off my blouse, then reach for his belt. He watches me, eyes locked on mine, breathing heavier by the second. I open his pants and find him already hard—thick and hot, the head swollen and flushed.

I wrap my hand around him.

He sucks in a sharp breath. "Fuck," he murmurs, low and rough.

Stepping back just long enough to strip my clothes off, I let him see all of me. My nipples already tight, my thighs slick with need, every part of me flushed and strung tight.

His gaze drags down my body, slow and reverent. My breasts, my hips, the soft swell of my belly, the gleam of wetness between my legs.

I climb into his lap. Knees braced on either side of his thighs, chest brushing his, heat pressed against the rigid line of his cock.

I reach between us, wrap my fingers around him, guiding him to where I need him most. I tilt my hips and sink down slowly—inch by thick, stretching inch.

My mouth drops open. "Oh my *God*—" I gasp, the pressure is almost too much. He fills me like he was made to. My walls stretch, tight around every inch of him, my inner muscles fluttering as I slide down and down and *finally* bottom out.

I feel everything. The thick ridge of his head dragging against my walls. The way his cock pulses inside me. The pressure so deep it feels like he's in my stomach.

He curses, hands gripping my hips, not moving, just holding me there while I adjust.

"Jesus, Talia," he growls. "You feel—fuck."

I move.

Slow at first. Grinding down, rolling my hips in lazy circles, letting every inch of him rub right where I'm aching. The ridge strokes against my front wall with every pass, hitting that perfect spot that makes my breath catch.

He tries to stay still. I *feel* him fighting the instinct to take over.

But I don't want him gentle. I don't want him careful.

I want to fuck him like I'm falling apart.

So I ride him harder. Lift and drop, over and over, thighs trembling, slick sounds filling the room as I take him deep, over and over, wetter and tighter and *messier* with every stroke.

He meets my thrusts—small, sharp movements up into me that punch gasps out of my lungs.

I reach between us, fingers sliding over my clit—swollen, soaked, desperate. I circle it fast and tight, matching the rhythm of my hips.

His hand closes around mine. He slides my hand away and replaces it with his.

My orgasm builds like a freight train. No warning. No brakes.

"Talia," he groans, voice wrecked. "Cum. Now."

I break.

My pussy clenches around him, pulsing hard, my whole body seizing as I cum with a cry that tears from my throat. I can *feel* myself fluttering around him, slick and hot and throbbing.

He lets go.

Slams up into me, hard and deep, teeth gritted, hips bucking as he spills inside. I feel the heat of it—thick, hot pulses flooding me, leaking around the base of his cock as he holds me down, buried deep, every muscle locked.

His skin is still hot and damp with sweat. He smells like sex and salt and that cedar soap he pretends isn't fancy.

I press my cheek to his chest and let my leg hook over his. My body's too loose to hold itself together right now.

My fingers trail across the slope of his chest, and I clock a scar near his ribs. Tight muscle under soft skin.

I like that about him.

I trace the edge of his abs, then the line of his hipbone, watching the little jumps under my fingertips. Lazy reactions. Nothing to prove now.

He doesn't say anything. Doesn't shift. Just lets me touch. Lets me *be*.

My hand glides down to where we're still a little messy. I drag my fingers back up over his stomach, smearing the reminder across his skin.

"What had you so upset?" he asks, fingers still moving down my back.

"My mother," I say, eyes fixed on the ceiling.

His hand stills, heat pooling under his palm. "What happened?" he asks, voice lower now.

I don't look at him. "She found out about the wedding, well the marriage. She lost her shit," I say, my fingers curling slightly against his chest.

He doesn't respond, but I feel it—his whole body shifts, bracing.

"She said I should've married the boy I dated in high school. She always thought I was a fool for dumping him, even though she seemed supportive at the time. That I looked bloated in the photos. That you weren't photogenic enough to ruin the family name over," I say, letting it land flat between us.

His body tenses under me.

"She brought up the pageants. Said I used to glow. That my thighs didn't touch. That now I'm soft. Comfortable. Boring. Said men get bored of soft," I say, mouth dry.

He moves.

I lift my head as he sits up, legs dropping over the side of the bed.

"Where's your phone?" he asks, already reaching for his.

"What?" I say, blinking.

"I'm calling her," he says, like it's a done deal.

"Stellan—no," I say, sitting up fast.

He rakes a hand through his hair, shoulders tight. "She talks to you like that and you want me to do nothing?" he asks, eyes flashing.

"She's my mother," I say, jaw clenched.

"'And you're my wife. Arranged or not, no one will speak to you like that,'" he says, voice clipped.

"I know," I sigh. "But in my defense, she has never said anything this harsh before."

"So that means she's done other things."

I open my mouth. Close it. I don't know what to say that doesn't make me sound like a cliché.

"It's not like that," I mutter, picking at the edge of the sheet. "She's just... always been intense."

Stellan raises an eyebrow. Just one.

I sigh. "She had high expectations. Still does. I was her only shot, you know? Her second chance. She wanted things to be better for me."

His expression doesn't change.

"She taught me how to walk in heels at six," I say, like that somehow softens it. "Made me practice my smile in the mirror until my cheeks went numb. She just wanted me to win."

"To win," he repeats, flat.

"Pageants were her world," I go on, fast now, like if I keep talking I won't think too hard about it. "She had plans. Schedules. Diets. I was never allowed to consume anything other than water the day before a pageant. Sometimes I passed out in the car, but that wasn't her fault. She just didn't want me to look puffy on stage."

Stellan doesn't interrupt.

"She'd tape my thighs at night. Said it would train them not to touch. Gave me appetite suppressants in Tic Tac containers so the judges wouldn't notice. She said beauty had rules, and I had to learn discipline if I wanted to matter."

I pause. My throat is tight, but I keep going.

"She never hit me. Never screamed. She just... adjusted things. Pointed things out. Like how my nose wasn't photogenic from the left. Or how I needed to stop laughing so loud—it made my face look wide."

I glance at him. "She meant well," I say, and even I can hear how weak it sounds. "She said I was her masterpiece."

I don't look at him now. I can't.

"That's abuse, Finch," he says, running a finger down my cheek.

I flinch involuntarily at that word. That name.

"Why don't you like that name?" He asks.

"Are you reading me now?" I say, defensive.

"You're deflecting," he responds.

I sigh and try to steel my spine. "She calls me Finch," I say, almost under my breath. "She has for years. Since I was little." The word tastes sour coming out. "I hated it," I admit. "Still do. But I never told her that. I thought if I ignored it long enough, it'd stop stinging."

I shift slightly, sheet dragging against my skin. My fingers find the edge of the duvet and twist.

"You know what a finch is?" I ask, not waiting for the answer. "It's small. Decorative. Caged."

I glance at him, but not for long.

"She used to say I was pretty, but noisy. That I fluttered too much. That I always needed attention. She said men didn't marry birds that chirped louder than they did."

I laugh once. It's empty.

"She said I was fragile. That I had to look delicate, but act contained. Because no one respects a girl who flaps."

I press my lips together.

"I used to draw birds when I was a kid. All the time. Escape fantasies, I think. Wings and air and freedom. I used to imagine I was one. That I could fly out of the house and never come back."

My voice drops.

"She saw one of my drawings once. A goldfinch. I was nine. She smiled, tapped the page, and said, 'You got the legs wrong. They're too strong. Real finches are fragile.'"

My stomach knots.

"That's what she wanted. Something small enough to cage and pretty enough to show off."

I exhale, slow.

"I worked my whole life to be that girl. And I never got there. I was always one step behind. So that name, Finch, is something that she used to get me to the place I could never be."

I don't realize I'm holding my breath until he speaks.

"That's not what it means when I say it," he says, voice low. "I didn't call you that to mock you," he continues. "Or to cage you. I wouldn't."

He keeps going before I can say a word. "Finches," he says, "are alert. Elusive. Smart as hell. I used to watch them out at my uncle's ranch—tiny fuckers. Always gone before you blink. Always one step ahead."

His mouth twitches. Almost a smile.

"They're underestimated. But they adapt to everything. Noise. Storms. Heat. You can't pin them down."

I blink.

"Yeah," he adds, softer now, "they're beautiful. But not in the porcelain way. In the wild way. The kind that doesn't ask for permission."

I press my lips together, hard.

"I didn't know she used it like that," he finishes. "But when I said it... it meant you were the one in the room I couldn't stop looking at. The one who could fly off at any second and I'd have no way to follow."

And for the first time... Finch doesn't feel like a wound.

"I didn't used to be like this," I murmur. "Not until after twenty."

He doesn't speak right away. But I can feel it—the way the air shifts between us. He caught it.

"What happened when you were twenty?" he asks, voice low.

That is something that I do not want to talk about. I never have. Only my parents knew.

I thought my mother was protecting me. She told me not to say a word and my father agreed. Don't report it. Just stay away, but when we broke up, she wanted to know why. When I told her, it became worse.

Stellan is opening my eyes. My mother was not intense or had high expectations. She was abusive. And I'm so tired of holding everything in.

"I never told anyone the whole thing."

Stellan doesn't move. Doesn't speak.

"I was twenty," I say, eyes fixed on the space between us. "Old enough to know what it was. Young enough to be told it wasn't."

Stellan doesn't interrupt. His hands are knotted in the sheets.

"It was a fundraiser at the club. Something for the scholarship board. Hunter was home from school. Clean-cut. Everyone's golden boy."

I laugh once. Dry. "He broke up with me after graduation, and my mother hated how it looked—so when he came back, she told me to win him back."

I glance at him. "I wore a red halter. Tight. Expensive. She picked it. Said it made me look powerful. He cornered me upstairs. In one of the guest rooms. Said I looked like a fucking dessert tray. That I owed him a taste."

Stellan's mouth goes flat.

"He didn't ask. Just pushed me inside, shut the door, and started talking—fast, low, like he'd done it before. Like he had a routine."

I shift. Sit up straighter.

"He said, 'Come on, we both know why you wore that. You've been eyeing me all night.' I told him no. He laughed. Said I was being dramatic."

I pause. My hands are cold now.

"He shoved me against the wall. Hard. I hit my head. He held me there with one hand and yanked the halter down with the other."

My stomach turns.

"He said, 'You don't have to do anything. Just stand there and let me take care of it.' And then he grabbed between my legs."

Stellan's whole body locks.

"I fought," I say. "I did. I scratched him. Kneed him. He said, 'Do that again, I'll ruin you.' And I believed him."

My breath stutters.

"He said he'd tell everyone I seduced him. That I got mad when he didn't want me. That I'd been drinking—even though I wasn't. That I was unstable."

Stellan speaks—barely above a whisper. "You weren't drinking?"

"No," I say. "I was there to help with the scholarship table. I was sober. I was trying to be perfect."

I blink back the burn in my eyes.

"He forced me down on the floor. Said, 'Don't scream. No one will believe you anyway. You're not exactly a virgin.'"

My stomach turns again. I can still feel the wood floor. The smell of his cologne. The pain. The worst part, I *was* a virgin.

"He shoved himself inside me and didn't stop. I bled. He didn't care. Just kept calling me his little prize. Said I'd thank him later."

His shoulders lock. Like he's bracing for the rage to pass through him before it breaks loose.

"When it was over, I couldn't move. He tucked himself back in, looked at me like I was trash on his shoe, and said, 'Don't ruin this for both of us.'"

I feel cold now. Frozen. But I keep going.

"I cleaned myself up with the hand towel in the bathroom. Walked back downstairs like nothing happened. Sat next to my mom. Smiled through speeches."

My voice cracks. "I didn't cry until I got home."

Stellan stands. He walks to the dresser, grabs his phone, and starts dialing.

"Stellan—"

"Kate" he says, voice like steel. "I want every asset tied to Hunter Grange flagged and frozen. I want his real estate, his licenses, his passports, his charity affiliations—everything. Start digging. He's going to lose more than his reputation."

He turns to me, eyes on fire.

"You don't have to do anything," he says. "I'll carry it. I'll bury him. I'll do whatever you need."

I stare at him, chest shaking.

"You believe me," I whisper.

"Of course I believe you, you're a good actress in front of the world, but you haven't lied to me once" he says, stepping forward, voice low and lethal. "And I'm going to make sure he pays for every second he thought you were his to take."

CHAPTER TWELVE

Talia

Shortly after our talk, we fell asleep. No nightmares. No tossing. Like my body finally shut the hell up.

But now there's this beeping sound. Some annoying, high-pitched thing pulling me up from the dark.

I blink. The room's pitch black, but that noise won't stop. Shrill. Sharp. Irritating as hell. I groan and reach for my phone, squinting at the screen.

2:03 AM.

What the fuck.

I try to sit up and can't. Because Stellan is wrapped around me like some kind of heat-trapping, overly muscled octopus.

One arm across my waist. One leg over mine. His whole chest pressed against my back, breathing slow and deep like he doesn't have a care in the world.

The man sleeps like a war just ended and he's the only survivor.

I elbow him. Hard.

"Stellan," I whisper. Nothing.

I try again, louder this time. "Stellan. Wake up."

He mumbles something into my shoulder. Incoherent. Half growl, half sigh. Then rolls tighter around me. I swear to God, he tightens his grip.

"Seriously," I hiss. "There's a noise. You are suffocating me with affection and also possibly a thigh cramp."

Still nothing.

I reach back and smack his chest—not hard, but enough to sting.

"Wake up, Rothwell."

He grunts again, finally blinking. "Mmm... what?"

"There's a noise," I say, squirming in his grip. "And you've wrapped around me like you're trying to pull me inside your skin."

"'S warm over here," he mutters, already falling back asleep.

I twist in his arms just enough to glare at him.

I swear the bastard's smirking—until the sound hits him too.

He rolls over and grabs his phone.

"Hello?" His voice is rough. "Kate? Do you know what time—"

He freezes. Okay. Something's up.

"What?" he snaps, already sitting up. "Who? Where?"

My heart starts racing, I'm fully awake now. "What's wrong?" I ask, pushing up on one elbow.

He doesn't answer, just holds up a finger, telling me to wait just a second.

"We're on our way," he says. "Yes. I'm bringing Talia."

He hangs up. Tosses the phone onto the bed, hands going straight to his face.

I stare at him. My stomach is in my feet

"What happened?"

"There was another leak," he says. "It's bad."

I don't waste a second.

I shove the sheets off, ignoring the fact that I'm naked, he saw everything last night anyway, and bolt to the closet. First thing I grab—jeans, T-shirt. Doesn't matter what. By the time I'm out of the bathroom, Stellan's dressed.

"Ready?" he asks.

"Yeah," I say, grabbing my phone.

We're out the door in seconds.

ONYX is still alive—slots humming, bars buzzing, music pulsing through marble and glass.

But as we move, it all goes hollow.

Like the noise gets sucked out, leaving nothing but purpose behind.

We're not here for the lights. We're going to war.

Kate and Erin are already there, moving fast, talking faster. Both on the phone, both looking like the floor's about to drop out from under them.

"Stellan... Talia," Kate says, stepping in fast. "Thanks for coming in."

"Client list's out," Erin says, barely glancing up from her phone. "The private list. Legacy elites. Offshore ties. Names that shouldn't exist on paper, let alone online."

"It's not just names," Kate adds, jaw tight. "There are notes. Preferences. Risk flags. What they pay us to keep buried."

"And that's not it," Erin continues, voice flat. "Someone sent a flash drive to every major news outlet. Anonymous. Same timestamp. No message. No trace."

"We don't even know what's on it yet," Kate says, shifting her weight. "But legal's already panicking. So it's big."

"And the breach," Erin cuts in. "Someone got into the network—deep. Wiped our servers, mirrored them, and dumped the whole thing. Internal docs. Black files. Suppression protocols. It's already on the dark web."

Kate exhales sharply. "Encrypted access codes are getting passed around like trading cards."

"This wasn't sloppy," Erin says, eyes on me now.

"And if it all hits at once," Kate finishes, "we're looking at a meltdown across the board. People are calling left and right. Clients from both sides are dropping like flies."

"Stop," I say.

Everyone freezes. Even Stellan.

I walk to the screen, eyes sweeping the data. "The breach wasn't rushed. It was sequenced. Every file pulled in a clean arc—PR first, ops second, client records third."

Erin blinks. "That's... true. I hadn't clocked that."

"Because it's not random," I say. "They wanted the client list to drop first. Make the story about secrets and scandal—before anyone catches the structural damage underneath."

I turn.

"Erin, the press release needs to hit three things. First—acknowledgment. We confirm the breach before they do. Second—accountability. Internal audit already underway, no excuses, no spin."

"And third?" she asks.

"We shift focus," I say. "We position this as an attack on *client trust*. Not our company—*everyone* who relies on discretion. We're the victim too."

Stellan folds his arms. Watching. Letting me work.

Kate steps forward. "We'll get the legal team in on it—"

"No," I cut in. "Not yet. Lawyers hedge. I want clarity. I want voice. I'll draft it myself."

Kate hesitates. Then nods.

I glance back at the breach map.

"Also—whoever did this? They knew our internal rhythms. The flash drives were sent twenty-five minutes after the breach, but right after our shift change."

Erin frowns. "So?"

"So," I say, "that means someone knew exactly when our security team would be rotating out. That's a timing leak."

"I want the employee logs," I say, eyes on Kate. "Anyone clocking in or out between 1:15 and 2:00."

She doesn't move. "You shouldn't know how to ask for that," she says, staring hard. "Not unless you've done this before."

I turn to Stellan. "She's clear," I say. "Tell her."

He hesitates. "Are you sure?" he asks.

"I know she is," I say. "Tell her."

Kate crosses her arms. "Tell me what?" she asks.

"The marriage is real—legally," I say. "But not personal. It was arranged. On record, I'm Stellan's wife. In reality, I'm here to find the leak."

Stellan nods. "We brought her in when the breaches started compounding. Quietly. No paper trail. No press."

Kate blinks. "Who the hell are you?"

"I used to work homicide and sex crimes with the Vegas PD," I say. "Transferred to behavioral intelligence two years ago. Embedded asset investigations. I see patterns before most people know they exist."

Kate's face shifts—calculating now.

"My brain holds expressions," I continue. "Every flinch. Every hesitation. Every lie that's too polished or too fast. I don't forget faces, and I don't forget fear."

Kate stares.

"I've been watching everyone in this building since the day I walked through the front door," I say. "And I already have ten possible points of failure. One name that stands out. But I need the logs to prove it."

"Okay," she says. "I'll go get them."

Kate leaves. I walk around her desk. I pull the keyboard close, open a blank file, and start typing.

Statement from Rothwell Strategic Holdings

At approximately 1:30 A.M., Rothwell Strategic Holdings experienced a coordinated cyberattack targeting legacy records, select client files, and internal operations documentation. Immediate containment protocols were enacted, and a full-scale investigation is now underway.

By 1:55 A.M., anonymous copies of compromised data were delivered to multiple media outlets. We are aware of the breach and its intent to erode trust through illegal exposure.

For decades, Rothwell has operated with discretion, integrity, and a global standard of client care. We have served individuals and institutions from across industries and sectors—guided always by confidentiality, not controversy.

That remains unchanged.

We have engaged independent security teams to assist with forensic review and are cooperating fully with cybercrime authorities. Clients affected by this breach have already been contacted directly.

We are not hiding. We are here. We are acting.

This is not the first time someone has tested us.

It will not break us.

"Perfect," Stellan says. "Send it."

It's been a few weeks since the massive leak, we got it under control relatively quickly, thankfully. Finally, we're all getting back into the typical swing of things around here.

We're getting up from lunch when Stellan grabs my arm, stopping me.

"Can I talk to you for a minute alone?" He asks.

"Sure," I reply.

He pulls me out of the chair and into the hallway, glancing around once, grabs my wrist and tugs me into the storage closet before I can argue. The door clicks shut behind us.

He turns me around and kisses my neck as he slides the zipper down, slow as sin.

He skims his fingers along the newly exposed skin, brushing the curve of my spine. "You knew exactly what you were doing the moment you put this on."

I don't answer. I can't. My voice would betray me.

The dress loosens, the straps sliding off my shoulders with a soft whisper of silk. Gravity does the rest, pooling the fabric at my feet like a sigh.

His hands glide from my waist up to my ribs, thumbs brushing beneath the lace edge of my bra.

"This isn't very professional," I whisper, trying for humor that falls flat under the crack in my voice.

He hums low. "Neither is the way you moan my name."

My stomach flips.

His lips find the curve of my neck, then my shoulder, each kiss slower than the last — a deliberate tease that makes my knees tremble.

"You always this reckless?" I manage, breath shallow.

"Only with you," he murmurs.

His hands find my hips, guiding me back against him. I feel him — solid, hot, impossible to ignore. My breath hitches as his mouth returns to my skin, trailing lower.

"We shouldn't—" I start, but the protest is weak. Embarrassingly weak.

"We're already here," he whispers. "Might as well make it worth the risk."

I shudder as his hands explore lower, his control maddening. The tension in the room coils tighter, hotter, until breathing feels optional.

And when he finally spins me to face him, eyes dark and hungry, I don't hesitate. I crash into him, mouth to mouth, devouring the last thread of restraint we pretended to have.

The storage room will never be the same.

"Shhh," Stellan mutters, pressing me gently into the shadows. "You want people to see you pressed up against a mop and a case of champagne?"

"I'd rather they see me doing that than see me shoved in here with you."

His breath ghosts against my temple. "Liar."

I shove at his chest. It's like moving a statue.

We shouldn't be doing this. Not now. Not when everything's falling apart — the leak, the files, the Lomier connection hanging over all of us like a loaded gun.

"We have too much going on," I breathe, voice catching. "This isn't smart."

His hand curls around my wrist, warm and steady, anchoring me like he can feel me slipping.

"I know." His voice is low, rough, like gravel under silk. "But I need you."

The way he says it knocks the air straight out of my lungs.

He needs me.

And God help me, I need him too.

I don't even register who moves first. One second I'm standing, pulse hammering in my throat — the next, his mouth is on mine, stealing every ounce of air.

The kiss isn't soft. It's not careful. It's everything we've been shoving down finally breaking loose. Rough hands on my waist. My back slamming into the wall hard enough to rattle the mop behind me. His body pressing into mine like he can't get close enough, like he wants to crawl inside my skin and stay there.

I grab fistfuls of his shirt like I might float away if I don't hold on. My body's already arching into his, desperate for friction, for contact, for more.

Clothes scrape. Fabric shifts. His mouth trails heat along my jaw, down my throat, leaving a path that makes my knees threaten to buckle.

There's no room for thought. No space for reason. Just want.

Just him.

The door clicks shut behind us as we step back into the hallway. My hair's a mess. His tie's crooked. We barely glance at each other — neither of us trusting ourselves to speak yet.

I don't regret a damn thing.

His hand brushes against mine like we can't afford to touch, but neither of us wants to break the connection entirely.

As we walk back to the office, Kate comes toward us—running, more like it.

Behind her are two people I recognize the second I see them.

"Rafe and Gareth," I say out loud.

Stellan glances at me. "Who?"

"Rafe Donnelly and Gareth Keane," I say. "Homicide detectives. I worked with them."

Stellan's eyebrows lift. Just slightly.

Kate skids to a stop. "We didn't call them," she says, breathless. "They came on their own."

"They don't move without a reason," I say.

Rafe locks eyes with me. I don't like what I see there. "Talia," he says. "Figured you'd be here."

Gareth nods. "We need to talk."

"That sounds personal," Stellan says, his voice unreadable.

"It used to be," I answer, calm. Honest. "It ended."

Rafe doesn't move. But his eyes stay on me longer than they should.

"It never really ended," he says, quieter now. "We just stopped pretending we could make it work in that job."

"Rafe," I say, my voice a notch lower. Warning.

But he steps half a pace closer. Not touching. Not threatening. Just inviting something that isn't coming.

"I still think about you," Rafe says. "You know that."

"I didn't know that," I answer, voice steady. Barely.

"Well, I do," he presses. "Maybe we could meet up. Grab coffee."

"Sounds like you're asking a married woman out," Stellan says, stepping forward and placing his hand on my waist.

"Maybe I am," Rafe counters, turning fully toward him. "We both know something else is going on. She wouldn't marry someone who doesn't love her like she deserves."

"We're here for a reason," Gareth says, taking a step between the two. "Let's stay on it."

Stellan's eyes move from Gareth to Rafe, then back to me.

"They're homicide," he says. Not a question.

I nod slowly. "Yeah."

"You working something for them?" he asks, voice thoughtful, like he's already fitting the pieces together but wants to hear it from me first.

"No," I say, sharper than I meant.

I turn to Gareth. "So why are you here?"

He pulls a folded document from his coat pocket. "Stellan Rothwell, you're under arrest for felony murder, obstruction of justice, conspiracy to suppress evidence, and unlawful influence over public officials," he says.

He steps forward and cuffs him.

"You have the right to remain silent," he says. "Anything you say can and will be used against you in a court of law…"

Stellan doesn't fight it. Doesn't speak.

"We'll get you out," Erin says, voice tight.

Gareth gives her a nod and starts walking Stellan out.

Rafe lingers, looking at me. "You could've told me," he says, shaking his head.

He doesn't wait for a reply. He turns and walks after Gareth, leaving me standing there, alone.

"Now what?" Kate asks.

"If they're charging him, they must think they've got enough to hold him," I say, turning to Erin. "What are we looking at?"

Erin nods, already flipping through papers. "Felony murder's serious—they won't move unless they've got something solid. But we'll force discovery, request bond, and start ripping their timeline to shreds before they even get to arraignment."

"Let's get going," I start. "Kate, call in reinforcements, but don't say where Stellan is. I want time to read people. I want to see who's behind this."

"You think it's from within?" Kate asks.

"Absolutely," I say.

Within the hour, the whole floor is alive. Buzzing. Moving. Hunting.

They're not just scrambling to protect Stellan. They're trying to save the company.

"We need to cross-reference internal comms with external log-ins," Dawson says, pacing with a tablet under his arm. "I want to know who accessed anything flagged Level Two and up in the last seven days."

"I already flagged five anomalies," Beckett says, spinning his chair toward a secondary screen. "One of them rerouted through a dead ISP. That's not clumsy. That's *hiding something*."

"I'm pulling all engagement files Opal and I marked high-risk last quarter," Frankie says, phone wedged between her ear and shoulder. "If we missed something, it's buried in those."

"I'm in comms with legal," Opal says, typing fast. "We're prepping a shadow report. Anything that helps question the credibility of the charge—we'll have it ready before the DA finishes breakfast."

Kate's walking between them, not flinching. "Good. Double it. Nothing gets out that we don't control."

Cal steps in from the hallway, arms full of printouts. "I pulled every flagged server trace from the past six months," he says. "Somebody buried something three layers deep. I've got an idea where to start."

Erin's in the center, eyes sweeping the room like she's tracking a battlefield. "Focus on the leak," she says, sharp and clear. "Everything else is noise until we lock down the source."

Everyone moves while I watch.

Dawson stalks the floor, reading code like it personally offended him. His hands clench and unclench at his sides. Sharp. Focused. Angry. But not reckless.

Beckett's a blur of motion at the corner terminal, tabs flying across three monitors. His mouth moves as he talks to himself, half-coding, half-interrogating the system. Jaw tight. Shoulders squared. Determined.

Frankie's on the line with someone—legal maybe. Her tone doesn't waver, but her typing has urgency in it. She doesn't sit. She paces. Her heels click like a clock counting down.

Opal's calm. Too calm. She speaks in short bursts, precise and polished, like she rehearsed it before anyone could ask. Her posture's closed. Shoulders tucked in. She's shielding something—I just don't know what yet.

Cal's at the back wall, sorting through printouts by hand. Methodical. Focused. His lips move silently, reciting names under his breath. His eyes never leave the paper. He doesn't even know I'm watching him. That tells me the most.

Kate moves like a metronome—checking screens, calling out orders, snapping things into motion. But I catch it. One moment. One crack. Her hand pauses on the glass wall near her office, pressing there just a beat too long before she pulls away.

I see it all.

Not because I'm suspicious. Because it's what I do. This is what I'm built for.

They showed up. They moved. They are fighting.

And for that—for the first time since this whole damn spiral started—I feel something real in my chest.

Gratitude.

Now it's my turn to fight for them.

CHAPTER THIRTEEN

Talia

I am so much better than this. One week. It's been one week since Stellan was arrested and I can't find anything to help.

Everything is tilting on it's axis. The judge said no bail, with his wealth and influence, he'd be a flight risk. I get it, but I know he's being framed.

Erin started investigating. The police have some really big evidence. Things that could actually convict him for life.

While looking through it, I notice the anonymous tip and file that away. I'm thinking this could match the leak. The same person could be behind both.

There are affidavits and surveillance of Stellan being close to where the alleged murder took place.

The number one file they have is something Stellan cleaned for a client where they were being framed for a murder. He worked tirelessly on this and if he can cover it for someone else, he can do it for himself.

There is one thing that the police don't have. A body. Or any physical evidence. Everything is circumstantial.

"Talia," Erin says, breath tight, "I just filed the injunction against the DA."

I stand. "What did you find?" I ask.

"She fast-tracked the bail denial on sealed evidence—no judicial review. And Stellan's been blocked from counsel contact for over thirty-six hours," she says, her voice low but urgent.

I don't flinch, but the chill in my blood is instant.

"That's pretrial misconduct," I say, already moving. "Due process violation, possible civil rights breach. Get me the intake logs—if he was processed without defense contact, we escalate. I want the original motion language from the bail hearing. Verbatim."

Erin nods, already dialing. "You want us to move for full judicial review?" she asks.

"No," I say. "Not yet. First, we subpoena the chain of custody for the sealed evidence. If there's even one tie to Lomier... we go nuclear."

"And the judge?" she asks again.

"If this connects, we don't file a complaint," I say. "We call the press."

I can hear pounding just outside. Running feet. Heavy. So male obviously. That's when Dawson rounds the corner in my office.

"We have a huge problem," he says. "Check out socials and turn on the news."

I don't ask. I cross to the wall-mounted monitor and flip it to the news feed.

The screen sharpens on Karolina Meade, blonde, poised, and deadly-serious behind the sleek Vegas Today anchor desk.

"Good morning. I'm Karolina Meade, and this is your Vegas Today Morning Report.

We're following a developing story shaking the foundations of one of Las Vegas' most powerful institutions."

The red banner rolls across the bottom.

BREAKING: STELLAN ROTHWELL ARRESTED — FELONY MURDER CHARGES SHAKE ROTHWELL STRATEGIC HOLDINGS

"Stellan Rothwell, CEO of Rothwell Strategic Holdings, was taken into custody by the Las Vegas Metropolitan Police Department. The arrest follows weeks of speculation after a series of anonymous leaks implicated Rothwell in the cover-up of a violent crime involving one of his firm's high-profile clients. Rothwell, long regarded as one of the city's most private and powerful corporate figures, is now facing four formal charges: felony murder, obstruction of justice, conspiracy to suppress evidence, and unlawful influence over public officials."

The feed cuts to shaky footage. Stellan, hands cuffed behind his back, jaw tight as he's led out of a restricted exit by plainclothes detectives. Cameras flash like lightning.

"While Rothwell's legal team has not issued a statement, the arrest has already triggered shockwaves across the city's political and financial networks. Even more controversial is the timing of Rothwell's recent marriage to strategic analyst Talia Cerny, now Rothwell—a union that some are calling a calculated move to secure spousal privilege during an impending investigation."

The camera cuts to a press line outside the LVMPD headquarters.

"Law enforcement officials involved in the arrest have released brief public statements."

[Cut to clip – Detective Gareth Keane]

"This remains an active homicide and obstruction case," says Detective Gareth Keane, LVMPD Homicide Division. "The charges are serious, but early. No conclusions until due process runs its course."

[Cut to clip – Detective Rafe Donnelly]

"The arrest followed internal review and procedural steps," adds Detective Rafe Donnelly. *"We're not speculating—we're following facts."*

[Cut to ADA Corinne Eddings, on courthouse steps]

"We've formally charged Mr. Rothwell with felony murder, obstruction of justice, conspiracy to suppress evidence, and unlawful influence over public officials," says Assistant District Attorney Corinne Eddings, standing behind a podium lined with microphones. *"This is about accountability. Power, money, intimidation—none of it puts you above the law."*

She leans slightly into the mic.

"For far too long, certain men in this city have hidden behind corporations and bought silence with threats and favors. That ends now. There are no special rules for the Rothwells of the world."

She smiles. It's not for the press—it's personal.

"And let this be a message to anyone who thought aligning with him would protect them: no name, no marriage, no legacy will shield you from the consequences of your choices."

I don't wait for the anchor's final word. The second Corinne Eddings' smug smile flickers off-screen, I grab the remote and cut the feed.

"This wasn't a press statement. It was a threat. And it wasn't about Stellan—it was about someone else entirely," I murmur, eyes still fixed on the blank screen, the shape of her smirk burned into memory.

I grab my phone and swipe open socials. The top trends are a disaster.

#RothwellMurder #VegasFixerGoesDown #CEOInCuffs

Clips of his arrest are everywhere—low quality, shaky angles, but they've already been slowed down, dissected, set to dramatic music like it's a trailer for a crime docuseries.

I scroll further. A post from a verified account.

Felony murder, obstruction, conspiracy. Vegas finally takes down its ghost king.

Another one that is even harsher.

Rothwell's always cleaned up messes. I guess this time, the body was his.

I did find something... interesting. A throwaway tweet buried in a thread.

"Look at this post," I say, turning the screen toward them. "I think this is something worth looking at. Eddings commented."

Dawson leans in. Erin does too.

It's a throwback photo someone posted—Grayson Lomier, arm slung over the back of a velvet couch, champagne in one hand, surrounded by shadowy figures at some club launch.

The caption's a joke.

Remember when Vegas royalty looked like this?

But it's the comment underneath that matters. It's Corinne Eddings.

Still the only man who ever knew how to play the long game. Everyone else just followed his lead.

Erin blinks. "Wait—is that—"

"She posted that two years ago," I say. "Before she was ADA. Before she was even in the courthouse full-time. And she hasn't deleted it."

Dawson frowns. "She's calling him a strategist."

"She's calling him a kingmaker," I correct. "We sent Gregory an email after Stellan cleaned up his mess for the tenth time, telling him that if he doesn't work on Grayson, we're dropping him."

"Maybe Kate can see what his email says," Erin starts, while Dawson grabs Kate. "Maybe Gregory responded."

I didn't think about that. If Gregory threatened Stellan, his company could try to retaliate.

"You asked for me?" Kate says, following Dawson in my office.

"Can we get into Stellan's email to see if Gregory Lomier responded?" I ask.

Kate glances up from her screen. "Yeah, but even I don't have deep access to everything," she says, voice tight. "There's a secondary layer on some of his flagged clients. Gregory's one of them."

That gets my attention.

"You mean he locked you out of his system?"

"Not completely," Kate replies, "but there are folders I can't touch without a clearance code. He built them that way—so if anything ever went wrong, only he could detonate it."

"Or protect it," I mutter.

Kate looks at me. "What are you thinking?"

"I'm thinking I know who can get in," I say, already opening my phone. "And it's time I call them."

"Who's 'them'?" Erin asks, one brow lifted.

"Juno and Iris," I reply, my fingers already flying across the screen.

I listen to the phone ring before Iris answers.

"This is early for our check in," she says.

I just had a check in with her yesterday. Since we only do it once a week now, it's not normal for me to call. Especially on the encrypted line.

"Is everything okay?" She asks.

"I need you and Juno," I start. "We need to get into Stellan's email. The secure section."

"Okay," she says. "I'm heading into Juno's office now."

A second or so later, Juno comes on the line.

"Hey, Talia. Iris told me you need into Stellan's server. I got it."

"Already?" I ask.

"You think his firewalls scare me? Please. I'm halfway through his comm logs."

Kate leans in. "Can she access the secure folders?"

"Already there," Juno says. "What exactly are you trying to find? Legal threads? blacklists? Encrypted security logs?"

"All of it," I say.

"All of it," she repeats, flat.

"Yes."

She pauses. "Okay. I'll open a back door. You'll have direct access from your device. Just don't trip the flags. He set a few watchdogs in there—if you hit the wrong trigger, the whole thing shuts down."

"I won't."

"Iris and I are off comms after this," she adds. "What you find is yours to deal with."

"Understood."

She disconnects.

I click on several folders and I don't need to enter anything. It just shows me everything I need to see.

I go where I need to be. His email. There are several unread ones that need attention. But the subject and sender that catches my eye is Gregory Lomier.

He responded to the email we sent about his son.

Subject: RE: Strategic Clarity – Immediate Containment Required

From: g.lomier@lomierholdings.com

To: s.rothwell@rothwellstrategic.com

CC: m.jameson@rothwellstrategic.com

Stellan,

Understood.

I won't insult your intelligence with excuses. What happened with Delphine is unacceptable, and Grayson's behavior has crossed the line—again.

I've made it clear to him that this will be the final incident. No more scandals. No more headlines. If he doesn't clean up immediately, I'll cut him off. Access. Funding. Name. Everything.

You will not lose Rothwell Strategic. I value our alignment too much to risk it on his recklessness.

Consider this message received. And acted on.

– Gregory Lomier

Chairman, Lomier Holdings

"Well that's interesting," Kate says.

"We always knew Stellan was set up. He wouldn't kill someone for no reason. Not unless it was earned," I say, rising to my feet.

I glance at Erin, then down at the folder in her hands. "It's not definitive," I say. "But it points to Grayson Lomier."

Erin scans the page, frowning. "Gregory threatened to cut him off."

"And Corinne?" I add, voice tightening. "She wasn't obsessed with the case. She was obsessed with *Grayson*."

The silence between us shifts, heavier now.

"She was circling him," I say. "Protecting him. Or trying to. That's not nothing."

Erin nods slowly. "It's not proof—but it's a hell of a red flag."

I look at Kate. "Can you call Gregory Lomier?"

"Of course," she responds, while walking out.

"Kate," I say before she can leave. "Make sure he brings his son."

"Got it," she says.

"Erin. I want you in the room when Cal and I confront them," I say.

She smiles like she is taking joy from this. "Absolutely," she says.

"About that," someone says from my doorway. I look to see Cal standing there. "We need to talk."

Everyone leaves Cal and I, Dawson closing the door on his way out. "What's up?" I ask.

He hesitates, shoulders tense like he's been holding something in too long. "I can't do it," he says finally, voice low.

I study him. "Do what?"

"Run the damn floor," he says. "Keep the team motivated. Keep things moving. I thought I could. Beckett and I both did. But…"

He trails off, shakes his head.

"Stellan made it look easy," he says. "And it's not. There are decisions stacking up faster than we can make them. Everyone's looking for direction, and I don't have it. I'm just trying to keep the lights on."

I stay quiet, letting him say what he came here to say.

"I know it's not your job," Cal continues. "But they listen to you. You walk into a room, and people stop spiraling. You talk, and they remember what they're doing."

He looks at me—really looks at me.

"Can you take the lead? Just until he's back. For him. For all of us."

I don't hesitate. I step forward and place a hand on Cal's arm.

"You did everything you could," I say. "No one expected you to carry all of it."

His throat works as he nods, eyes fixed on the floor like he's trying not to fall apart.

"I've got it," I say gently. "Just breathe. I'll take it from here."

I see the real Cal—not the one always cracking jokes or pushing too far.

Just a man who's tired. Who tried.

Subject: Interim Executive Leadership

From: t.rothwell@rothwellstrategic.com

To: All Staff

Team,

Effective immediately, I will be serving as Acting CEO of Rothwell Strategic Holdings until Mr. Rothwell's return.

Operations will not pause. Stability remains our mandate. Department leads will receive updated directives within the hour. For any cross-functional or client-level concerns, route them directly to my office.

This company has always operated under pressure. We don't flinch. We don't fold. And we do not let an external narrative dictate who we are.

You have a job to do.

So do I.

Talia Rothwell

Acting CEO | Rothwell Strategic Holdings

t.rothwell@rothwellstrategic.com

"Hey," Kate says, popping her head in. "Lomier will be here within the hour."

"Wow. That's quick," I reply.

"He sounded... concerned about the summons. I'm guessing that's what lit the fire under his ass."

I nod and turn back to my screen.

The next hour is a blur of check-ins with department heads over company chat—restructuring teams, reaffirming priorities, holding the tone Stellan set, even if everything under it is shifting.

When Kate returns, she doesn't have to say much.

"They're in the conference room," she says. "Erin's with them."

Erin's already seated. Gregory Lomier sits at the head of the table, polished and cold. Grayson lounges beside him like he's the one doing us a favor.

"Thank you for coming," I say, taking my seat across from them. "We have some things to clarify."

Gregory folds his hands. "We're here because I don't want this to escalate further."

"It already has," Erin replies. "And you know why."

Kate cues the monitor.

Opal's compiled file spills across the screen: screenshots, blog archives, recovered posts—Corinne Eddings' digital obsession with Grayson Lomier. Photos. Comments. Mentions. And a timeline that leads straight into her current position in the DA's office.

"She was fixated," Kate says. "And this wasn't passive."

Grayson scoffs. "She was annoying, not dangerous. I mean—yeah, I slept with her. Once. Maybe twice. She got weird about it."

Gregory's gaze sharpens. "You said it was nothing."

"It was," Grayson says quickly. "But she kept showing up. Kept talking about how Rothwell was in her way. How I needed to be out from under it. From under you. From under Stellan."

"And you thought that wasn't worth mentioning?" Erin snaps.

Grayson shrugs. "She wasn't the only one talking. Gen was worse."

"Gen?" I ask.

"Genevieve Redgrave," he mutters. "Corinne's best friend. She's the one who told Corinne to go after someone big. Said Rothwell was untouchable until someone made him bleed in public."

I glance at Erin. Her eyes are already locked on mine.

"Did Genevieve have access to anything on our end?" Kate asks.

"Maybe," Grayson says. "She and Corinne used to share every-thing. Said we were soft. Said Stellan played too clean."

Gregory stands, hands gripping the back of his chair.

"I'm done," he says. "I've protected you long enough. You had Rothwell watching your back, and you sold that out for pillow talk."

"I didn't sell anything," Grayson says, rising now, voice pitching higher. "I just—she was there. I didn't think she'd actually—"

"You didn't think at all," Gregory says. "I'm cutting you off. Effective immediately."

Grayson blanches. "No—Dad, don't—"

"Access. Trusts. Shares. Gone."

"I'll fix it. I swear. Just—just don't do this. I didn't know—please."

I stand.

"If he's still on payroll, if he still has a badge, if he even has a seat in one of your boardrooms—Rothwell is done with Lomier."

Gregory nods once.

Grayson turns toward me, face blotched red. "You bitch—"

He takes a step forward. Dawson is there before I need him, a wall of muscle with one hand to Grayson's chest.

"Don't," Dawson says evenly.

Grayson seethes, fists clenched. But he doesn't move. Kate opens the door, "Out."

Gregory doesn't speak again. They leave together—Grayson cry-ing, Gregory ignoring him.

"Do you think Grayson is behind the leak?" Kate asks, with Erin listening intently.

"Not Lomier. I think Corinne and Genevieve are who we need to look into," I say.

"Both?" Erin asks.

"More Genevieve. It sounds like she was using Grayson and Corinne. She wants Stellan in ruins, but something doesn't add up," I say.

"What do you mean?" Kate asks.

"Well, all this didn't start until after I came," I say, eyes still on the file, "but the leak itself started before."

Kate frowns. "So it's not Gen?"

"No," I say. "She didn't start it. She's not that careful. The leak is clean—controlled. Whoever did it knew exactly where to plant every thread."

Erin leans in. "Then what's she doing?"

"She's feeding it," I say. "Hard. Every whisper, every half-truth, every convenient detail—she's pushing it out like it's gospel. She's loud on purpose. A distraction."

Kate blinks. "She's the smoke."

"Exactly," I say. "The louder she screams, the harder it is to trace the source. She didn't light the fire. But she's making damn sure no one sees who did."

Erin exhales slowly. "So we've been chasing the wrong one."

"Not wrong," I correct. "Just second. And now it's time to look past the noise."

We get back to work. Our only goal is to free Stellan, so when we got enough on that damn ADA, we called in reinforcements.

"This better not be bullshit," Gareth says, walking into the building with Rafe following closely behind.

"We wouldn't have called if it was," I say.

"Let's hear it," Rafe says.

Kate doesn't wait. She pulls up the screen and starts scrolling through the compiled files. "Corinne Eddings. Assistant District Attorney. History of association with Grayson Lomier. Multiple social connections. Public posts, private accounts, indirect financials."

Erin takes over. "Six months ago, she filed a complaint with the DA's office targeting Rothwell. No action taken. Two weeks later, she requested investigative clearance and began laying groundwork for sealed evidence review. No oversight. No judicial transparency."

I step forward. "She's been in Grayson's orbit for over a year. We pulled post history, donations, a trail of small but consistent financial ties to people connected with Lomier Holdings. We're not speculating. We're showing you a pattern. And a motive."

Rafe glances at Gareth.

"Is any of this even legal?" Gareth asks. "You're not feeding us some illegally hacked bullshit, are you?"

"No," I say. "Everything here was pulled from public records, campaign disclosures, social posts, and court logs. No backdoors. No surveillance. We built this clean."

Kate nods. "It holds up."

Rafe stares at the screen like he wants to punch it.

"So she weaponized us," he mutters. "Used the badge, used the system, and used us to take down a man who wasn't guilty."

"She used your reputation," I say.

Gareth's hands are fists now.

"She built a case on garbage," he says. "And we put our names on it."

"I know," I say. "But this time? You get to take the shot."

Chapter Fourteen

Stellan

I'm free.

Well—not exactly. Out on bail, waiting to see if today's the day the charges get dropped. If Erin's motion hits, it will be. She's earned extra vacation days after this.

We step out of the car and the flashbulbs hit like lightning.

Talia's arm is looped through mine. Security flanks us like shields. Erin's ahead, already barking at someone in a DOJ windbreaker.

I think about Rafe. I shouldn't care.

He's no threat. A flirt with too much bravado and not enough brain.

I know how people like him look at women like Talia. How easy it would be — a laugh too long, a touch too familiar. How she might have smiled back just to keep the peace. How he might have convinced himself it meant something.

My jaw tightens.

I keep my head up. Keep moving. But every step feels like it's grinding bone.

The press starts screaming.

"Mr. Rothwell, do you have anything to say about the felony murder charge?"

"Mrs. Rothwell, why are you still standing beside him?"

"Is it true you're planning legal action against the DA's office?"

"Why target the ADA? Isn't this just retaliation?"

I don't look at them. I don't look at her either.

We walk into the courtroom and see Corinne Eddings already seated at the prosecution's table—tight bun, navy suit, eyes locked on a screen in front of her. She's leaning in toward the man beside her.

District Attorney Marshall Strand.

He's not watching the room. He's talking. Corinne nods, sharp and fast, like she's taking instructions from God Himself.

He never shows up for trials. So they're not backing off. No dismissal. I'm a headline they want framed on the damn wall.

The judge enters. Gavel drops. Showtime.

Erin stands first. This isn't just a courtroom. It's a crucifixion.

"Your Honor, we're moving for immediate dismissal of all charges against my client with prejudice. The state's case isn't just flawed—it's poisoned. And the prosecution knows it."

Strand rises, measured. "We'll be contesting that. The murder charge was based on testimony, timeline, and motive."

The judge narrows his eyes. "You're claiming misconduct, Counselor. Show me your proof."

Erin doesn't blink. Doesn't smile. Just steps forward like she's been waiting to drop the hammer all week.

"Let's go down the list," she says.

She clicks the remote.

First, the screen shows transcripted messages between Detectives Gareth Ellison and Rafe Donnelly. A formal report. Timestamped. Admissible. One line highlighted.

I told them the truth. The timeline. My alibi. But they buried it. Now they want to help? They made me feel somewhere deep down, that maybe I deserved it.

"Rothwell was never at the scene. Security logs confirm he was two buildings over, with video. We cleared him within 48 hours. ADA pushed back. Said it wasn't relevant."

Murmurs ripple. The judge leans forward. Corinne stays silent.

Erin clicks again.

"Second, your motive's gone. The prosecution's narrative relies on a manufactured conflict between my client and the deceased. The supposed witness? Grayson Lomier."

Erin clicks again. The screen comes to life—**Deposition: Grayson Lomier – Exhibit C**.

Grayson lounges at the table like it's just another board meeting. Cool, detached, too casual for what's about to come out of his mouth.

"Mr. Lomier, please confirm. Did you have a personal relationship with Assistant District Attorney Corinne Eddings?" Erin asks, voice crisp and direct.

"Sure. We slept together. Once or twice," Grayson replies, leaning back in his chair, casual.

Of course he's smug. He's always smug. The kind of arrogance only born sons can afford. And Corinne—God, I should've seen it. She wasn't prosecuting justice. She was chasing a boy who never promised her anything.

"Would you define that as a romantic relationship?" Erin continues.

"Not really. I mean, I didn't," he says, shrugging without hesitation.

"I think she thought it was something. She used to act like we were exclusive—messaging all the time, checking where I was. But to me, it was just casual. She was a number," he adds, indifferent.

"And during that time, did she ever discuss Stellan Rothwell?" Erin asks.

"Constantly," Grayson answers, almost amused.

"Can you be more specific?" she prompts.

"She hated him. Said he got away with everything. She'd get all worked up when we'd talk about Rothwell. Her and Gen—they'd joke about taking him down. Like... get rid of him for good," he says, tone flat and dismissive.

"Did she ever imply she'd use her legal position against Mr. Rothwell?" Erin asks.

"Yeah. She told me flat out she'd bury him if it came down to it. Said I had too much to lose and she'd make sure I didn't," Grayson says, matter-of-fact.

The video ends.

The sound cuts. Gasps. Cameras flash. Strand mutters something. Corinne doesn't move.

The room is still echoing with Grayson's last words when the judge leans forward, voice low but firm.

"Ms. Harding, the court would like to see the corroborating statement you referenced."

Without missing a beat, Erin reaches into her folder and lifts a sealed envelope. The wax insignia is unmistakable—the Redgrave crest, gold and sharp against blood-red lacquer.

My heart doesn't race. It hardens. Because now, finally, the tide is turning. I don't know if I can come back from what it cost to get here.

She hands it to the clerk, who delivers it to the judge.

"I'll read the full statement for the record," Erin says. She clears her throat and begins.

To whom it may concern,

I, Genevieve Redgrave, provide the following statement of my own volition, without coercion or incentive.

I have been present for multiple personal conversations with Assistant District Attorney Corinne Eddings in which she expressed personal animosity toward Stellan Rothwell. These statements were often emotionally charged and involved both criticism of his professional standing and speculation about his influence in the city.

I have also personally witnessed her ongoing attachment to Grayson Lomier. While Grayson and I are not close, I can attest to Corinne's belief that their relationship held more significance than he implied. Her fixation was evident in the way she spoke about him—possessive, defensive, and increasingly erratic.

Given the nature of her commentary and the pattern of behavior I observed, I would not be surprised if she allowed her personal motives to compromise her objectivity in legal matters involving Mr. Rothwell.

Signed,

Genevieve Redgrave.

Gen. The very woman who would sell silence for power, now handing Corinne's downfall on a silver platter.

Before the judge can even set the letter down, Corinne's chair screeches against the floor as she stands—too fast, too loud.

"That statement is baseless," she snaps, voice rising. "Genevieve and I haven't spoken in weeks. She's bitter and manipulative and—"

"Ms. Eddings," the judge warns, tone clipped.

She ignores him. There it is. The crack. Not in her case. In her. The obsession, the desperation. She wanted to ruin me for a man who won't even claim her.

"You're going to take the word of a Redgrave? Of a woman who has made it her life's mission to—"

"Ms. Eddings, sit down," the judge says again, louder.

Corinne keeps going, now visibly rattled.

"This entire defense is built on gossip and personal vendettas. They're twisting everything. I built this case by the book. I didn't even bring charges until—"

"Until what?" Erin Harding asks, quietly.

Corinne turns, eyes flashing. But she says nothing.

And that silence? That's the nail.

The judge nods once. "All charges against Mr. Rothwell are dismissed, with prejudice. This court finds the prosecution's actions not only unsupported by evidence, but clouded by personal conflict and ethical failure."

He slams the gavel, stands, and exits through the side door, robes sweeping behind him like the curtain falling on a play gone off-script.

Flashbulbs explode the second the gavel hits wood. The reporters shout questions over each other, pushing toward the gallery rail.

Corinne moves to gather her files, jaw clenched. Marshall Strand stands without looking at her.

"You're done," he says, not quietly.

"What?" she snaps.

"You're fired, Corinne. Effective immediately."

"You can't—"

"Try me," he cuts in. "And if you push it, I'll press charges. Interference. Abuse of authority. You want a trial, you'll get one. Just not from the prosecution table."

She's frozen. Jaw twitching. Hands still.

Corinne is still frozen when a hand appears at her elbow.

"Corinne Eddings," Rafe says, voice neutral as he hands her a sealed envelope. "You've been served. Civil suit. Defamation. Filed this morning."

She grabs it reflexively, fingers twitching like she might throw it back.

Erin steps forward, heels silent against the marble floor.

"On behalf of Mr. Rothwell and Rothwell Strategic Holdings," she says coolly, "we look forward to discovery."

Erin doesn't wait. She turns, heels sharp on marble, and leads the way to the doors.

Talia falls in beside her, flanked by Dawson—eyes scanning the press, already managing their exit route.

Erin stops just outside the courthouse steps. The press swarms, cameras rolling.

She faces them head-on.

"Mr. Rothwell has been cleared of all charges. The state's case was baseless, corrupt, and pursued with prejudice. Our legal team will be pursuing additional action, and Rothwell Strategic remains fully operational under Mr. Rothwell's leadership."

Questions fly. Flashbulbs burst. Talia's voice is quiet in the chaos.

"You okay?" she asks.

My eyes track the press, the guards, the doors.

"Yeah," he says.

But I'm not. I'm not free.

They dropped the charges, but I'm still standing here alone. It doesn't feel like I won. It feels like I survived something I shouldn't have.

I'm avoiding Talia. I know it. She knows it.

Her eyes are always on me. Every time she looks, it feels like a spotlight I didn't ask for.

She's at the kitchen island when I come out of the bedroom. Reading something on her tablet, coffee within reach. The picture of calm.

"I'm heading to work," I say, adjusting my cufflinks like that fixes anything.

Her head lifts. "It's been two days."

I hate how soft she says it. Like it's concern.

"Yeah. And it's still my company," I say, jaw tight. "Or is it yours now? You seem comfortable enough in my chair."

That gets her attention. The tablet goes down.

"I stepped up because someone had to," she says. "You were in a cell. The company was falling apart."

"You're good at keeping things alive, Finch. Even things that aren't yours," I say, the words cut before I can stop them.

Her lips press together. The name hits. I know it. And still—I twist the knife.

"You may be my wife on paper," I add, voice dropping, "but stop acting like you care."

"That's not fair," she says.

Fair. What a fucking word.

"Neither was felony murder, but here we are," I bite back.

I see the hurt flicker. Not big. Barely there. But it's enough to make me feel like the worst version of myself.

And yet—this is easier. Anger is easier.

She crosses her arms. "You're spiraling, Stellan. I see it. But you're not going to make me hate you just because you hate yourself right now."

That lands. Hard. I should apologize. But all I do is shrug into my jacket.

"I'll be late," I mutter. What I don't say is, if I stand here with you any longer, you'll see how scared I really am.

I just go to work. The lobby hasn't changed.

The floors gleam. The glass walls catch every beam of morning sun. People pass through security, phones in hand, heads down, moving like this is any other Monday.

But today, it feels like they're all watching me.

Every glance feels sharper. Every quiet murmur sounds like my name.

"Rothwell's back. Did you hear? Felony murder. Suppression. Corruption."

Words they're not saying out loud, but I hear them anyway.

I tell myself it's not real. Just paranoia. But paranoia doesn't make your chest this tight.

I keep walking. Past the reception desk. Past the security team that didn't save me. They nod. Smile, even. Like nothing happened.

"Aaron." My voice scrapes more than it should.

"Good to have you back, sir," he says, giving me a respectful nod. His tone's easy. Professional. Like we're still playing the same game.

I used to feel ten feet tall when my people greeted me like that. Today, it feels like sandpaper.

Stacy catches my eye next. She's all bright lipstick and customer service warmth. "Morning, Mr. Rothwell. How are you today?"

The question is harmless. Routine. But it lands wrong.

I shake my head. Manage something like a smile. The walls are glass, but today they feel like mirrors. But the reflection isn't mine anymore.

I'm moving. Breathing. But it feels like watching someone else wear my skin.

I hear my shoes click. I see the smiles. The waves. But it's all underwater.

I step into the elevator. Doors close. *Maybe I should've stayed gone.*

The elevator pings. My office waits. But it doesn't feel like mine.

"Stellan," Kate says. She doesn't look surprised to see me.

"How did you know I was coming in?" I ask.

"Talia called," she says, not looking up. "She said you're heading in."

"Of course she fucking did," I mutter, shouldering past. "She doesn't remember what she's here for."

Kate's fingers pause over the screen. Just for a beat. But she doesn't argue. She just presses play on her professional smile and gets back to work.

"You have a meeting in the conference room in 20 minutes," she says. "Talia will be there too since she brought in the client."

"Fine," I say.

I close my office door like it'll keep everything out. It doesn't. The second the latch clicks, it's not my office I'm standing in.

It's that cell.

Gray walls. Fluorescent lights that never shut off. Cold so sharp it felt personal. You'd think it's the noise that gets you—the clatter, the shouts. But it's the quiet. The hours where nothing happens. No one looks at you. No one says your name.

It gets inside your bones.

They didn't rough me up. They didn't need to. A week's enough to gut you from the inside out.

There was this guard—called me "corporate scum" like it was my legal name. Didn't raise a hand to me. Just smiled. Every day.

Now I'm standing here, in the middle of everything I built, and it feels like trying on a suit that doesn't fit anymore.

My hands curl into fists at my sides.

I think of the day they moved me to protective custody. Two guards. No explanations. No warnings.

"Security concern," one said.

The walk felt longer than the cell time. Down a corridor lined with faces—some sneering, some silent, but all of them watching me.

The whispers weren't whispers. "Rothwell's scared. Rothwell's hiding."

They put me in a smaller cell after that. A kindness wrapped in a cage.

That was when it hit me. Not even my name could protect me.

I remember sitting there, knees apart, elbows on my thighs, staring at my own hands. Hands that used to shake those of kings in this city.

It's choking me now.

It's time for the meeting. So I walk to the conference room.

Talia's already there, standing where I should be. She's poised, collected, a folder in hand. The client sits across from her. I don't catch his name. Don't care.

She's speaking. The words are all there—strategy, discretion, brand integrity. I've said them a thousand times. But now, they sound like hers.

Erin interjects with a figure. Kate pulls up a projection. I hear none of it.

All I see is Talia. Leaning in, voice low, eyes locked on the client. Like he's the only person in the room.

I'm in the chair beside her. Supposed to lead. But I feel like a guest.

The client nods, impressed. Pens scratch. Deals are made.

Without me.

Talia closes the folder with a quiet click. Stands. Offers her hand.

"I trust this meets your expectations," she says.

Of course it does.

The client thanks her. Thanks Erin. Nods politely at me. I don't return it.

"Anything you want to add, Mr. Rothwell?" Talia asks, her voice so neutral it burns.

I look at her. At the team behind her. At the empire I built now running without me.

"Nope," I say, pushing back from the table. "You took over."

She doesn't react right away. Just gathers her notes like my words don't cut.

But before she turns, she says it. "It's too soon, Stellan. You're not ready to come back."

"Excuse me?" My voice pitches higher.

Her gaze lifts to meet mine. Calm. Level. Like she's defusing a bomb.

"Your head's not here. You need time. Space. You've been through—"

"Don't," I snap out, harsher than I intend. "Don't stand there and act like you know what I need. Like you're the only thing keeping this place afloat. You were sent to find a leak, Talia. You didn't. But congratulations, you kept the lights on. Must feel good."

"I never said I was replacing you."

"You didn't have to," I snap. "Every time you sit in my chair, every time you speak for this company—you say it."

She holds my stare. No anger. Just that same infuriating calm.

"I'm not your enemy, Stellan."

"Funny. It sure feels like it," I grunt.

I decide to go home, but I should've known she was going to follow me.

"What's the endgame, Talia? Rich. Respected. Famous. Just like your mother wanted for you."

That lands.

I see it in her shoulders. The way she goes still. But she doesn't break.

"You don't know a goddamn thing about what my mother wanted for me."

I don't stop. I can't.

"You're a placeholder, Talia. That's all you've ever been," I say gesturing to the space around us. "This? It was never yours. Maybe you got too caught up playing the role and forgot what you're supposed to be doing."

Her breath catches.

And when she speaks, it's soft. The kind of soft that's lethal. "My mother wanted me to marry power. Wear it. Smile through it. No matter how much it hurt." She meets my eyes. "You think you're any different?"

That stops me. But only for a second. "Clearly not. Because you're still here."

That's when she picks up her bag. "I'm done, Stellan."

She shakes her head. "You're so busy trying to prove you don't need anyone, you're pushing away the only person who gave a damn."

She doesn't slam the door when she leaves. But it feels like she did.

CHAPTER FIFTEEN

Talia

I've been staying at the ONYX, tucked away in one of the executive overflow suites the Harrington family keeps immaculate for VIPs and inconvenient employees. Beckett Harrington's name isn't on the welcome packet, but his signature's in every detail—polished wood floors, slate-gray fixtures, a view that whispers old money without needing to shout. Comfortable. Impersonal. Exactly what I need.

It also keeps the press from asking questions. Keeps Rothwell's hands clean. Keeps me visible, but only to the right people.

I haven't been back to my own place since the fallout began. Not because I can't. Because it sends a message. Subtle, but deliberate.

This isn't home. But home isn't Stellan's, either.

Beckett hasn't said a word about my stay, which says everything. He's the kind of man who understands leverage isn't always loud. His family plays the long game. So do I.

I avoid Stellan during the day. We arrive together, leave together, and in between, there's a mutual silence that feels like walking a razor's edge. My office has never looked more organized. His has never felt more fortified.

By now, it's a rhythm. A detente. And at night, when the city softens into neon glow and quieter sins, I head back to the office.

Most nights around nine, Erin and Kate are already there.

The conference room has turned into our war room—screens glowing, coffee cooling, takeout containers lined up like we're hosting a very specific, very uninvited dinner party. They've been helping me piece things together, tracing threads no one else wants to pull. For now, we keep it to just us. Away from Stellan's desk. Not out of defiance. Just... until we're sure of what we're holding.

"Anything new?" I ask, dropping my bag into the chair that's unofficially mine now.

Kate doesn't look up. She just nudges two boxes my way. Lo mein and orange chicken. Predictable. Boring. Exactly what I'd have chosen myself.

"Nope," she says, chopsticks in hand. "Same old same old."

Erin raises a brow without lifting her eyes from the screen. "If 'same old' counts as corporate espionage and asset manipulation."

Kate grins around her next bite. "Minor details."

I settle in, flipping open the lo mein. We're used to this now—late nights, half-spoken thoughts, chasing a ghost through data trails.

Half an hour in, the pattern starts to form.

At first, it's a flicker. A credential pinging from a department that should be dark. Then another. And another. Logins at hours that don't make sense. User IDs tied to shifts that never existed. Some names I recognize—real employees, wrong place, wrong time. But others?

Too clean.

Spotless HR files. Crisp digital profiles. On paper, they're perfect. But I know every single person on our roster. Their faces. Their quirks. Who takes their coffee with too much cream. Who always calls IT because they forget their password.

These names don't belong.

"They built them," I murmur, sitting up straighter. "Fake files. Fabricated records. Someone's been busy."

Erin looks up, sharp. Kate pauses mid-bite.

"How deep does it go?" Erin asks, already shifting to a new screen, fingers flying.

I scroll further, pulling up employee directories, cross-referencing schedules. The list grows. Too many to be coincidence. Too precise to be random.

"Deep enough to slip through every surface check," I say. "But they missed one thing."

"What's that?" Kate asks, leaning in now.

"I'm Employee Relations. I don't need a system to tell me who's on my floor."

Erin's already digging into access logs, muttering under her breath. Kate abandons her food entirely, drawn into the gravity of what we're seeing.

I keep going.

Each file is a shell—built to pass every standard scan, but hollow underneath. No history. No real interactions. Just placeholders. Like someone made them to be seen, but not known.

My pulse kicks up.

"This isn't sabotage," I say. "It's leverage. Someone wanted Rothwell compromised, but still usable."

"It's time for us to start compiling a list of people who'd have the access, the know-how, and the sheer nerve to pull this off," I say, dropping my chopsticks onto the empty carton. "There aren't many."

"Start with IT," Erin says, not looking up from her screen. "Kylie Brent. She lives in the backbone of this place."

Kate snorts. "Kylie's too smart to get caught, but she's also the kind who'd do it just to prove she can."

"Exactly," I say. "Keep her on the board."

Erin taps her stylus against her lip. "What about O'Malley? Data compliance. He's got clean hands, but he's the guy who decides what gets buried and what doesn't."

"Liam O'Malley," I echo. "He'd make it look like procedure."

Kate leans back, arms crossed. "Connor Price. Strategic Risk. Ambitious. Still sore from getting passed over on that internal audit lead. He'd jump at the chance to prove a point."

I nod. "And he knows how to cover his own tracks."

"External vendors?" Erin prompts.

"Nara Quinn," I say without hesitation. "She's got Lomier ties through her last job. Knows how to grease paperwork until it's invisible."

Kate whistles low. "Subtle sabotage with a smile."

"And Bellamy," Erin adds. "Special Projects. He's charming as hell, but no one ever knows what he's really working on."

"Bellamy Cocalyn," I confirm. "He'd have the infrastructure to bury a shadow program."

Kate's expression turns sharp. "What about HR? Someone had to build those profiles."

"Chris Maddisson," I say. "If anyone could weave fake identities into our system without a ripple, it's him."

"No," Erin says, shaking her head. "Not Chris."

Kate lifts an eyebrow. "You sure about that? Feels like he checks a lot of boxes."

"He does," Erin says. "But Chris is a purist. The system's his baby. Breaking it? That'd be like torching his own house. He'd rather throw someone else under the bus than leave fingerprints on his architecture."

"So, he wouldn't do it himself," I say, leaning back.

"Not directly," Erin says. "But if someone came through him—slipped in under a maintenance update, piggybacked on his access—he might not even know."

Kate smirks. "So he's either clean, or the perfect blind spot."

"Exactly," Erin says, meeting my eyes. "He's still worth watching. Just not for the obvious reasons."

I sit back, letting the silence stretch. My gaze flicks over the list. Kylie. Liam. Connor. Nara. Bellamy. Chris. All of them fit. All of them don't.

Someone's hiding in the spaces between.

My fingers drum once, sharp against the table.

"What about Opal?" I say.

Kate's head snaps up. Erin's fingers freeze mid-type.

"Opal?" Kate says. "Absolutely not."

"No way," Erin agrees, shaking her head like the thought is offensive.

"Why not?" I ask, keeping my tone even.

"Because she's close to Stellan. All of us!" Kate exclaims, throwing up her hands. "She's in the trenches with us. You think she'd risk that?"

"She's green, but she's loyal," Erin adds. "Genuinely. She works late. Picks up the slack. This isn't her."

I lean forward, elbows on the table. "She's exactly who none of us would suspect. That's the point."

Kate's eyes narrow. "That's a reach, Talia."

"Is it?" I say. "She started her promoted position right before the leak. Never asks for more access than she needs—but somehow, always has enough."

Erin frowns. "That could just be good onboarding."

"Or it could be deliberate placement." I don't raise my voice, but the weight is there. "Proximity is opportunity. If someone wanted to slip in unnoticed, they'd need the right face. The one no one would question."

"Stop," Kate says sharply. "It's Opal. Maris' little sister. You know how hard she's worked to get here."

"She didn't get handed this job, Talia," Erin adds. "She fought for it. She's one of us."

I sit with that, giving the loyalty a chance to settle.

"I know that," I say. "Doesn't change the timing. Doesn't change the access. I'm not accusing her. I'm asking a question no one wants to."

Kate's glare softens. "Because it feels like a betrayal to even consider it."

"Exactly," I say. "Which makes it the perfect blind spot."

Erin groans loudly. "You really think she could be playing us?"

"I think she's the one person no one would see coming," I say. "That doesn't make her guilty. But it makes her worth looking at."

Kate lets out a sharp laugh. "You're really not going to let this go."

"No," I say. "Not until we know."

I don't go through company systems first. I start with the human places.

Social media. Public records. Opal Greer's life, in snapshots and fragments. Family photos tagged by Maris. A graduation post. Volunteer work. Employee of the Month three years ago—earned, not gifted.

Promotions that line up with company timelines. Friends, colleagues, harmless likes and follows.

On the surface, it's exactly what it should be. But surfaces lie.

I pull deeper. Cross-reference timestamps. Match locations. Every innocuous post gets weighed. Every network connection examined. I map her digital footprint, thread by thread. Travel records. Vendor liaisons. The little things no one hides because they don't think they matter.

Patterns emerge.

By midnight, my screen's a mosaic of tabs and files. My pulse hasn't slowed.

I want this to be nothing. But what if it isn't?

I pivot, searching sideways.

Maris.

Public posts about her divorce. Threaded through are glimpses of something raw. The toll it's taken. The balancing act with her kids. The cost of trying to keep a life upright while it all falls apart.

Photos from last year's Christmas party at the company she works for. Maris smiling, glass of champagne in hand, but the caption talks about "new beginnings" and "letting go."

And then there's Opal.

Not in the photos, but in the comments. Small, easy to overlook. A string of casual interactions—likes, emojis, the usual surface-level noise. Until they're not.

You deserve better than someone who couldn't even keep his promises. First loves never really go away, do they?
Funny how some people get chance after chance while the rest of us have to fight for scraps.

No names. No direct mentions. But the subtext hums.

Old wounds. Resentments folded into casual words.

I lean back, staring at the screen.

This isn't corporate sabotage. This is personal. The kind of personal that simmers. The kind that waits. I don't want to believe it. But if anyone would slip through the cracks, unnoticed, with a perfectly human motive... it'd be someone standing in the shadow of all this history.

I call Juno. She needs to try to break into her socials without her knowing.

"You wouldn't call if it wasn't something."

"I need a dive. Deep. Full spread on Opal Greer." I rub a hand over my face. "Socials. Digital footprint. Anything that's not company-logged."

Another pause. Longer this time. "Maris Greer's sister?"

"Yeah."

"Talia, what the hell are you looking for?"

"I don't know. But I can't let it go." I breathe out slowly. "There's history there, Juno. Personal. I've been scrolling through her comments. Posts. Little jabs that aren't directed, but they cut."

"Give me an example."

I click through the posts, reading aloud. "First loves never really go away, do they? Funny how some people get chance after chance while the rest of us have to fight for scraps. And my favorite. You deserve better than someone who couldn't even keep his promises."

Juno whistles, low. "That's... pointed."

"Exactly. It's never direct. No names. But we both know who she's talking about."

"Maris and Stellan," Juno says.

"Stellan never talked about it. But you can see it plain as day. The distance. The tension." I scroll further. "Opal's been on the sidelines of that fallout for years. Watching. Learning where the cracks are."

Juno's voice sharpens. "You think she's the leak?"

"I think she's been holding onto a grudge for a long time. And if someone wanted to bleed Rothwell from the inside, they wouldn't need to recruit her. She'd already have her reasons."

Juno hums for a moment. "Okay. I'll dig."

"Thanks." I lean back, staring at the screen. "And Juno? Don't leave fingerprints."

"Please," she scoffs. "Amateur hour."

The call ends, but I don't move. Just watch the clock bleed past midnight, the city humming beneath the building.

Fifteen minutes later, my phone vibrates. It's Juno.

> Check your inbox. You owe me coffee. Fancy coffee.

I open the file.

Access logs. Cloud-sync patterns. Screenshots of internal reports Opal shouldn't have been saving off-grid. Not high-level intel. Not enough to trigger alarms. But personal. Specific.

Maris_Notes

It's not company data. It's screenshots of social posts, old photos, snippets of comments—bits of digital debris no one would think to trace.

Pictures of Maris. Her divorce announcement from a few months ago. Candid shots Opal took from company events. Even ones where Stellan's in the background from family events when she was a kid. They're not saved for sentiment.

The captions tell the real story.

Some people forget their wedding day. Others remember every crack.
Funny how no one mentions the price of being someone's almost.
It's easy to celebrate a marriage when you weren't the one left behind.

Bitter. Careful. Aimed like knives with no names attached.

And Opal's comments—small, sharp jabs threaded through the years.

You deserved better.

They never look back. But we never forget.

Wish I'd gotten my shot before you got hurt.

It's heartbreak. Plain and raw. But it's also fuel.

Maris moved on. Built a life. But the cracks from Stellan never quite healed. And Opal? She's been carrying that loyal anger ever since. Watching. Remembering. Wanting justice no one asked for.

I lean back in my chairs, stretching for a moment. This isn't corporate espionage. It's personal.

Opal didn't have to be recruited. She made herself useful.

Because some betrayals don't need bribes.

"It's Opal. She did it," I say, flat and certain.

Kate's head snaps up. "No. Come on, Talia."

Erin's already shaking her head. "That's a hell of an accusation. You sure you want to say that out loud?"

"I wouldn't if I wasn't sure." I turn my laptop toward them. "You wanted proof. Here it is."

Kate crosses her arms. "Show me."

"Start with this," I say, pulling up the access logs. "These are off-grid pulls. Internal reports saved to her personal cloud. Low-level enough not to flag IT. But systematic. Repeated."

"Could be sloppy habits," Erin says, but her voice wavers.

I click again. "Then there's the email. Dormant for six years. Reactivated two months ago. Used to forward internal data. Not through Rothwell. Through an old personal account. Looks harmless. Feels deliberate."

Kate leans in, eyes narrowing. "Still sounds thin."

"Fine." I open the folder labeled Maris_Notes. Screenshots of old social posts, comments. The digital graveyard of resentment. "She's been cataloging every crack in Maris and Stellan's history. Watching it. Holding onto it."

Erin's lips press together as she reads aloud. "'Some mistakes wear tuxedos.' That's not subtle."

"She never names him," I say. "But we don't need her to. This isn't a grudge she let go. It's one she's been feeding."

Kate's listening now. Erin too.

"You know her," I say. "You've seen how close she's kept to Maris. To Stellan."

Erin sighs, rubbing her temple. "God. I didn't want it to be her."

"None of us did," I say. "But here we are."

Kate's shoulders slump. "Alright. You've convinced me."

"Good," I say, straightening. "Because now we bring it to Stellan."

That gets a reaction.

Kate's head snaps up. "You sure that's the play?"

"Do you have a better one?" I ask.

Erin leans back, skeptical. "You think he's going to take this well? You're not just naming a leak, Talia. You're naming Maris' sister."

"I know exactly what I'm naming," I say. "But this isn't a decision we get to sit on. He needs to know."

Kate's frowning. "It's going to blow up. Big."

"It already has," I say, standing. "We're just the ones who get to light the match properly."

I grab my tablet, gather the files, the evidence. "Let's go tell him who's been bleeding his empire from the inside."

The room sways a bit as I open the door. Behind me, chairs scrape back.

And just like that, we walk straight into the storm.

Chapter Sixteen

Talia

As I get ready for the day, indecision knots in my chest. I don't want to hurt Stellan. But he needs to know. I'd hoped to catch him in the penthouse. Somewhere less busy than the office.

My phone buzzes on the vanity.

Kate

> He came in early.

Of course he did. That's the worst thing I could've read. Office hours mean ears everywhere. This conversation doesn't deserve any of that.

But we're out of options.

The ride over is a blur—too much time to think, not enough to feel.

By the time I step off the elevator, the air in Rothwell feels different. Kate's waiting by my office, tablet in hand.

"He's alone," she says, voice low. "Doors closed. No one's been in."

"Thanks," I say, even though there's nothing grateful about this.

I reach his office, raise my hand.

And knock. Once.

"Come in," Stellan says, muffled behind the door.

I open the door.

"Do you need something?" He asks, not looking up from his desk.

"Yes," I say, shutting the door behind me. "To talk."

He sets his pen down, leans back, studies me with that unreadable expression he's so good at.

"You haven't said a word to me in days." His voice is quiet. Not cold. Not yet. "Why now?"

Because this can't wait. Because what I'm about to say will change everything. But I don't flinch. I meet his eyes. "Because it's Opal," I say. "She's the leak."

For a second, he just stares at me. Like I've spoken in a language he doesn't understand.

All of a sudden, he laughs. A loud disbelieving laugh. "You can't be serious."

"I am," I say, standing tall. "And I have proof."

"No," he says, rising from his chair. "No, you think you have proof. You have scraps. Circumstance. You don't know her."

"I have more than that," I say, pulling the tablet from my bag. "I'm not here to guess, Stellan. I'm here because I've done the work. You need to see this."

"I don't need to see anything." His tone cuts like glass. "Especially not from you. Not when you're so ready to believe the worst."

"I'm not ready to believe anything," I snap. "I wanted to be wrong. But the facts don't care what you want."

He moves around the desk, sharp, deliberate. "Opal has been with this company for years. She's earned her place. She's loyal."

"She's loyal to Maris," I fire back. "And that loyalty has a cost. One you've been too comfortable ignoring."

"You don't know what the hell you're talking about." His voice rises, a rare crack in his control. "This is personal. You think you can walk in here with your files and your outsider logic and tell me that someone I'm close to is the leak? That my friend is doing this to me?"

"I'm not telling you anything you don't already suspect," I say, holding the tablet out. "But you're too proud to look."

His jaw clenches. "Put it away."

"No," I say, stepping forward. "Look at it. Look at the access logs. Look at the files she's pulled, the email accounts she's used. Look at the way she's been bleeding you while smiling to your face."

His gaze locks on mine, furious. "I hired you to stabilize. Not to gut my inner circle."

"Maybe your inner circle is the rot," I say, voice low, but sharp. "And maybe the reason you can't see it is because you're too busy protecting your pride."

"Get out."

I lower the tablet, but my grip stays tight. "You can hate me for this," I say. "But that doesn't change what's true."

I turn, heading for the door.

Kate gets out of her chair. "What did he say?"

"Kate!" Stellan bellows from his office.

"I think you get the picture now," I say while walking towards the exit.

By the time the elevator doors close, my hands are already dialing.

Iris picks up on the second ring.

"I solved it," I say, cutting straight to it. "It's Opal. I have everything. Proof, logs, patterns. He won't even look at it."

"Of course he won't," Iris says.

"So now what?" I ask. "I did my job. He won't do his."

There's a pause. "You did your job, Talia. That's the end of your obligation."

"It shouldn't be," I say. My throat feels tight. "I want to release it. Take it public. Force his hand."

"That's your call," Iris says. "But if you're asking me? Release it. And leave him. File for divorce. Seriously. I know it's been less than a year, but you already solved it with all of the proof. Let him deal with the backlash."

She knows what I've been dealing with. Our weekly check ins have officially turned into nightly ones. Things with Stellan... they're not simple. But lately, they're harder in a way I don't know how to fix. He's pulling away—or maybe I am.

I stare at my reflection in the elevator glass.

"Whatever you choose, Talia, make sure it's for you. Not for him. Not for Rothwell. For you."

I hang up without answering. The truth is, I don't know who I'm fighting for anymore.

I go straight to my room and pack everything. I think I made my choice. So I grab my phone and open the group chat.

Talia

It's done. I'm releasing it. Stellan won't move, so I will. You deserve to know. You've had my back through all of this. Thank you.

The three dots blink.

Erin

Are you sure?

Kate

You don't owe him your silence.

Talia

I'm sure.

Kate

We're with you.

Erin

Let it burn.

I sit on the edge of the bed, phone in hand, thumb hovering. I call Mirelle. She answers on the first ring.

"Talia. I've been expecting this."

"The job's done," I say. "Opal's the leak. I have everything. Logs, files, the whole trail."

"I assume Stellan took that news with his usual grace."

I let out a breath. "He refused to see it. Wouldn't even look at the evidence. So now I'm handling it."

There's a pause. "Meaning?"

"I'm releasing it. Quiet if I can. Loud if I have to."

Mirelle's voice sharpens. "Good. Then we're done here."

"I—what?"

"You're done there, Talia. Grab the rest of your things. Come straight to our office."

"I can finish this from here."

"No. You've done your job. You don't sit in the fallout. That's his mess to clean up. You don't stay."

The finality in her tone leaves no room for argument.

"This isn't about him," Mirelle says. "This is about you knowing when enough is enough."

I close my eyes. "I wanted to believe in what we were building."

"And now you believe in facts. That's what matters."

There's a softness there, but only for a breath.

"Gather your things. Be out of the ONYX in twenty minutes. You're done."

She hangs up before I can answer.

And that's that. I don't dawdle. I move through the suite, grabbing what's left. Minimal. Efficient. The choice is made now.

By the time I step into the ONYX lobby, it feels different. Less like a cage. More like a place I'm leaving behind.

The car ride to Mirelle's office is the first breath I've taken in days. I'm out.

Now it's time to finish this on my terms.

Juno's the first to spot me, waving me into the war room at La Fondation Noirel with her coffee in hand. Iris is already at the table, scrolling through her tablet like she's been waiting for this. Brenna's leaning against the wall, arms crossed, a quiet smirk playing on her lips. And at the head of it all, Mirelle sits, calm and in control.

"Talia," Mirelle says. "Welcome back."

I drop my bag beside the table. "Let's get this done."

Juno spins her laptop around. "Files are ready. The release plan is clean. Minimal fallout for Rothwell. Maximum pressure where it hurts."

"Circulated through the right channels," Iris adds. "No press storm, just quiet suffocation. The kind that forces response."

Brenna nods. "Surgical strike. No drama. Just facts."

I take a breath. "Stellan had every chance to fix this. He didn't."

"And that's why we're here," Mirelle says smoothly. "You did your job. Now we do ours."

She gestures to the laptop. The final confirmation prompt waits on the screen.

"One click," Juno says. "Your call."

I don't hesitate. I press send.

It's done.

There's no applause. No dramatic sighs of relief. Just a shared understanding.

The job is finished.

"What happens next is his problem," Mirelle says, standing. "You? You're free."

I don't argue when they send me to the safe house.

Keys. An address. Mirelle's final word. "You're done. Go breathe."

The brownstone is nothing like the ONYX. The walls here aren't trying to impress anyone. The floors creak. The air smells like rain and old wood. Lived-in. Human.

I drop my bag by the couch and don't bother unpacking. I won't be here long.

I sink into a leather chair by the window, watching the city breathe outside. No skyscraper glow. Just fire escapes and rusted brick. Honest in a way Rothwell never was.

My phone vibrates.

The first headline hits.

Internal Leak Identified at Rothwell: Analyst Opal Greer Implicated in Sabotage Scheme.

There it is.

I open the article.

Sources confirm Rothwell Industries has identified mid-level analyst Opal Greer as the primary figure in the internal data breach. Utilizing her trusted position, Greer systematically extracted sensitive informa-

tion over several months. Company officials are managing the fallout, but the betrayal has struck close to home.

It lands like a punch. Another notification pings.

Betrayal from Within: Opal Greer Tied to Rothwell Leak Scandal."

New details reveal Opal Greer, a long-serving analyst and sister to former Rothwell executive Maris Greer, as central to the leaks. Known for her discretion and work ethic, Greer's involvement highlights a deep-seated personal vendetta. Rothwell's board remains silent on disciplinary actions.

They're threading the narrative carefully.

No firestorm. Just slow, deliberate exposure.

Another headline.

Rothwell Crisis: Family Ties Exposed in Sabotage Scandal.

The fallout from Rothwell's internal breach intensified today as Opal Greer, sister of Maris Greer, was officially named as the source. The betrayal underscores how personal history and unresolved grievances can erode corporate trust. Analysts commend Rothwell's swift containment response.

Personal history. That's polite code for *Stellan.*

Another one follows.

Trust Broken: Opal Greer Named in Rothwell Breach.

Multiple sources confirm Opal Greer leveraged her analyst access to facilitate the leaks. Though exact motives are unconfirmed, ties to Maris Quinn and historical friction within Rothwell leadership are cited as contributing factors. The board is reviewing internal protocols.

I lock my phone and let it drop to the table beside me.

Outside, life moves on. Traffic hums. Lights flicker. None of it stops.

I finally let myself breathe.

Chapter Seventeen

Stellan

"Fuck," I say. "Fucking Talia!"

I punch the wall next to me leaving a massive hole. She really did it. She released it. A lie.

Opal did not do it and now I have to do damage control to clear it. I will *destroy* Talia for doing this to her.

"Kate!" I scream out of my office.

People scatter left and right. No one wants to be around me right now.

"Erin?" I ask, trying to keep my voice from snapping, though something in my gut coils tight. "What are you doing here?"

"Ms. Noirel and Hallie Whitlock have sent over divorce papers," she says, holding the envelope like it weighs nothing.

Stellan straightens. "How the hell is that ready already?" I ask, voice tight.

"It was drafted the day you got married. For when she found the leak and could leave clean," Erin replies.

"She didn't find the leak," I say, stepping forward.

"You're wrong," Erin says, calm, but the steel's there.

"Take that back to Noirel. Get Talia's ass back here. Tell her to apologize to Opal. Then she can keep looking," I say, every word clipped.

"You're still not seeing it," Erin says, with that no-more-bullshit edge she gets when she's done pulling punches.

"Seeing what?" I ask, the edge in my voice sharper than I intended.

"Opal *is* guilty," Kate says. "Look at the evidence."

"I don't have to," I say. Don't they understand? Opal wouldn't do something like this.

Kate steps forward. "Then listen. We found a video from the employee scan room. The one where credentials are made for new hires," she says, voice clipped, businesslike.

"That proves nothing," I say.

"It proves everything," Kate says. "Talia showed us how the leaks came from those credentials—emails, access points, all routed through them. Untraceable on the surface."

Erin adds, "But the cameras for that timeframe? The footage was scrambled. Deliberately."

My jaw tightens. "Easy enough to manipulate."

"Talia called Juno to fix it before she left," Kate says. "Juno pulled the raw data. The timestamp shows someone scanning in. The cameras didn't shut off by themselves."

There's a heavy pause.

"Who was it?" I ask, though part of me already knows.

"Opal," Kate says.

"That doesn't mean anything," I say, shaking my head. "She works in that department. Of course her credentials would show up there."

Kate's jaw tightens. "Watch the video."

She taps her tablet, holds it up.

The image is grainy, but clear enough. The scan room. A figure swipes in. No hesitation. The timestamp matches. The camera glitches right after she enters.

"She could've been doing her job," I say.

"You're not listening," Kate says, frustration sharp. "That room was off-limits at that time. Only authorized during scheduled entries. She wasn't scheduled. She wasn't supposed to be there."

"That's not proof of sabotage," I snap.

Erin steps in, pulling up another file. "Look at this. These are the emails tied to the leaks. All traced back to the fake credentials Talia flagged. Clean on the surface. But Juno pulled the embedded data."

Kate flips to another screen. "The IP routing, the bounce patterns—this is how she masked it. Layered. Smart. But not perfect."

I stare at the screen. The evidence is all there.

And still, the words come out. "Talia's looking for a scapegoat."

"No," Erin says. "Talia's the only reason we even found this. She did her job when you refused to listen. When you shut us all out!"

"I don't need a lecture," I say, cold.

"Good," Kate snaps. "Because we're done giving them."

She steps forward, slamming her badge onto my desk. "You want loyalty? Start with giving a damn about the people who earned it."

Erin's not far behind. She places her badge beside Kate's. No slamming. Just final. "You treated her like a pawn. Used her. Questioned her. She deserved better."

"She made this personal," I say, standing.

"No, *you* did," Erin fires back. "She fought for you. For this company. You turned your back because it was easier than facing you were wrong."

Kate's jaw is set. "Talia didn't fail you. You failed her. And you failed this company."

Their words hit harder than I want to admit. "This is bigger than her ego," I say.

Kate shakes her head. "This was never about ego. This was about respect. You should try it sometime."

Erin gestures to the files still glowing on my screen. "Everything you need is right there. But you've already lost the one person who cared enough to save you."

The door swings open before they can get far.

Dawson steps in, blocking their exit. "You're really going to walk out now?" he asks, eyes flicking between them.

"Damn right we are," Kate says, folding her arms.

"Think about this," Dawson says, calm but firm. "You've both put years into Rothwell. Into him." He jerks his chin toward me. "You don't want to throw that away over one bad call."

"One bad call?" Erin's laugh is sharp. "This isn't one bad call, Dawson. This is a pattern."

"She's right," Kate says. "Every time someone sticks their neck out, he cuts them off."

Dawson holds up his hands. "You've seen what happens when the wrong people get power. You want to let Rothwell burn because you're angry?"

"I want no part of a place that lets true loyalty get punished," Erin says, her tone like ice. "Especially when the only person doing the job was pushed out for telling the truth."

"She didn't fail," Kate adds, leveling Dawson with a look. "She gave him every chance to see it. He chose not to."

"This isn't personal," Dawson says, but even he sounds like he's trying to believe it.

"It always was," Erin says. "We're done."

They brush past him.

I look at Dawson. He's been with me the longest. If anyone's going to hand me a way to clear Opal's name, it's him.

"Say something," I tell him.

Dawson crosses his arms. "What do you want me to say? You want me to give you an out?"

"I want the truth," I say, jaw tight.

"You've had it. You just don't like how it sounds."

"She wouldn't do this," I say. "Opal's loyal. To Maris. To—"

"To her version of you," Dawson cuts in. "The one where you're the villain who broke Maris and never looked back."

"That's not what happened," I snap.

"Doesn't matter." Dawson pulls out his phone, swipes, holds it out. "This is how she tells it."

You deserved better.

They never look back. But we never forget.

Wish I'd gotten my shot before you got hurt.

"That's not the truth," I say, but it sounds thin. Hollow.

"Truth's not the issue," Dawson says. "Perception is. And she's been stewing in hers for years."

Before I can argue, the door swings open.

Frankie strides in like she owns the place. Cal's right behind her, Beckett trailing, a bottle of champagne in his hand.

"Well, well," Frankie says, her smile bright. "Looks like the leak's officially nailed down."

Cal leans against my desk, grinning. "Thought you'd want to celebrate."

Beckett stays back, arms crossed, watching.

Frankie's smile sharpens. "Since we're all here, maybe you should tell them about Talia."

I glance at her. "What about her?"

"Oh, don't play dumb now," Frankie says. "You've been playing chess with your feelings for months. I'm just moving the board."

She turns to Cal and Beckett. "Talia wasn't just here for Rothwell. She was his damage control. A contract marriage. PR fix. Keep the shareholders happy. Clean exit plan."

Cal's brows lift. "Seriously?"

Beckett doesn't flinch. "Figures. Explains why he looks like someone kicked his teeth in every time she walks away."

"It was business," I say, voice flat.

Frankie laughs, humorless. "Sure. Until it wasn't. She fought harder for this company than anyone in this room. Including you."

Cal shakes his head. "You're in love with her. And you're too damn stubborn to admit it."

"She knew the terms," I say, but even to my ears, it sounds like a weak defense.

"Yeah, and she still gave you everything she had," Frankie fires back.

Beckett's tone is quieter, but it cuts sharper. "You're the only one pretending it's not obvious."

I feel it...the crack.

All the pride. All the control.

Useless.

I hired her to fix the damage. I broke the one thing she didn't come here to save—me.

"They sent me divorce papers," I say.

"What!" Frankie exclaims, eyes wide, like I just told her the building's on fire.

"Hallie Whitlock and Mirelle Noirel had them ready," I add. "Prepared the day we got married. For when Talia found the leak and could leave clean."

Cal whistles, low. "That's cold."

Beckett's voice is even. "They?"

"The Society," I correct, mouth flat. "This was never about us."

Frankie snorts. "Bullshit. It *was* about you. From the second you started looking at her like she was more than a fix."

I meet her eyes. "Doesn't change the facts."

"No, but it sure as hell changes what you're doing about it," Frankie snaps. "You gonna sit here and mope, or are you gonna stop being a coward and go get her?"

Beckett adds, quiet but final, "Time's ticking."

Cal just shakes his head. "You've lost everything else by trying to protect yourself. Don't lose her too."

Frankie steps closer, jabs a finger into my chest. "You want the last word? Fine. Here it is. You love her. She's not your shield. She's not your savior. She's your match. And you're too damn scared to see it."

Before I can even respond, the office door slams open.

Opal storms in, eyes wild, voice sharp enough to cut glass. "Where is she?"

No one has to ask who she means.

"Talia," Opal spits. "That lying little snake. You're all so blinded by her, but she's nothing. She doesn't belong here. Never did."

Frankie turns slowly, like a predator who's been handed dessert. "Say that again."

"I said," Opal snarls, stepping forward, "Talia used you all. She sunk her claws into this company, into him, and you're too pathetic to see it."

Frankie's laugh is sharp and dangerous. "Sweetheart, if anyone's been playing the long game, it's you."

Opal doesn't hesitate. She lunges. Frankie meets her halfway.

Frankie grabs Opal by the collar, slamming her back against my desk. Papers scatter. Beckett moves to intervene but Cal stops him with a shake of his head.

"This was overdue," Cal mutters.

"You think you're protecting her?" Opal snaps, shoving Frankie. "She's the reason this is all falling apart."

"No, darling," Frankie says, fists clenched. "You are. Talia cleaned up your mess while you were too busy playing victim."

Opal swings. Frankie's faster.

The crack of palm against cheek echoes through the office.

"Enough!" I bark.

Neither of them flinch. Opal's breathing hard, hair wild, fury radiating off her. Frankie's smiling like she just won a prize.

"Still think Talia's the problem?" Frankie says, brushing her hands together like she's done with the trash.

Opal glares at me. "She's going to ruin you."

Frankie's grin sharpens. "Funny. You said the same thing about Maris."

Opal's hands ball into fists. "Maris didn't deserve what happened. Neither did I. And now Talia's doing the same thing—digging where she shouldn't. Poking into files, into people that were never meant to exist."

My head tilts. "What people, Opal?"

Her mouth snaps shut. Too late.

"You know what I mean," she says, voice tight. "If Talia hadn't been here, those files would've stayed buried. No one would've questioned the employee logs. No one would've looked at the credential scans."

Frankie's smile fades, sharp and cold. "Talia never mentioned the credential room to you."

Beckett straightens. Cal's gaze sharpens.

But it's me she's looking at. Daring me to see it.

I do.

"Talia's the only one who brought up those fake profiles," I say, voice low. "The only one who connected the credentials to the leaks."

Opal's eyes widen.

And there it is.

She just admitted it.

"You've been cleaning up your own mess this whole time," Frankie says, stepping in. "Planting fake employees. Masking leaks. And now you're mad you got sloppy."

Opal's breathing goes shallow.

I don't need more. "Talia was right," I say.

Admitting it means owning every time I shut her down. Every time I called her wrong. Every time I watched her walk away and let my pride hold the door open.

"I was a goddamn idiot," I say, slamming my hand down on the desk.

Frankie doesn't gloat. Neither does Dawson. I don't need anyone else telling me what I already know.

"Frankie brought her in," I say, louder now. "And the second she made this place stronger, I tore her down. I didn't trust her. I didn't protect her. I let her walk out like she was nothing."

"You still have time to fix it," Cal says quietly.

"No. I had time. I wasted it," I snap.

The silence after is deafening. But it's not guilt sitting in my chest anymore. It's regret.

Because Talia was right. About the leak. About me.

"You used me," I say, turning on Opal. "You used Rothwell. You dragged Maris' name through this mess to justify every lie you told."

Opal's chin lifts. "I protected what mattered."

"Don't dress it up as loyalty," I snap. "You gutted this company from the inside because you couldn't stand being overlooked."

"My actions didn't happen in a vacuum," she fires back. "You built this place on people you used and discarded."

"You think sabotaging Rothwell fixes that? You think this makes Maris whole again?"

Opal's smile is thin. Sharp. "No. But at least now you'll know what it feels like to lose something you never appreciated."

My fists clench. "I never owned her. And I sure as hell don't owe you."

"No, but you broke her," Opal says, voice like glass shattering. "And I wasn't going to let you forget it."

The office door opens.

There she is.

Maris.

"You have got to be shitting me," Frankie says, exasperated.

"I heard about the leaks," Maris says, her voice soft but clear. "When I saw Opal's name tied to Rothwell, I knew what must've happened. So I got on the first flight."

She looks at Opal, not with anger—just pity.

"You've only ever known Mom's version, haven't you?" she says. "How Stellan broke my heart and stole my business plan."

Opal stiffens.

"And it's time you heard the truth."

CHAPTER EIGHTEEN

Stellan

"I didn't know there was another story going around besides the truth," Maris says, her tone gentle, like she's not here to fight, just to set the record straight.

She glances at me before moving to Opal.

"Stellan and I... we were never what people wanted us to be," she says. "In college, we were ambitious. Both of us. We worked well together because we challenged each other. Because we didn't let up." She smiles, soft but distant. "We were good at the same things. Bad at the same things, too. Mostly communication."

That gets a small huff of breath from Frankie. But Maris stays focused.

"We built a project together. I had the vision. He had the strategy. We pushed each other to make it better. But somewhere along the line, people—Mom especially—decided that meant we were building a future together. The kind with rings. She wanted me to marry Stellan before I ever met anyone else. And for a while, I think she believed it would happen. Until I didn't."

She doesn't look at me when she says it.

"I cared about him. Of course I did. But I didn't want the life everyone mapped out for me. I wanted my own. And Stellan wanted his. We didn't fit in the way that matters."

My hands curl into fists at my sides. Because she's right. But I never fought the story that said otherwise.

"I ended it. Not him. Me. Because staying would've been dishonest. To him. To me. It wasn't going to last," Maris says, turning back to Opal. "He didn't want marriage. Or children. At least not then. And I did. Just... not with him."

Opal flinches.

"I wanted the picture our mother painted. But not at the cost of forcing it where it didn't fit," she says, her voice staying kind, not a shred of venom. "Walking away wasn't easy. But it was right," she adds, soft but certain.

Frankie's arms are still crossed, but her mouth twitches like she's impressed. Beckett and Cal stay quiet. And me? I'm standing here, watching the narrative I let fester finally unravel.

"That's not true," she says, her voice sharper now, brittle. "You loved him. I remember. I saw you crying."

Maris turns to her, gentle but firm. "I did love him, Opal. But loving someone doesn't always mean you're meant to stay."

"You were heartbroken," Opal says, shaking her head like she can't reconcile the memory. "I remember how hurt you were. I was little, but I saw it."

"I was hurt," Maris says, voice soft. "Because endings hurt. Even the right ones."

Opal's hands are fists at her sides. "It wasn't fair. What he did. What he took."

Maris' smile doesn't waver. "Stellan didn't take anything from me. I chose to leave."

The words are gentle, but they leave no room for argument.

Opal's fists tremble. "No," she says, but it's not sharp anymore. It's breaking. "You don't understand. Mom said—she said you gave up everything for him. That he used you. That he left you with nothing."

Her voice cracks, years of belief shattering all at once.

"She made me believe it was my job to fix what you couldn't. That you were too soft, too trusting. That I had to be smarter. Stronger."

She shakes her head, tears brimming. "I wanted her to be proud of me. I thought if I fixed this—if I took him down—you'd be proud too."

Maris steps forward, slow, deliberate.

"Opal," she says, her tone soft but unflinching. "Mom loves a certain picture of what we need to be. She needed someone to blame when my choices didn't match her picture."

Opal's shoulders shake. "But you cried. You were hurting."

"I was," Maris says, with a sad smile. "But not because of Stellan. Because I disappointed her. Because I chose myself over the version of life she wanted for me."

Opal's breath stutters.

"Mom needed a villain. She made one. And you were too young to know the difference," Maris says, kind but cutting through the fog. "This isn't your fault."

"Well, damn," Frankie says, crossing her arms. "That's a hell of a lot of mess to carry on your own." Her voice isn't cruel. Just matter-of-fact.

"You can't keep living someone else's life, sweetheart," she adds. "No matter how much you think you owe her."

Maris glances at Frankie, soft but grateful.

Frankie shrugs. "Someone had to say it."

"So are you going to press charges, Stellan?" Maris asks, looking directly at me.

"No," Cal says before I can answer. "Stellan, she's just a kid. What she did was wrong. No question. But her heart was in the right place."

Opal flinches again, but this time, it's not from guilt. It's from hearing someone defend her without justifying the damage.

"No," I say, voice flat. "I'm not pressing charges."

Maris nods once. "She'll issue a public apology. Full accountability. No excuses."

Opal's breath stutters, but she doesn't argue.

"Actions have consequences," Maris says, her tone kind but final. "But punishment doesn't always have to be destruction." She places a hand on Opal's arm. "And I'm taking her home," she adds, gentle but leaving no room for a comeback.

Beckett's voice echoes in the office. "Heard about your divorce, Maris. Sorry it came to that."

Maris turns her head, a soft smile tugging at her lips. "That's the man I left Stellan for. Funny, isn't it?"

She pauses, then adds, her tone light but sharp, "Turns out, I learned something from Stellan after all. I don't need a man to be successful. Or happy."

Cal leans back, shaking his head. "Look at us. One big, sweet family moment."

Frankie huffs a laugh. Beckett smirks.

Dawson steps forward, placing a firm hand on Opal's shoulder. "Come on, kid. Let's get that statement done."

Opal nods, small and tired, but she follows.

As they leave, Maris turns back to me. "Now," she says, her smile sharp, "let's talk about your wife."

"She's not my wife," I say, flat. "She came to help the business. That was the deal."

I shouldn't think about that night.

But I do.

The lights are lower than usual. The kind of softness I don't typically allow in this place. Two plates, two glasses. Real food. My food. Not something plated by Jean, but something I made with my own hands.

Talia steps into the dining room and freezes for half a second. Just enough for me to catch the surprise flicker across her face.

"You cooked," she says.

I nod. "Don't sound so surprised."

She pulls the chair out and sits warily. It almost makes me laugh. Does she think I'm going to poison her or something?

I don't want to make her uncomfortable. So I pour us some wine.

"You've never done this before," she says. It isn't a question.

"No." I meet her eyes. "But I wanted to."

The words are simple. But they cost more than I want to admit. Her gaze drops briefly to the plate. I made the only thing I could think of. Salmon, roast potatoes and sauteed greens. It was easy enough.

"You're staring," I say, stabbing a potato with my fork.

"So are you," she counters.

I allow the corner of my mouth to lift. "That's fair."

She studies me like she's turning the tables. I'm not used to being the one under the lens.

"I'm not good at this," she says, voice low.

"At eating?" I ask, though I already know that isn't what she means.

"At—" she gestures loosely, frustrated. "This."

"Being taken care of."

Her throat works around the lump she doesn't want to name.

"I can learn," she says finally, softer now.

I lean forward, my elbows resting on the table, locking my gaze onto hers. I let her see that I mean every word of it. That this is the truth.

"Then so can I."

Maris raises a brow. "Funny, for a business deal, you've got that glazed-over look people get when they're replaying memories they shouldn't admit to."

Cal grins. "You do realize you've been in love with her since week two, right?"

Beckett folds his arms, deadpan. "Week two's generous. I had it pegged by day three."

I exhale sharply. "This is not a team meeting."

"Could've fooled us," Frankie says, laughing. "You're just mad we're right."

"Well, she filed for divorce," I say.

Maris blinks. "What did you do?"

"Why does it have to be me?" I ask, though we all know the answer.

"Because it's always you," Frankie says, not missing a beat.

Maris steps closer, her voice soft. "Stellan, you love her. Anyone who's seen the two of you together can see it."

I say nothing.

"I've seen the photos," Maris adds, a small smile tugging at her lips. "Public events. Candid shots. You don't look at anyone else the way you look at her."

I shake my head. "It's not that simple."

"It is," Frankie says. "You're just the last one to admit it."

"It's not easy," I snap. "Admitting it means losing control. It means—" I stop, jaw tightening. "It means she could leave. And it wouldn't matter how much I want her to stay."

Beckett stays silent. Cal doesn't. "Newsflash, Stellan. She already stayed," he sighs like he's tired of spelling it out. "Longer than she had to. Longer than anyone would've, if they didn't care."

I run a hand through my hair, throat tight. "She sees me. And I've spent every damn day trying to pretend I don't want that. Because wanting it means needing her. And needing her means she could tear me."

The words are ugly. Raw. But they're true.

Maris' smile softens. "That's exactly why it's not too late."

I look at her, skeptical.

"You see the photos of you looking at her," she says, stepping closer. "But you missed the ones of her looking at you."

Frankie crosses her arms. "It's written all over her face. Every boardroom. Every event. She looks at you like you're worth the fight."

"And you are," Cal says, serious now. "She loves you. Probably more than you deserve. But definitely enough to give you a second chance—if you stop wasting time."

"Why are you so damn scared, Stellan? What's the worst that happens? She loves you back?" Frankie asks, eyebrow raised.

"The last person I let in was Maris," I say, voice low, not looking at anyone. "And when it ended, it wasn't a fight. It wasn't ugly. But it broke something in me," I add, the words heavier than I expected.

I glance at Maris. She doesn't flinch. "I learned how easy it is to confuse building something together with building a life," I say, shaking my head. "I told myself I wouldn't make that mistake again. Wouldn't get blindsided by wanting more than what was on paper."

I exhale, sharp and bitter.

"So I buried it. Every time Talia challenged me. Every time she saw more than I wanted her to. Because if I kept it business, it couldn't hurt when it ended," I say, the truth scraping its way out.

"But it hurts anyway," I finish, blunt.

I scrub a hand down my face.

"She makes me want to be better," I say, voice rough. "Not for the company. Not for show. For her. For me."

The words feel foreign. But right.

"She's not impressed by the suits or the titles. She calls me out. She doesn't flinch. She sees every flaw, and still... still, she stayed."

I exhale, slow, like it might steady me.

"I don't know how to be the man she deserves. But I want to try. And that scares the hell out of me."

I look down, shaking my head.

"Because with her, losing wouldn't be about pride. It would be about losing... something real."

I swallow hard.

"I love her," I say, quieter now. "And I think I've loved her from the moment she stopped being afraid to challenge me."

"Get off your ass and go fight for her, you dumbass," Frankie says, rolling her eyes like this is the most obvious thing in the world.

Maris smiles, softer. "Consider this your official permission slip," she says, tilting her head. "Go get your wife."

The room doesn't press. They don't need to.

But I don't move. I don't know where she is.

For the first time in my life, I'm ready to beg. "I need to find her," I say, voice rough. "I'll search heaven and hell if I have to."

Frankie pulls out her phone, putting it on speaker. "Let's skip hell and start with Mirelle," she says, tapping the call button.

The ring feels longer than it should.

"Mirelle Noirel," the woman answers, crisp as ever.

"It's Frankie. Don't play dumb. Where's Talia?" Frankie says, straight to the point.

I blink. "Why do you even have her number?"

Frankie rolls her eyes. "Stellan, please. Focus."

Static crackles as Mirelle sighs.

"Ms. DeLuca, this isn't your concern," Mirelle says, cool.

"It is when your concern just confessed his undying love and looks ready to burn the city down," Frankie shoots back.

My throat's tight. "Mirelle. I love my wife," I say, stepping closer. "I love Talia. And I need to see her."

"My responsibility is to Talia's privacy," Mirelle says, calm but firm. "Not your feelings."

I step forward, planting my hands on the desk. "Mirelle, I'm not asking as a Rothwell. I'm not asking as a client. I'm asking as a man who loves her. And who's failed her."

Frankie's watching me now, but she stays quiet.

"I know I hurt her. I know she left because of it. But she's not just walking away from a job. She's walking away from me. And I can't let that happen."

Mirelle exhales, slow, through the speaker. "Words are easy, Mr. Rothwell."

"I'm not giving you words," I say, voice rough. "I'm giving you everything I've got. I'll walk to her if I have to. Crawl, if it means making this right."

Frankie raises an eyebrow, impressed.

"She's not a project. She's not a fix. She's—" my breath hitches "—she's the only thing I've done right in years. Even if I was too much of a coward to admit it until now."

Another pause.

Mirelle says, "She checked out of the ONYX this morning."

"Where is she now?" I ask, barely breathing.

"I shouldn't—" Mirelle starts.

"She loves him, Mirelle," Frankie cuts in. "Don't punish her for his stupidity."

"She's at a safe house," Mirelle says, finally. "I can ask her if she'd like to see you, but I won't force her."

Maris steps up beside me.

"Go get your girl," she says, giving my arm a squeeze.

Cal leans back, watching me like he's waited for this moment. "Don't screw this up, Stellan. You've already learned the hard way—people like her don't come twice."

This is my last shot.

And I'm not wasting it.

CHAPTER NINETEEN

Stellan

The second my phone buzzes, I'm on it.

"Mirelle," I say, without even checking the screen. I've been waiting—hoping—she'd call.

"I spoke to her," she says. No preamble. "She didn't sound thrilled, but she didn't say no either."

My breath catches. "She'll see me?"

"Yes." Mirelle doesn't make me work for it. "I'll send you the address."

"I appreciate it."

"I didn't do it for you," she says, and hangs up.

The message comes through two minutes later.

Just the address. Nothing else. Mirelle doesn't waste words, and she knows I don't need them. Not for this.

I stare at the screen for half a second, then I grab my keys. I don't think. I don't pace or change clothes or run through a speech in my head. I just go.

By the time I pull up to the safe house, the sun's dipping low. I get out of the car and cross the walkway, bracing to knock.

But before I can, the door opens and Talia is standing there.

She must've heard the car, or maybe she was watching for it. I don't know. I don't care. She's here.

"Hi," she says, voice small, but not timid. More like wary.

"Hi," I echo, and it feels like not enough, but it's all I've got right now.

I shift from one foot to another, hands loose at my sides. "Can I come in?"

She nods once and steps back.

"So what did you want to talk about?" she asks, folding her arms, guarded but curious.

"I love you," I blurt out, no finesse, no build-up.

Talia freezes. It's like she didn't hear me. Or maybe she's trying to convince herself she didn't.

"I'm sorry—what?" she says, blinking, like she's waiting for the punchline.

"I love you," I repeat, softer now, but not backing down.

"No, you don't," she says, shaking her head. "You love control. You love being right. You love comfort. But me? You don't get to say that."

"Talia—" I start, but she barrels on.

"You didn't love me when I told you the truth," she says, her voice sharp. "When I gave you everything I had, you looked me in the eye and said I was wrong. You chose Opal. You made me the villain."

Her words cut because they're true.

"I was wrong," I say, voice low. "I know that now."

"That's convenient," she says, folding her arms tighter. "Now that it's safe. Now that it costs you nothing."

"It costs me everything," I say, stepping closer. "You're not a fix. You're not an asset. You're the first person who ever looked at me and didn't flinch at what you saw. And I was a goddamn coward."

She shakes her head, retreating a step. "You don't love me, Stellan. You love what I can do for you. That's not the same."

"I love you," I say, the words scraping out. "Not as an employee. Not as a contract. As you. Every bit of you."

Her breath catches.

"You're lying to yourself," she says, but her voice wavers.

"No. For once, I'm not," I say, stepping into her space. "You're brilliant. You're infuriating. You make me want to be better because you deserve better. And you terrify me, Talia. Because you made me want things I thought I didn't get to have."

She shakes her head, arms wrapped tight around herself like armor.

"You think you want me because you lost control," she says, voice sharp but trembling. "But when you get it back, you'll regret this."

"I'm not here for control," I say, softer now. "I'm here because losing you is the one thing I can't come back from."

She swallows, throat working hard.

"I know how to rebuild companies. I know how to salvage reputations. But I don't know how to live without you," I say, every word like tearing something open. "And I don't want to learn."

Her walls are crumbling, but she's still holding the last piece.

"You said I was wrong," she whispers. "You said I was wrong about Opal. About everything."

"I did," I admit, no defenses. "Because I was afraid. You saw things I didn't want to see. Things I couldn't face. And instead of trusting you, I pushed you away."

She turns her face slightly, blinking hard.

"I thought if I kept it all surface, it wouldn't matter when it ended," I say, stepping closer until there's barely space between us. "But it did. It does. Because it's not business. It's not a game. It's you. It's always been you."

Her breath stutters.

"I don't want a life that looks good on paper," I say, voice low. "I want a life with you. Messy. Real. Ours."

Her arms fall, slowly, but she doesn't reach for me yet.

"You hurt me," she says, voice breaking.

"I know," I say, heart in my throat. "And I'll spend every day making it right. Not because I owe you, although I do. But because I love you, I want you. All of you."

She looks up then.

"It's easier when I don't feel anything. I don't know what to do with this," she says, voice raw.

"You don't have to do anything with it," I say. "You don't have to manage it or justify it. Just feel it. With me."

She finally looks at me, and it's like watching a wall try to decide whether it wants to fall.

"No contracts. No deals," I add, softer now. "Just us. Because I've already lived the version of my life without you in it. And I'm not going back."

She breathes in sharply.

"I don't know how to be something else," she says, voice trembling.

"Neither do I," I say, with a small, helpless laugh. "But I want to learn. With you." I reach for her hand, not pulling, just holding. "So let's do this. For real. Scared. Messy. Together."

For a long moment, she just looks at me. "I want to believe you so badly," she whispers.

"Let me prove it," I say, squeezing her hand. "Every day. As long as it takes."

She stares at our hands, like she's trying to make sense of this new version of us.

"What happens when I tell you something you don't want to hear again? Do I get shut out?" Her voice is tight, but I thank God, or whoever is out there, that she's talking to me, giving me the chance to prove it to her.

"No," I say, no hesitation. "Because this time, I won't be the man who's afraid of hearing it."

She searches my face. "And when you don't have control?" she presses. "When things don't go the way you planned?"

"If it's with you, I'll take every unexpected, unplanned second of it."

Her defenses are still there, but they're cracking.

"What if I can't go back to the way things were?" she asks. "What if I don't want to?"

"I don't want that either," I say. "I want something new. Something we build together. No more pretending."

She swallows hard. "Stellan, this isn't a small thing," her eyes are bright. "It's not just your heart on the line."

"I know," I say, stepping closer. "I'm not asking you to risk yours alone. I'm giving you mine, too."

Her breath stutters. "You're really doing this," she murmurs.

"For you? Always," I say.

"Okay," she says, voice trembling. "One more chance. But it's a leap, Stellan. For both of us."

"I'm ready," I say, because I am.

She doesn't wait. She grabs my lapels, pulls me down, and kisses me.

Not tentative or unsure. Like she's staking a claim. Like she's tired of running from what's always been ours.

Her hands slide up, fisting in my shirt, dragging me closer like she's done being careful. Like she's done letting me keep distance between us.

"Talia," I breathe against her lips. It's a plea.

She kisses me harder. Every ounce of anger, hurt, want—right there, between us. I grip her waist, anchoring her to me, because letting go isn't an option.

"This isn't careful anymore," she says, breathless.

"I don't want careful," I say, my voice rough. "I want you."

Her laugh is sharp, gasping. "Good. Because I'm not leaving."

That's all it takes. The dam breaks. My mouth crashes into hers, not gentle, not soft. This is every missed moment, every swallowed word, every time I almost told her.

Her fingers thread into my hair, pulling, demanding. I walk her back until her spine meets the wall, but she doesn't yield. She meets me head-on.

When we break apart, her pupils are blown wide, lips swollen, breath uneven. "I'm still mad at you," she says, but her hands say otherwise.

"Good," I say, pressing my forehead to hers. "Stay mad. Just stay."

Her lips curve and she's kissing me again.

But this isn't the same as before. This kiss isn't about anger. Or power. It's about choice. Her choice.

Her fingers thread into my hair, nails dragging against my scalp as her mouth claims mine—hungry, insistent. Every move says she's done letting me hold back. And I'm done pretending I can.

"I love you," I say against her lips. "Every fucking inch of you."

She shivers and lets out a small moan, one I'm willing to do anything to hear more of.

I back her toward the nearest surface, but she beats me to it—shoving my jacket off, working open my shirt with sharp, impatient hands. Buttons scatter. Neither of us cares.

"Talia—" I start, but she's already unbuckling my belt.

"Stop thinking," she says, breathless. "For once, just feel this."

I don't argue. I've never wanted anything more.

Her dress slides off her shoulders, pooling at her feet. No bra. No panties. Just her. Bare. Beautiful. Mine.

"Jesus, Talia," I breathe, my gaze devouring every inch of her. "You're going to ruin me."

"Good," she whispers, tugging me down into another kiss.

"Bedroom," I say, voice wrecked. "Now."

She doesn't argue.

I carry her through the house, her nails fucking embedded in my shoulders, her mouth trailing fire down my throat. Every step is hell. Every step is heaven.

By the time we hit the bed, we're half-undressed and fully feral.

I drop her onto the mattress, watching her bounce—hair wild, lips swollen, pupils blown wide.

"Off," she says, breathless. "All of it."

Fuck, I love her like this. I strip fast. Shirt ripped open. Pants shoved down. My cock's hard, heavy, already leaking and aching for her.

Her legs fall open. No shame. No hesitation.

And Christ, the sight of her—bare, flushed, glistening—is enough to bring me to my fucking knees.

I crawl over her, slow enough to make her squirm.

"This isn't going to be soft," I warn, dragging my cock through her wetness, teasing her slit, just to hear that sharp little gasp.

"Good," she pants. "I don't want soft. I want you to fuck me like you mean it."

That breaks me. I drive into her in one brutal stroke. She screams—high, sharp, perfect.

"Fuck, Talia," I groan, bracing myself as her heat clamps down, sucking me in in the best goddamn way.

Her nails bite into my back, dragging me closer. "Move, Stellan."

And I do. I fuck her hard. Deep. Every thrust a vow. Every slam of my hips a goddamn declaration.

"You're mine," I snarl into her ear.

"I've always been yours," she gasps, writhing beneath me.

I pin her wrist above her head, my other hand gripping her thigh, angling her up as I hammer into her.

The slap of skin echoes in the room. Wet. Slick. Sinful.

But it's her—her breathy moans, the way she chants my name—that undoes me.

"You love this," I grit out. "You love me filling you up. Ruining you."

"Fuck, yes," she cries, hips bucking. "Don't stop."

I drop my mouth to her breast, sucking her nipple hard, teeth grazing, making her arch, making her shudder.

Her thighs tremble. She's close.

So am I.

"Say it," I demand, biting at her throat. "Say you're mine."

"I'm yours," she sobs, breath ragged. "Always."

I slam into her, deep and punishing, until her body locks up—her orgasm ripping through her, pussy spasming around me.

That's it. I snap. I spill into her with a growl, hips jerking, buried so deep I never want to leave.

Her name's a curse and a prayer on my lips.

We ride it out— desperate and perfect.

When we finally collapse, it's not sex anymore. It's us. Breathless. Real. Loved.

Her head rests on my chest, her fingers tracing lazy circles over my ribs. Every touch feels like a grounding wire.

"Move back in," I say.

She huffs a breath, not quite a laugh. "You're serious."

"I've never been more serious in my life."

She shifts, props her chin on my chest, eyes narrowing. "What happens when I annoy you again? When I push too hard, ask too many questions?"

"Then you'll annoy me in our kitchen. In our bed. In our goddamn home," I say, brushing her hair back. "And I'll love you through every second of it."

Her lips part, but no argument comes.

"I don't want to fall asleep in a place that doesn't have you in it," I say, the words tasting like truth. "Not anymore."

She blinks, throat working.

"I'm not a charity case, Stellan," she says, quiet but firm.

"I know exactly what you are," I say, leaning in. "You're mine."

A long breath escapes her.

"Okay," she says, soft but sure. "I'll come home."

Relief punches through me.

I kiss her again—slow, deep, claiming.

Because I'm finally home.

CHAPTER TWENTY

Talia

My first day back at Rothwell feels strange. This time, I'm not alone.

It's been a couple of weeks since I moved back into the penthouse and we decided to stop pretending and actually be together.

Stellan didn't ask me to be in his office today. Instead, he made sure there was an extra chair pulled up to his desk. Made sure my laptop was already there. And made sure no one else would dare step foot inside.

He hasn't said it. But every glance—every time his hand brushes mine when passing papers, every time his eyes track me like he's counting the seconds I'm still here—it's loud. He's afraid of me not being here tomorrow.

Kate and Erin are back too. They'd call it loyalty, but I'd call it insanity. The last thing I wanted was for them to quit their jobs over me. But clearly, no one cared what I thought.

"You know I'm going to have to go back into my office at some point, right?" I chuckle. "I will have to take calls at the same time as you."

"But not today, Finch," Stellan says.

The look in his eyes makes me sit back in my seat. He looks... guilty maybe? I can't even describe this one. He's never looked this way before.

Erin and Kate walk in at that moment.

"Awwww," Kate says, batting her eyelashes. "You're so cute."

"We're just working Kate," Stellan says, while laughing.

"Still. You're adorable," Kate says.

"Did you guys see Opal's response?" Erin asks, business as usual.

"No," I say. "I know she recorded one. Stellan told me."

"Yeah," he says. "Dawson did it."

Erin walks over to them and shows us her tablet. She presses play.

Opal appears on screen, seated against a plain backdrop. Neutral tones. Nothing flashy. Her posture is perfect, hands folded neatly in her lap. But her eyes—her eyes are wrecked.

"My name is Opal Greer," she begins, voice shaking slightly. "For the past three years, I have been employed at Rothwell Strategic Holdings. During this time, I engaged in actions that violated the trust of this company, its leadership, and its employees."

She's not being dramatic. There isn't any edited music over the video.

"I accessed and manipulated internal credentials to leak sensitive information. I created fabricated employee profiles. I compromised the integrity of Rothwell's internal systems."

Stellan's jaw ticks.

"I did this of my own accord," Opal continues. "No outside influence. No financial incentive. This was a personal vendetta—rooted in my own misplaced anger and family history."

She exhales, slow.

"My sister, Maris, has always been the example I measured myself against. When her and Stellan Rothwell ended their relationship, the story I was told left me bitter. That bitterness guided my actions."

Opal glances down for a beat. When she looks up, her voice softens.

"But stories aren't always the truth. And my actions were mine alone."

My fingers tighten around the edge of the desk.

"I apologize to Rothwell Strategic Holdings. To Stellan Rothwell. To the employees whose work I undermined. And to Talia Rothwell—for questioning her integrity and involvement."

That last line lands heavier than the rest.

"I take full responsibility. No one else."

The screen fades to black.

"Did she write that or PR?" Kate asks.

"She didn't write anything down," Stellan says. "Dawson took her to the other room and recorded it."

"I just have a hard time believing she meant it," Kate says.

"Her body language shows remorse and her tone of voice is genuine," I say.

"That's kind of creepy," Kate says.

I just shrug. It's who I am. "So that's it?"

"What's it?" Erin says.

"The leak is out and neutralized," I say.

"Yeah, but our story is only beginning," Stellan says, while leaning in to kiss me.

"What the fuck is this?" Frankie says, crashing into my office.

"What?" Stellan says.

"I thought the leak was taken care of," she says.

"It is," I say.

"If that's the case, why did Opal release another thing saying that Talia is a fake?"

"Wait what?" I say.

Westwood Investigates | By Rhys Westwood

The Talia Cerny Effect: Rothwell Strategic Holdings' Most Strategic Acquisition

When Talia Cerny quietly married Stellan Rothwell, CEO of Rothwell Strategic Holdings, the business world recognized it for what it was: an optics maneuver. The company was bleeding reputation. A well-timed union offered the illusion of stability.

"She wasn't brought in for her business acumen," says a former Rothwell consultant. "She was brought in because she looked good on paper."

Yet somehow, Cerny remains.

In the wake of Opal Greer's confession to orchestrating internal data breaches, many have pointed to Cerny's involvement in uncovering the deception. But not everyone is convinced it was her brilliance at play.

"Sleeping with the CEO opens a lot of doors," one executive remarked bluntly. "Let's not rewrite history. She got access most of us earned with years of work."

Others within the company echo the sentiment.

"She didn't solve the leak. She stumbled onto it because she was too close to the right people," says an anonymous insider. "Right place, right pillow talk."

Everyone's thinking it. No one says it out loud.

"Her job was to fix the PR nightmare. She did. So why does she need to stay?"

While public perception has warmed to Cerny's involvement, internally, questions persist.

"It's leverage, not love," a former board member commented. "She was a strategic hire. A face. But now she's tangled in places she shouldn't be."

Even after Greer's admission, there's a lingering belief that Cerny's role at Rothwell Strategic Holdings remains precarious.

"She's efficient at cleanup, sure," says another source. "But don't mistake that for leadership. This isn't her world."

For now, Cerny stays. Whether as a fixture or a placeholder remains uncertain.

"I'll handle this," Stellan says, voice flat, but there's a tension in his jaw that says more than words.

I watch as he types. Usually, statements like this are passed off to comms teams, polished until they're safe. But not today. Not with my name on the line.

"Where are you planning to release that?" I ask, though I already know.

"Everywhere," he replies without looking up. "But first—directly to Rhys Westwood."

Official Statement from Stellan Rothwell, CEO of Rothwell Strategic Holdings

To Rhys Westwood, and anyone else questioning the credibility of my wife, Talia Rothwell:

Let's set the record straight.

Yes, I used a matchmaking service. After years of public relationships that served headlines more than happiness, I chose a different approach. One with discretion and wasn't a waste of time.

Talia Rothwell was matched to me through that service. Not because of optics or convenience. Talia wasn't hired to "fix" Rothwell. She wasn't a strategic pawn. She walked into a storm she didn't create and rebuilt a foundation most of you were content to watch crumble.

Every board member quoting anonymity should remember: they were in those rooms. They saw the leaks. They saw the damage. And they did nothing—until Talia forced them to act.

I paid for a matchmaking service.

I didn't pay for the woman who would end up saving this company.

Her name is Talia Rothwell. And she is mine.

—Stellan Rothwell

"You didn't have to do that," I say, shaking my head.

"I did," Stellan says, like it's the simplest truth in the world. "Because it's your name now. And they'll learn to use it properly."

I open my mouth with no idea what's about to come out. That's when the office doors slam open.

"Good," Genevieve announces, her voice all silk and venom. "Glad you're all here."

She doesn't slow down. Doesn't hesitate.

One moment, she's striding across the room. The next, her hand whips through the air, slicing across my cheek with enough force to rock my skull.

Pain blooms—hot, immediate, electric—fanning out from my jaw, across my face, down my neck.

My head snaps to the side, vision flashing white at the edges.

But I don't fall. I don't flinch. I anchor myself, spine straight, feet planted, swallowing down the taste of copper blooming in my mouth.

She wants a reaction. She's not getting one.

"What the fuck do you think you're doing?" Stellan growls, stepping between us.

But I'm not hiding behind him.

"You want to try that again, Gen?" I ask, voice low, the sting on my cheek nothing compared to the heat rising under my skin.

"I always knew you were a fake," Genevieve says, voice dripping sweet. "A paid prop in a dress. Hired help who got too comfortable playing house."

The words land with precision. She means to belittle me.

"That all you've got?" I ask, tilting my head. My cheek throbs with every syllable, but it's nothing compared to the heat curling low in my gut. "Because you're going to have to do better."

Genevieve's eyes narrow, mouth curling into something ugly.

"You think a marriage certificate makes you one of us? That wearing his ring gives you power?" She laughs, but there's no humor in it. "You'll always be the woman who was bought to fix a problem. Just another name he'll erase when you stop being useful."

Behind me, I feel Stellan move. A ripple of fury.

But I don't need him for this.

I take a step forward, closing the space between us.

"I wasn't hired to fix him, Gen," I say, voice low, razor-sharp. "I was matched with him. And somewhere between your schemes and his pride, I did what you couldn't."

Genevieve's smile sharpens, going for the throat. "I'm glad you're so confident," she says, voice dipped in sugar. "But when he's done playing house, when he remembers he never wanted the mess of a family, where does that leave you, Talia?"

She turns, aiming it at Stellan like a dagger.

"You don't want kids. You never did. You told me that, remember? No strings. No legacy. Just power on your terms." Her smile twists. "She's a temporary fix. You'll get tired of pretending."

Genevieve's lips curve into something ugly. "Well," she purrs, reaching into her bag, "since we're playing so honest today…"

She pulls out her phone. Tilts it just enough for me—and Stellan—to see.

One tap.

And there we are.

Grainy footage. The two of us. Private. Intimate. My nails digging into his shoulders. His mouth on my throat. Movements raw, desperate, ours.

The sound is mercifully muted, but it doesn't matter.

She's not showing this for shock.

She's showing it to shame.

"To think," Genevieve says, voice soft, dripping. "For all your pride, Stellan, you let her degrade you in your own office. On your own desk."

She turns off the video.

"You're disgusting," I say.

Stellan's voice cuts through, low and lethal. "You broke the law, Genevieve."

She lifts her chin, unbothered. "You're sleeping with your wife. Hardly scandalous."

He doesn't blink. "Exactly. My wife."

But she's not done.

"And what if she's pregnant?" Genevieve asks, eyes gleaming. "You never wanted kids. You said it yourself. And now? You're going to rewrite your entire life for a woman you barely know?"

She thinks she's landed the blow.

But Stellan just reaches for my hand, and laces his fingers through mine, anchoring us to one another.

"With her," he says, voice steady, raw, real, "I want everything."

"Fine," Gen says. "Prove it."

She reaches into her purse and pulls out a pregnancy test, handing it to me.

"You really woke up and chose delusion today, huh?" Frankie says, letting out a low whistle.

"You know, for someone bold enough to break federal law with a sex tape, this is a weird pivot," Erin adds, deadpan.

"Also, Gen, who carries a pregnancy test in their purse? Seriously. Are you okay?" Kate asks, tilting her head.

"I don't need to prove anything to you," I say, feeling Stellan's grip on my hand tighten. "But if it makes Stellan feel better, I'll take it."

Before anyone could talk me out of it, I grab the test and head into the bathroom in my office. There's one here, but I don't want people listening to me pee.

I take the test and walk back out, putting it on the desk. "I'm on the pill, not that it's any of your business. So not pregnant."

These are the worst three minutes of my life. I'm not nervous, but annoyed. A timer goes off.

"Really, Gen?" Kate says. "A timer?"

She just shrugs. "Read the test."

Fine. I pick it up, turn it over. One line. Negative. A pin could drop.

"See?" I say, holding it up. "Negative. Crisis averted."

But Frankie's brow furrows. She steps closer, plucks it from my hand.

"Look again, genius," she mutters. "There's a second line. Faint, but there."

My stomach flips.

I take it back. Bring it closer. There it is. A thin line of pink. Barely visible, but there.

"No way," I breathe.

Stellan's beside me before I realize. His breath ghosts my ear as he leans in.

"That's not nothing," he says, voice low, threaded with something raw.

He sees it. Clear as day. His hand slides around my waist, pulling me into his side.

He laughs. Not mocking. Not disbelieving. Relief. Joy. Something fierce and real.

"We're having a baby," he says, pressing his forehead to mine.

"What!" Genevieve exclaims, snatching the test. "You're happy about this?"

He slides his hand to my lower back and says, "Of course I'm happy."

The way he says it... it's the one thing Genevieve can never refute or take away from us.

"I love her," he adds. "I love every hard-earned, infuriating, brilliant part of her. And this?" He gestures to the test. "This is ours."

Genevieve opens her mouth again, but Erin's voice cuts in—smooth and lethal.

"You should leave, Genevieve. While you still have a few clients left."

Genevieve stiffens. "Excuse me?"

Kate folds her arms. "Word gets around. The little things you've been saying. Gossiping to other clients that happen to be clients of ours as well. Hinting that Talia trapped him. That she's not stable. That the marriage isn't real. They told us everything."

"I never—" Genevieve starts, but Frankie's already stepping forward.

"You did," Frankie says with a sharp smile. "The problem is, you said it to people who care more about their reputations than your bitterness."

"Rothwell Strategic doesn't tolerate anyone who threatens the family image," Kate adds. "Neither do our clients. And after this? They're done with you."

"You can't blacklist me," Genevieve snaps.

"We don't have to," Erin says, cool as ice. "The clients are doing it for us."

Frankie leans in, voice honey-sweet. "Vegas is built on power and proximity. And you just got cut off from both."

Genevieve's jaw tightens, but she sees it—there's no way back from this.

She turns, heels clicking across the marble as she storms out. No one watches her leave.

Because the second the door clicks shut, Frankie spins back to us, eyes bright.

"Well," she says, clapping her hands once. "Now that *that* trash has been taken out, can we talk about the *actual* good news?"

She points at the test still in my hand.

"You're having a damn baby! Holy shit, Talia."

Stellan's laugh rumbles through me as he pulls me into his side.

Everything is right in the world.

CHAPTER
TWENTY-ONE

Talia

I'm leaving Rothwell a little early today. Just a routine doctor's appointment. Nothing urgent, nothing dramatic. I wish Stellan could come, but something came up—completely unavoidable, he said.

He promised he'll be at all the rest. I believe him. He always keeps his promises.

I tuck my phone into my purse, step into the elevator, and ride it down to the main lobby.

It's busy—noisy, bright, full of movement. People rushing in and out, laughing, talking, tapping on phones. Just a normal afternoon.

I spot Rafe near the security desk, chatting with someone. He sees me and gives a small wave, cutting across the lobby with that easy energy he always carries.

"Talia," he says, smiling. "You're headed out?"

I nod. "Doctor's appointment."

"Need a ride?" he offers without hesitation. "I'm heading out any-way, could drop you."

I almost say yes. It would be easier. Safer.

But something in me wants a little space to think. A quiet car. A moment alone.

"I'm good, thanks," I say, smiling back. "Appreciate it though."

"You sure?" He glances toward the parking structure.

"I've got it," I assure him. "I'll see you later."

I start to move past him.

But his hand catches my elbow.

Not roughly. Just enough to stop me.

"Talia," he says again. Lower this time. "Come with me."

I blink at him, confused. "What—?"

I feel it. The press of something cold and hard beneath my ribs. Subtle. Hidden under his jacket.

A gun.

"I don't want to hurt you," he says, voice still calm. Almost gentle. "But I will if I have to."

The floor drops out from under me.

The lobby is full. People everywhere. But no one notices.

Rafe's smile doesn't slip. He looks like he's just escorting me to the door.

He takes me to his car and opens the passenger door like a gentle-man.

"Get in," he says.

I do. Not because I trust him, but because I don't want to know what a bullet feels like.

The door closes with a click.

He gets in behind the wheel, starts the engine like this is routine. Like he's driving me to lunch.

For a minute, neither of us speaks.

I press my hands to my thighs to keep them from shaking. My heart's hammering, but my voice stays measured when I ask, "Where are we going?"

"You'll see," he says, eyes on the road. "Just sit tight."

"That's not an answer."

"No," he agrees, glancing at me. "It's not."

We hit the freeway. The city thins. My pulse doesn't.

"You know this is a mistake," I say. "Whatever you think this is—it isn't."

"I think it's exactly what it looks like," he replies, tone flat. "You need a reset. And I'm the only one willing to do what's necessary."

I stare at him, stunned. "Necessary for what?"

"For getting you out. From under him. From all of this," he says, gesturing vaguely. "You don't even see it anymore. What he's done to you."

My throat tightens. "I'm not trapped, Rafe."

He actually laughs. It's humorless. "You don't think I saw it? The way you flinch when he walks in the room. How you make yourself small to keep the peace."

I want to scream, to tell him he's wrong, but I stay motionless.

Outside the window, the landscape changes. The clean lines of the city give way to rougher edges—industrial lots, empty side roads, dust curling in the heat.

I recognize none of it.

"Where are we?" I ask, my voice tight.

He doesn't answer.

The car turns off the main road, gravel crunching under the tires. I see it—a small, squat building ahead. He pulls up and puts the car in park, the engine dies, and for a second the silence is so loud it presses against my ears.

"Get out," he says.

I hesitate.

He draws the gun again, just enough to remind me it never left. "Now."

I open the door and step out. Heat rises off the pavement. My legs feel like wire. Every nerve is too loud. He walks beside me, like this is a favor. Like he's escorting me into safety, not locking me away.

When we reach the door, he pauses.

"You'll understand soon," he says. "I'm doing this because I care."

He opens the door and shoves me inside.

But it's not what I expected.

The lights are low, warm. The air smells like something cooked too long—meat, maybe. There's a table set. Two chairs. Plates. Real ones. Wine glasses. A vase of dead flowers in the center.

"You're hungry," he says, brushing past me to the kitchen. "I made lamb. It's not perfect, but it's better than whatever garbage they feed you in Rothwell's little world."

He's trying for casual, like this is some dinner party and I just forgot to RSVP. But the energy under his voice is too tight—too rehearsed.

I stay frozen by the door. My hands twitch at my sides.

He sets down a plate like we're on a date. Like this isn't real.

"Sit," he says, nodding to the chair across from his.

I don't move. Not because I'm frozen. Because I'm watching.

His eyes don't narrow. That's good. He doesn't like defiance. His tells are subtle, but there—they're always there. That shallow inhale, the pulse tick just under his jaw.

His voice softens. "Talia. Please."

Soft voice. Open hands. Controlled posture. He thinks softness works on me. That's his read. And maybe, right now, it needs to be mine too.

I sit.

The fork is heavy in my hand. He pours wine—red, too much, no coasters. Trying to make this look like something it's not. He's playing house. And he thinks I'll play too.

"I always knew we'd come back to this," he says, cutting into the food. "You were never meant to end up with him. That's not who you are."

I don't answer. I keep my eyes on the plate. He's testing me—poking for cracks, watching how I react to the rewrite of my life.

"You think I don't see it?" he says, sharper now. "How miserable you look with Rothwell. How cold he is to you. You don't have to lie here. Not with me."

Control slipping. He's waiting for me to deny it. He wants to feel justified.

"You don't know what you're talking about," I say, quiet. Neutral.

"I do," he insists. "They've forced you into this. Blackmail, contracts—your mother, the Society. You think I don't know what they do to women like you?"

That's the second time he's said "women like you." It's not about me. It never was. It's about power. About the story he's already decided I belong in.

I blink at him. Let him fill in the blank.

His smile twitches, almost fond. "You were brave. You were the first one who didn't flinch when I said no to them. That's why I knew. You were mine before either of us understood it."

"I was never—"

"Don't," he snaps. "Don't rewrite it."

There it is. The crack. His hands clench around the knife, white-knuckled now. The story is sacred. Any deviation is betrayal.

"That night, you kissed me. You did. You looked at me like I was the only one who saw you."

He's rewriting it in real time. Out loud. Trying to convince himself more than me.

"I said no."

"You said you were scared." His voice cracks. He believes this. He's not posturing—he's pleading with a version of me that never existed.

"You said no because you didn't want to lose control. Because I made you feel something real."

"No," I say again, and it feels like my voice has to claw its way out of my throat. "You hurt me. You held me down."

"I loved you!" he explodes, slamming the knife into the table hard enough that the plate jumps. "I still do! And you—you act like it was nothing. Like I didn't matter."

My flinch is manufactured, he needs it. He needs to see fear. That's what keeps the fantasy intact. If I fight, he breaks.

His breath heaves. He drags a hand down his face. The next words come quieter.

"You're just scared. That's okay. You'll remember soon."

He walks around the table, and crouches beside me like I'm breakable.

"I know how hard it's been. Pretending with him. Living in that house like a prisoner. But you don't have to anymore."

I go still. Not out of fear. Out of focus.

"I'm going to make it better. I'm going to fix everything. And when this is over—when they can't touch us anymore—you'll marry me. The way it should've been from the start."

When he reaches up to run a hand through my hair, I let him.

"Don't worry, Talia," he whispers. "I'll keep you safe."

That's when I let the mask slip on. The one he wants to see.

I lower my lashes. Let my voice soften. Let myself sound small. "I didn't realize how much I missed this," I say. "Being seen."

He stills. I feel it—the exact moment the delusion swells in his chest. "I knew you'd remember," he breathes.

"You were right," I say. "About Stellan. About the house. About... everything."

His shoulders loosen. His smile is reverent now, like I've just answered a prayer he's waited for for years.

"You don't have to say it yet," he says. "You don't have to mean it all. Not right now. I know you will."

He stands, and lets out a sigh like it's over. Like I've surrendered.

"I want to show you what our life will be," he says, beaming. "Dinner. Next we'll talk. Then we start over." He lifts his glass. "To second chances."

My hands don't shake as I pick up my own. "To second chances," I echo.

I drink. Because this is a performance. He's smiling when I place my glass gently back on the table.

I give it ten seconds before I start feeling it.

Not in my mouth. Not in my stomach.

My fingertips.

A slow warmth seeps into my skin where they touch the armrests. Not heat—numbness. Like I've been outside too long in the cold.

My heartbeat spikes.

I flex my fingers. Nothing. They don't move the way they should. I try to lift my hand. It's sluggish, foreign.

It's not the wine.

My eyes flick to the glass. No residue. No bitter aftertaste.

He's watching me too closely.

The chair.

He drugged the *chair*.

The fabric—it's soft, but treated. Infused. Topical. Absorbed through contact. I didn't even think. I sat when he asked. I wanted him calm.

"You're tired," he says gently. "It's okay. Just rest your head."

My vision sways, the edges feathering. I press my lips together. Hard. Anchoring myself in sensation.

"I don't..." I start, but my tongue feels thick. My head tilts.

He moves closer. Stands behind me, hands on my shoulders.

"You've been carrying so much," he murmurs. "Let me take it from you."

The room's not spinning—it's melting. My thoughts slide off each other, frictionless.

"You were always so tense," he says, voice low. "Even when you wanted it, you didn't know how to let yourself have it."

He crouches beside me, thumb tracing the edge of my jaw.

"There she is," he whispers. "There's my girl."

He presses a kiss to my temple—slow, reverent. I don't move.

"I know you're scared," he whispers. "You don't have to be. I'm not him."

His hand drifts to the back of my neck. He doesn't grip, doesn't pull. Just rests there, like he's comforting me. Like this is a moment we agreed on.

I let my eyes close halfway. I let my body slump an inch deeper into the chair.

"Come on," he says softly. "Let's get you comfortable." He stands, hands moving to the buttons of his shirt.

One. Two.

He doesn't rush. He's not aggressive. This is a ritual for him. A fantasy he's played out in his head a hundred times.

The fabric parts down the center. He shrugs it off, folds it over the back of a nearby chair with eerie precision.

He walks toward me, bare-chested now, eyes locked on mine.

"You're beautiful like this," he murmurs. "Soft. Quiet. Open."

I feel it in my legs now. The numbness. The weight. Like I'm sinking into my own body, like it's turning into something unresponsive.

He kneels in front of me again, hands moving to my ankle, fingers brushing the strap of my shoe.

"You always made everything so difficult," he says, not unkindly. "So much noise. So many shields. But now... now you're finally letting me in."

That's when I move.

My leg snaps up—every muscle screaming, every nerve burning—and the heel of my shoe slams into his chin with a crack that vibrates up my spine. Something splits. Bone or tooth. Maybe both.

He reels back with a guttural sound, spit and blood flying from his mouth in a spray.

I don't wait.

I hurl myself forward, the chair scraping against the floor as I collapse to my knees. The impact is brutal—my bones jolt, skin tears on impact—but I don't feel it. My eyes are locked on the shards.

The wine glass. Splintered, jagged, glinting under the table like a trap. I grab the longest piece—my fingers slice open along the stem, blood mixing with blood—and I rise just enough to swing.

It catches him across the face. A wet, meaty rip. Cheekbone to jawline. The flesh peels, a raw flap of skin hanging as he screams—a high, cracked, animal sound.

"Still too much noise for you?" I rasp, my voice shredded.

He lunges. I don't flinch, don't think, just drive the glass into his side, deep and merciless. I feel it punch through tissue, muscle, something hard—maybe a rib. My whole hand disappears in blood.

He howls, eyes bulging, body convulsing as I twist. He makes to grab me, but it's clumsy, panicked—fingers scrambling over my collarbone, nails digging in. We collapse again, a mess of limbs, slipping in his blood.

I punch him hard across the jaw and drive my elbow into his cheekbone as he reels. When he stumbles, I grab the back of his neck and slam his face into the floor until blood smears across the wood in jagged streaks.

His nose folds sideways. Something bursts. He makes a sound like choking on gravel.

Flesh rips beneath my teeth—his skin separating in stringy bursts—and the taste floods my mouth, copper and bile and something rancid.

He screams and jerks back, hand dangling useless, blood pouring from the torn meat of his wrist.

Half crawling, half sliding across the floor, I try to spit as much of him as I can out. If I can get to the chair, I might be able to reach the knife still stabbed into the table.

Behind me, he's sobbing, gagging, swearing through shattered teeth.

My fingers wrap around the knife handle just as the click sounds.

Not a door. Not a footstep. A trigger.

I freeze.

Slowly, I turn.

Rafe's on one knee, face smeared with blood, shirt off, and his hand—his fucking hand is wrapped around a gun aimed straight at my chest.

His mouth is trembling. His eyes wide. But his finger?

Rock solid.

"Talia," he breathes, voice raw.

I don't blink. "Put it down," I say, inching sideways, keeping the table between us. "You don't have to do this."

He shakes his head, but the gun wavers.

"You don't understand," he mutters. "You don't know what it's like—watching someone love a version of you that doesn't exist."

I soften my voice, slow my breath, and let the knife fall from my fingers and clatter to the floor.

"I do," I say. "I know exactly what that's like."

His gaze locks on mine, confused. Vulnerable. The barrel dips another inch.

"You wanted to be seen," I continue, soft and sure. "To matter. And you do. You always did." His breath hitches. "I see you, Rafe."

He blinks. His hands begin to tremble. His face changes. Hardens.

"You're doing it again," he growls. "That thing. That voice. That *fucking act.*"

"Rafe—"

"Don't!" he shouts. "You stall. You soften. You *disarm*. That's your trick, right? Make us think we're special. Make us *confess*." His lip curls, and something wild flares behind his eyes. "You really think I didn't study you too?"

He snarls and lifts the gun again. "You think I'm that fucking *stupid?*"

The gunshot rips the air in half.

Pain explodes in my side—hot, searing, like a flame being driven into bone. I hit the wall, then the floor, breath gone, blood already spilling under me.

I clutch the wound, choking on air.

"I loved you!" he screams, pacing in short, feral bursts. "I *protected* you! I gave you every chance, and you—goddamn you, you *used* it!"

I press my palm to the wound, every breath a battle.

"You don't get to walk away," he growls, stalking toward me, gun still raised. "You don't get to win."

The floor tilts beneath me.

My hands are soaked. My breath's coming shallow. The edges of the room are curling inward, black is creeping in like smoke under a door.

I press harder against the wound, but it's not enough.

He keeps coming.

I can't feel my fingers anymore.

I think of Stellan.

Of the baby.

Of the name I'll never get to say out loud.

Suddenly, everything goes dark.

CHAPTER TWENTY-TWO

Stellan

This has been the longest day of my life. It was meeting after meeting. Coming back means a ton of extra work.

I hate that I missed Talia's first doctor's appointment. She was so excited and I wanted to go with her. Honestly, I'm lucky she's not more mad than she was when I told her I had to work.

"Talia!" I yell, walking in the penthouse. I drop my keys and bag on the table that she added by the front door, just like I do any time I get home after her.

My brow furrows when I'm met with silence. It's not like her to be silent. She's been tired lately, but she usually takes naps on the couch until I get home.

"Jean," I say.

She turns around and smiles at me. "Good evening, Mr. Rothwell. Is Mrs. Rothwell joining you for dinner tonight?"

I freeze at that. *Joining me for dinner?*

"Isn't she home?" I ask, dreading the answer.

"No," she says, turning to look at me fully. "I thought she had a doctor's appointment today."

"Yeah. I couldn't go to this one," I say.

"She isn't back yet," she says. "Maybe it's taking longer than she thought. What time was it?"

"12," I say.

She was going to lunch after with Kate and Erin. Maybe they're still with her. I need to text them. Something doesn't feel right about this.

Stellan

> How was lunch with Talia? She didn't text after.

Kate

> She didn't come. Figured she was swamped.

Erin

> Or having pregnancy brain. Probably went home to crash. Girl was wiped.

Stellan

> She's not home. Jean says she never came home.

Kate

> ...That's not right.

Erin

> She would've told us.

Stellan

> Something's wrong.

Kate

We're coming. Bringing Dawson.

I'm worried now. They're right. This isn't like her at all.

I pace the living room until I hear the elevator come up. In walks Kate, Erin, Dawson, Frankie, and Beckett.

"What are you guys doing here?" I ask, scanning Frankie and Beckett as they step into the penthouse.

"Kate called us while they were in the car," Frankie says, arms crossed, tone clipped. "Said Talia never came back from lunch."

"That's not like her," Kate adds, frowning. "She doesn't just vanish."

"She's not at home," I say, jaw tight. "Jean said she never came back after her meetings."

The room goes still.

"Maybe she's laying low," Erin offers, but even she doesn't sound convinced. "Resting. Headache. Something small."

"No," I say, already moving. "Something's off."

I turn toward the hall. Beckett follows. So does Frankie.

"Where's Cal?" I ask.

Beckett glances at his phone. "He had back-to-backs all afternoon. Strategy deck. He's probably still buried."

And then the door opens.

Cal walks in, loosened tie and a coffee in one hand. He stops when he sees us.

"What's going on?" he asks, frowning.

Beckett doesn't sugarcoat it. "Talia's missing."

Cal's entire posture shifts. Coffee forgotten. "What do you mean missing?"

"She left Rothwell around noon for a doctor's appointment," I say. "She never showed for lunch after."

Cal sets the cup down, already reaching for his phone. "I'll pull footage. See who she was talking to."

"We already saw her with Rafe," I say, stepping in closer. "But check everything. Who else she passed. Who was watching her. I want eyes on every damn hallway she touched."

Cal nods, already moving toward the console. "Beckett, grab the east elevators. I'll take the lobby."

Frankie's typing something on her phone. Probably sending Iris after comms. Erin's pacing. Beckett taps a few keys and brings up the lobby feed. We all lean in. "There," he says. "Talia. Right at twelve-oh-seven."

She's walking out, head down, focused. Purse on her shoulder. No hesitation.

Rafe steps into frame. He's too close. Smiling. Not creepy at first glance—just casual. But we all see it now. Predatory.

"She talks to him for twenty-five seconds," Beckett mutters, scrubbing slowly. "Then—"

"Right there," Cal cuts in, switching angles. "They go out the side doors. She doesn't even text first."

"Hold up," Erin says, leaning forward. "Zoom in."

Cal tightens the frame.

Rafe's hand is on her back. "Son of a bitch," I breathe.

"Do we have parking lot coverage?" Cal asks, already switching feeds.

Another screen pops up. Black sedan. Rafe opens the passenger door. Talia gets in.

"I need plate tracking," I say. "Now."

Cal's already dialing. "Security's flagging it. If he used his own car, we'll have him on traffic cams in fifteen."

But fifteen is too long. Talia's been gone for hours.

I grab my phone and call Gareth. "Rothwell?"

"You seen Rafe?" My voice is already fraying.

"No. Why?" Gareth sounds like he's still catching up.

"He left with Talia around noon. Said something about giving her a ride. She hasn't been heard from since."

There's a beat of silence, then, "Shit."

I press a hand to the back of my neck, trying to breathe around the heat rising in my chest. "Talk to me."

"I didn't think it was anything serious," Gareth says, voice low, I can hear him pacing. "He's been... off. Staring too long at her photo. Keeps it on his desk like it's nothing. Talks about her like they've got some history."

I close my eyes. "You should've told me."

"I know," he says. "I should've. But I didn't think he'd act on it. He's not violent. Obsessive, maybe. But not..."

"We pulled security footage," I cut in. "He walked her out. Put his hand on her. Put a gun on her. Got her into his car. She never came back."

"I'll get ahold of him," Gareth says, and he sounds different now. Grim. "One way or another."

The line goes dead.

"So now what?" Frankie asks.

"We need to call him," I say. "Now."

"Are you sure?" Erin says, ears perked.

"Absolutely," I respond. "I'll call him now."

I hit the number. It rings once.

"You never call me," a voice drawls on the other end. Smooth. Dangerous. "It's me calling you. That's how this works."

"Not today," I say, voice flat. "I need you."

"Talk," he says, all business.

"My wife's missing," I say, pacing. "Rafe Donnelly took her. But the police won't move—they can't see past his badge. They think it has to be a misunderstanding. That it can't be one of their own." My grip tightens around the phone. "I need eyes. I need muscle. We're not waiting."

"You're lucky I like you, Rothwell." His tone shifts, lethal now. "I'll be there in ten. Bringing some friends."

Before I can say more, the line goes dead.

"Who did you call?" Frankie asks.

"Dante Valera," I say, dropping the name like a hammer.

That gets everyone's attention. Beckett whistles low. "The Dante Valera? You've been holding that ace?"

"He doesn't get called in unless the city's bleeding," I say, pacing. "And when he moves, it's surgical."

"Runs Obsidian like it's his playground. But underneath? He knows where every body's buried. Half of them because he put them there," Beckett says. "He's also the one person who'll find Rafe faster than any cop."

"Ten minutes," I say, glancing at my watch. "Be ready."

He wasn't kidding when he said he would be here in ten minutes.

Dante Valera does not rush. He doesn't need to. His pace is calculated to suggest indifference, the kind of careless ease that takes years to perfect. Tailored charcoal suit, sleeves pushed just far enough to imply he's capable of getting his hands dirty—if he ever desired to. Open collar, no tie.

There are two men flanking him.

Not bodyguards. Not associates.

Blood.

Massimo Bianchi. The king of the southern syndicates. Charisma weaponized. Fire in his smile, steel in his spine. He didn't inherit his power—he took it. Built it with bare hands and ruthless charm. The kind of man who makes you believe deals are handshakes until you realize he never promised fairness.

To his left, his son. Alessio Bianchi. Younger. Colder. Where Massimo commands with presence, Alessio does it with silence. His power isn't announced. It's calculated. Surgical. Every inch of him is precision, from the cut of his suit to the quiet, assessing weight of his gaze.

Legacy in real time.

By Kate's gasp beside me, I know the rest of the room has caught up.

"Nice to see you, Dante" I say, extending my hand for him to shake.

"Stellan," Dante says, taking my hand in a tight grip. "I trust you know Massimo and Alessio."

"I do," I respond, nodding my head and shifting my gaze to the men. "But I'm afraid we've never been formally introduced."

Massimo's smile is a slow, wicked curve. "No need for formalities, Mr. Rothwell. You're a hard man to miss."

"They're looking to contract your services," Dante continues, his tone casual. "I told them you're the best."

Of course he did. Dante doesn't make introductions without making business deals.

"We'll talk about that," Massimo says, stepping into my space. It doesn't feel like a challenge, but as a reminder why they're really here. "After we find your wife."

"I filled them in," Dante adds, smooth as ever. "They're here to help."

"At what cost?" My question is direct. I'm not about to sugarcoat anything now.

Desperation is a luxury I can't afford. The mafia never does anything for free.

Massimo laughs. Low, rich, like he enjoys the question more than the answer. "I like him. He asks the right questions."

Next to him, Alessio's voice is quieter. "We want you to take us on as clients. When we call, we expect the best you have."

"My son." Massimo claps a hand to Alessio's shoulder, pride cutting through the moment. "Always so business-minded."

His tone is indulgent. His eyes are not. Legacy breeds ambition. But it's the quiet ones who play the long game.

"I don't make promises for 100% success," I say. "And I don't work on good intentions."

"Neither do we," Alessio replies, meeting my gaze without flinching.

"We saw how you handled Lomier's boy. Impressive. With us, you won't have that problem," he says, tone shifting, his smile gone. "We don't breed fools."

Massimo shifts, voice low, almost conversational. "But speaking of fools... Rafe Donnelly, the cop."

"He kidnapped my wife," I say.

"We know him," Alessio says, voice like a blade sliding free of its sheath. "We know who he's been speaking to. Who he's selling to. And how many bodies are stacked under that little crusade of his."

I don't respond right away.

I believe him.

Alessio steps forward, smooth as ever, expression unreadable. "You think Rafe's some rogue agent? Misguided idealist? He's not. He's a parasite. He feeds off institutions like yours. Uses your language—order, ethics, structure—and then bends it until it snaps around your throat."

Massimo doesn't bother with preamble. "He's been peddling false evidence to anyone who'll listen. Law enforcement. Intelligence groups. NGOs. A few of ours."

"And if you dig deep enough," Alessio adds, "you'll find at least two internal complaints with his name tucked into the margins. Nothing coordinated. Just sloppiness—flagged interviews, missing timestamps. The kind of thing that only stands out in hindsight."

"Because he's not clever," Massimo says. "He's entitled. He thinks proximity gives him power. And when that doesn't work, he turns messy—emotional. Desperate. The danger isn't in what he plans. It's in how far he'll spiral when no one sees him."

"And now he's got my wife," I say, my voice flat and dangerous.

"Yes," Massimo replies. "Which means he's moved past leverage. This is personal now."

Erin crosses her arms. "So why didn't you do something sooner?"

Alessio looks at her like that question's cute. "Because we needed him to step over the line. And kidnapping your wife? That'll do it."

"Let's roll," I say.

We all head out to our cars. Massimo and Alessio go in theirs, Dante in his. Erin and Kate go in the third row while Cal and Beckett get in the backseat. I climb in the front with Dawson behind the wheel.

The last thing I want to do is tell the women they can't come. They are part of our team too. But I do have one stipulation for them.

"You need to stay in the car," I tell them.

Erin nods and Kate doesn't blink. But Frankie? Frankie bristles.

"What—excuse me?" Her hands go to her hips, chin lifting like she's gearing up for a fight. "Since when do I—"

"I agree," Beckett cuts in. His tone is calm, but final. "You stay."

Frankie's head snaps toward him. The betrayal is palpable.

"Of course you do," she mutters, jagged enough to cut glass.

"Frankie." My tone is clipped, final. "Not now."

She opens her mouth—then slams it shut. Smart. For once.

The desert doesn't hide things. It exposes them. No noise. No cover. Just open land, cracked and dry, the air sharp enough to cut skin. Darkness settles here differently— heavy, with nowhere to go.

The cabin sits squat against the scrub, its outline jagged against the pale wash of headlights. Weathered wood, tin roof, the kind of place people drive past without looking. Which makes it perfect for men like him.

The door bursts open.

Rafe staggers out, blood slick down his throat, soaking into the collar of his shirt. Dark, wet, fresh. More on his hands. Smudged across his ribs where he tried—and failed—to stop the bleeding.

The Bianchis move first. Firearms drawn without theatrics. Dante follows, slower, his draw casual but sure. Their backup fans out, forming a wall.

Rafe laughs. A raw, broken sound.

"You're too late," he chokes. "She's already dead."

For one brutal second, I believe him.

"What do you want to do with him?" Dante asks, twirling his gun with a kind of lazy menace.

"I want to kill him," I say, and mean every word.

"Alessio, let's take him to the blacksite," Massimo says smoothly.

"Sure, Father," Alessio replies, already moving. His fist slams into Rafe's face with a wet, sickening crack. Cartilage crunches. Bone gives way.

Rafe collapses, blood spraying in a sharp arc as he hits the dirt.

"Go see to your girl, Stellan," Massimo tells me, voice quiet, calm. "We'll take him to the blacksite. You can meet us there when you're ready."

They drag Rafe off, his head lolling, body limp. Still breathing. For now.

I run.

The cabin door is cracked open.

And when I step inside, I see her.

She's crumpled on the floor beside the bed.

Blood is everywhere.

Pooling beneath her hip, smeared across the warped floorboards in dark, sluggish streaks. It clings to her hands, her face, soaked through what's left of her shirt. Fresh and dried, layered like a map of what he did to her.

For a moment, she doesn't look alive. She looks like a body.

My heart is breaking, shattering, I've never known an emotion like this. Without thinking, I drop to my knees next to her, lifting her head to lay in my lap.

"Talia," I shake her. "Baby stay with me."

I press my fingers to her throat, relieved when the pulse kicks beneath my fingers.

Until I feel it. Wet. Hot. Spurting against my hand.

Blood. Too much. Too fast.

My hand presses to her side. The warmth spills between my fingers like sand through a fist.

"She's been shot!" My voice snaps out.

"Ambulance ETA five minutes out!" Dante calls back.

"Stay with me, Finch."

My hands are slick with her blood, sliding, failing. I press harder. Too hard. I don't know anymore.

"You're not done. You don't get to be done."

Her lashes flicker. Barely. But it's enough to wreck me.

"You're stubborn. Don't you dare stop now."

The pulse beneath my hand stutters, faint and fragile.

"I need you to fight." My voice is rough, splintering. "Because I can't—"

The world shatters.

"I can't lose you, Finch."

A breath. A truth I never said.

"I won't survive it."

Not like this. Not when I was too late.

CHAPTER
TWENTY-THREE

Talia

E verything hurts. Breathing. Thinking. Existing. Pain isn't sharp
anymore—it's dull, constant, like the world pressing down on
every inch of me.

I try to claw toward consciousness, but the abyss keeps dragging me
under. It's thick, suffocating, a weightless kind of drowning. There's
no light, no sound. Just the echo of my heartbeat, slowing. Fading.

But one thought cuts through.

I need to see Stellan. Not want. *Need*. Like oxygen. Like blood.

Darkness coils tighter, wrapping around my chest, pulling me
down.

I can hear his voice, like he's right next to me. So close. So broken.

"Finch," he whispers, his voice frayed, barely holding together. "I'm
here."

It shouldn't matter. It should be just another sound swallowed by the dark. But it isn't. His voice pulls at me. A thread tugging against the undertow.

But the darkness pulls harder. It doesn't want to let go.

I don't know how long I've been out, but I feel myself starting to wake.

It's like swimming through molasses—every breath heavy, every thought slow. My body feels foreign. Bruised. Like I've been fighting a battle I barely survived.

"I've got you, Finch," Stellan says, his thumb brushing over my knuckles. The motion is steady, almost desperate, like he's memorizing the shape of me in case I slip away again.

I latch onto his voice, letting it anchor me. I sync my breathing to his cadence. His touch feels real. Safe.

The door swings open, shattering the fragile quiet.

"Vitals spiking," a nurse says, already at my side, her tone clinical, detached.

"BP's climbing," another adds, fingers cold against my wrist, like I'm a chart to correct.

But Stellan doesn't move. Doesn't flinch.

"Stay with me," he says, softer now, but every word lands like a lifeline.

"Where am I?" I ask, my voice raw, scraping out like it's been locked away too long.

"You're in the hospital," Stellan says, his thumb never stopping its slow circles over my skin. Like if he stops, so will I.

"How long?" I whisper, staring at the ceiling because looking at him feels too dangerous.
I'm afraid of what I'll see in his face.

"Two days," he says, quietly, as if the words might crack the fragile thing holding us together.

Two days. I swallow hard. It feels longer. It feels like I've been gone forever.

"I should be dead," I say. The words hang between us, brittle. I don't know if it's a statement or a question.

His jaw tightens. The muscle jumps. "You're not," he says, but it sounds like a vow. Like a warning. Like a prayer.

I close my eyes. He's not telling me something.

For a moment, all I hear is the machines.

Beeping. Mocking. I'm alive. I'm breathing. But something vital—something *mine*—is gone.

"We lost the baby," he says, and it sounds like he's confessing to murder.

The words don't hit all at once. They seep in. Slow. Drowning me inch by inch.

I don't feel the bed beneath me anymore. I don't feel his hand. All I feel is the emptiness.

"I couldn't stop it, Finch."

His voice breaks.

"There was too much blood. Too fast. And I—" He drags a hand through his hair, fingers trembling. "I was right there. I was holding you. And I still couldn't save you. I still couldn't save him."

Him.

A sob claws its way up my throat, but it doesn't come out soft. It's raw. Violent.

My arms wrap around my stomach. But there's nothing to hold.

No soft curve of life. No heartbeat under my skin. Just... nothing.

"I would've given you my blood, my heart, anything," he says, voice splintering. "But it wasn't enough. I wasn't enough."

A sound tears out of me. Not human. Not words. Grief in its purest, ugliest form.

I curl into myself, but there's no safety in it. Only the hollow where my baby should be.

I should have protected him. My body should have been his shelter. Instead, it became his grave.

I'm choking now. On air. On truth.

"I'm sorry," I gasp, but I don't know who I'm apologizing to.

Our son.

Stellan.

Myself.

It doesn't matter. The word feels useless.

Because no apology can fill this emptiness.

"I lost our baby," I whisper, a sob curling into the words. "He killed our baby. He tried to kill me. He ripped him from me."

I'm shaking now, the fury pulsing through me, drowning out the machines, the walls, even Stellan.

"I hope he suffers. I hope every breath hurts. I hope when you end him, Stellan, it's not fast. *It's not merciful.*"

My fists slam into the mattress, useless, but I want to break something. Anything.

"He doesn't get to take this from me. He doesn't get to walk away from this." The words blur with tears, but I don't stop. "He took my baby. He took *our* son. And I want him to bleed for it."

I'm gasping now, each breath a fight.

That's what breaks him.

Stellan's head bows, his shoulders shaking as everything crushes down on him. No quiet, composed unraveling—this is raw, brutal grief, the kind you can't disguise.

I don't wait. My hands reach for him, pulling him in, clinging like he's the only thing tethering me to this broken, bleeding world. And when he folds into me, when his arms wrap around me so tightly it hurts, it's not careful. It's desperate.

We cry like we've both been shot, like we're still bleeding out on that cabin floor. There's no control, no mask, nothing left between us but shared devastation. His breath stutters against my shoulder. My fingers fist into his shirt. We hold on, because if we let go, we'll shatter.

In that moment, we're not Stellan and Talia Rothwell. We're just two broken people mourning the life that should've been ours.

"I don't know how to do this," I rasp, but it's not a whisper now. It's a confession torn from somewhere deeper. Darker. "I was supposed to protect him. I was his mother. And I failed."

Stellan's jaw clenches. His grip on my hand tightens, bordering on pain. "You didn't fail him. You loved him. You carried him. This wasn't you."

But I can't stop. The words are bile in my throat. "My body was supposed to be safe for him. And it wasn't. He died because of me."

"No." His tone is lethal now. Not at me. At the world. At himself. "If you're going to blame someone, blame me. I didn't stop Rafe. I didn't see it coming. *I failed both of you.*"

The silence after feels like impact. Like breathless, brutal truth.

"We lost him, Stellan."

My voice cracks. Splinters.

"We lost our son."

His forehead presses to mine. His breath is ragged. "I know." The words barely form. "God, Finch, I know."

There's nothing left to say.

Grief folds us in, brutal and suffocating. We don't cry pretty. We shatter. Together.

There's no blame left. Only loss. And we hold onto each other like that's enough to keep breathing.

But it's not enough.

The sobs won't stop. They rip out of me, harsh and relentless, until every gasp feels like knives in my ribs.

I can't catch my breath. I can't stop seeing him—what he could've been. What we'll never have.

My fingers clutch Stellan's shirt, twisting the fabric like it might hold me together.

But my body has limits. It always did.

The room tilts. My vision blurs. My heart's still racing, but my body can't keep up.

I'm slipping.

Stellan's voice is still there, calling my name. "Finch. Stay with me. Finch."

But it's distant now.

The darkness pulls me under again. This time, I don't fight it.

The world filters back slowly. Not with light. With sound. Voices, muffled at first, like they're coming from underwater. I blink, and the ceiling sharpens into focus. The phone is in Stellan's hand with the speaker on.

"How is she?" Alessio's voice crackles through the speaker.

"She woke up this morning," Stellan replies. "Still weak. Still hurting. But she's here."

There's a pause on the other end. "Good. She's stronger than most." Alessio's tone is clipped, but there's respect threaded through it. "It's been two days. You've waited long enough."

Stellan doesn't answer immediately.

"He's contained," Alessio adds, as if to fill the silence. "Exactly where you wanted. No noise. No eyes. He hasn't said much since we put him under."

I lie still, listening, pulse beginning to rise as the pieces start clicking into place.

"He won't be talking at all when we're done," Stellan says. His voice is calm. Too calm. It chills.

"One last thing, Rothwell." Alessio's voice drops lower. "Do you want to do it yourself?"

Stellan doesn't answer right away.

His gaze shifts to me. Our eyes lock.

"Yes," he says.

The line goes dead.

"What are you going to do, Stellan? Where's Rafe?" I push, needing—no, *aching*—to hear it from him.

"Awaiting punishment," Stellan says, his voice flat, but the undercurrent of violence is impossible to miss.

A shiver runs through me. It's not fear. It's rage. A slow, burning ember catching flame.

"Are you going to kill him?" I ask, my throat tight, each word scraping out like a dare.

"Yes," he says simply, with no hesitation, like it's already done.

"Good. Make it hurt," I bite out, the heat of it blistering past the crack in my voice.

My hand drifts to my stomach, to the place that feels so achingly empty, the loss sharper than any wound.

"For our son," I whisper, and the words scrape through me like broken glass.

The ache in my side is nothing compared to the hollow cavern where he should have been. It's not just emptiness. It's absence. A piece of me ripped away, leaving edges too jagged to heal.

I thought I'd have more time. Time to feel him grow. Time to see his face. Time to be what my mother never was.

But time was never mine to keep.

A sob tears out of me, sharp and punishing. My hands press against my stomach, desperate to hold something that's no longer there.

"I'm sorry," I whisper, but I don't know if it's to Stellan, to our son, or to myself.

The grief isn't soft anymore. It claws, it burns.

And beneath it all—rage. Stellan's vow was calm, but mine is alive. Breathing. Demanding.

I don't see him move, but I feel the shift in the air. The scrape of his chair. His promise settling into place.

When he leaves, it's not as Stellan Rothwell, CEO.

It's as the man carrying the fury I can't wield from this hospital bed.

God help Rafe Donnelly when he delivers it.

CHAPTER
TWENTY-FOUR

Stellan

Dante picks me up from the hospital to take me to the black site where Rafe is being held.

Her voice follows me.

Make it hurt.

I will. He's going to die today.

Dante glances at me from the driver's seat for a long moment without saying a word.

"You know this doesn't come with a way back, right?" he says, tone low. "You do this yourself... it'll mark you. The first time always does."

He's not wrong. But this isn't about firsts.

"I'm not asking if he deserves it. We both know he does," Dante continues. "I'm asking if you're ready to carry it. That kind of darkness doesn't wash off, Rothwell."

I meet his gaze in the rearview mirror.

"I don't need it to wash off," I say quietly. "I need it to stay. As a reminder." A reminder of what happens when I let mercy outweigh precision.

Dante nods once, like he understands more than he says.

"This is soul-cost shit," he says. "You sure you want it?"

He's going to die today. "I'm sure."

The road disappears under us. We drive through the desert, the main road stretching flat and empty for miles. Predictable. Contained. Until it isn't.

Without warning, Dante veers off onto dirt. No signs. No markers. Just open land that doesn't belong to anyone.

But it belongs to us now.

Every mile is another layer of insulation. Another assurance this will never touch the outside world.

A fence cuts across the desert. Unremarkable. Chain-link. Easy to ignore.

But that's the point. The most dangerous things never announce themselves.

At the gate, there's a speaker box. No cameras. No visible security. But we're seen. Catalogued. Processed.

We pull up. Dante rolls down his window.

"Bianchi authorization. Artemis Four," he says.

Static hums, before a voice responds. "Confirmed. Proceed to Bay Three."

The gate slides open without sound.

Permission granted.

An ATV rolls up from one of the side tracks. The driver's uniform is discretion. Black clothes and mirrored sunglasses despite the dusk.

He jerks his chin, signaling for us to follow. Efficient. Impersonal. Perfect.

"This is how they do it here," Dante says. "Minimal footprint. Maximum control."

Control. That's what this is. Control restored.

The facility unfolds in a grid of low, squat bunkers, half-buried in the desert floor. No windows. No names. Just concrete promises that no one leaves without permission.

Above each entrance, a single light glows. Blue. Red. Blue. Blue. Red.

"Blue means unoccupied," Dante says, not needing to be asked. "Red's in use. Active rooms."

Each red light marks a quiet end.

We pull up to a bunker with a red light above it. This is it. The bunker Rafe is in.

Before the engine cuts, the door to the bunker opens. Alessio steps out first. Relaxed. Hands in his pockets. As casual as if we were here to talk numbers.

Massimo follows. Slower. But heavier. A man who never needs to raise his voice to be heard.

"Rothwell," Massimo greets, voice like gravel sliding. "You came yourself. Good."

Of course I did. There's no subcontracting this.

Alessio's grin widens. Knowing. "We kept him breathing. Just like you wanted."

Not mercy. Logistics.

Alessio gestures toward the entrance. "Bay Three's ready. All yours."

Time to finish this. I walk into the bunker. It's colder inside. Purposefully so. Cold sharpens focus. Weakens resistance. Makes people brittle. The walls are reinforced concrete, lined with acoustic panels. Soundproofed. There's no chance of anything leaking out.

Fluorescent lights hum overhead, their glare relentless. White. Surgical. Designed to leave no corner untouched. No shadows for liars to hide in.

I move further in, my steps muted by the concrete floor. The walls close in around me—plain, reinforced slabs, lined with matte acoustic panels. Soundproofed. Purpose-built. A place for screams to die before they can echo.

To my right, the wall is a testament to efficiency. Floor-to-ceiling racks welded straight into the concrete, gleaming under the lights. Not chaotic. Not crammed. Curated.

My gaze drags over the blades first. Thin, scalpel-precise knives hang beside heavier cleavers—tools designed not just to cut, but to shatter bone, to peel a man apart piece by controlled piece.

Beside them, batons wait. Weighted. Ridged grips. Some designed to break ribs clean, others for soft tissue. A specialist's selection.

Lower still, rows of pliers. Wire cutters. Bone spreaders. Not the kind you find in a hardware store. These are finer. Meaner. Built for precision in destruction.

At the center of the display, the electrical rigs gleam. Portable. Compact. Wires coiled like snakes. A control box sits docked beneath—dial, trigger, nothing more. No learning curve. No mercy.

Hooks and chains hang further down. Some are restraints. Some are for suspension. None are decorative.

To the far left, a workstation gleams under its own directed lamp. Stainless steel trays lined with scalpels, clamps, syringes. Packs of gauze. Antiseptics. Surgical gloves stacked with care.

This isn't a dungeon.

It's a correctional suite.

In the center of the room, the chair waits. Bolted down. Heavy-duty restraints gleam against worn leather padding. Not for comfort. For efficiency. Keeps the subject from thrashing. Keeps the work clean.

Beneath it, a drain sits flush with the floor. Stainless steel. Wide enough to handle anything.

Rafe is already there. Slumped, but breathing.

"How long has he been out?" I ask.

"Two hours," Alessio replies, casually, like he's talking about a client running late to a meeting. "He needed a little... recalibration."

Massimo's gaze sharpens. "He came in loud. Mouthy. Thought this was going to be a negotiation. We educated him otherwise."

"Lesson one was bones," Alessio says, his grin sharp, unbothered. "Arms first. Keeps them conscious longer." He gestures lazily toward Rafe's slumped frame. "Lesson two was breath," he continues, voice light, almost conversational. "How much you can take away before the body panics. That one's always fun."

Rafe stirs, barely. A twitch of fingers against cold metal.

"He's not broken yet," Massimo says, tone even. "But we brought him to the edge. You asked for him breathing. That's all we promised."

"Everything else is yours," Alessio adds. "We made sure of that."

"Well, look who finally showed up," Rafe rasps, lips splitting into a bloody grin. "Took you long enough, Rothwell. What's the matter? Had to grow a spine first?"

I don't answer.

He shifts in the chair, testing the restraints. They don't give.

"That little wife of yours—" he starts, but the words slur. He's bleeding from the mouth. Still playing the same hand, even as it burns.

"You're not in control here, Rafe," I say, voice flat.

He huffs a bitter laugh. "Aren't I? You came all this way to see me. Feels like I'm still calling the shots."

He's wrong. But he needs the illusion.

"You'll talk," I tell him. "The only variable is how cleanly this ends."

"What if I don't?" he mutters. "What then?"

"I don't mind blood," I say, taking off my jacket and rolling up my sleeves. "You took something from me," a single step closer. "It's time you pay."

His grin doesn't reach his eyes. "Is she dead?" he asks. "Did you lose her?"

"She lived," I say evenly. "Despite you." That flickers. A twitch in his brow. Not regret—jealousy. "You failed," I add. "So now you get to tell me why."

"I love her, Rothwell." He leans forward, defiant. "From the moment she walked in. The way she looked at people. The way she made you feel like you mattered. She saw me."

"She tolerated you," I correct. "Because she's kind. That's not the same thing."

"You don't get it," he says, voice rising. "She was supposed to be mine. She *was.* I was going to get her out. Away from you. From this."

"She was never yours," I say.

He shakes his head. "You think she loves you? You think what you two have is real? It's not. It's programming. It's pressure. She chose you because she thought she had to."

"She chose me," I repeat. "Even when she didn't have to."

His face twists.

"I would've given her everything," he says. "Safety. Freedom. A life where she could be *herself.*"

"You drugged her. You chained her. You shot her."

"I panicked," he snaps. "She wasn't listening. She was lying. Saying she didn't feel it. But I know she did. She *had* to."

"You think obsession is love?" I ask.

"I *know* what love is," he snarls. "It's sacrifice. It's risk. I risked everything for her."

"You risked her life for your fantasy," I say. "That's not love. That's delusion."

He doesn't answer.

"You were never part of her story, Rafe," I add, low and final. "You were a footnote she was kind enough not to erase."

That breaks him.

His breath stutters. His hands flex in the restraints.

"She looked at me like I mattered," he whispers.

"No," I say, turning away. "She looked at you like you were human. That's the part you never understood."

I roll the tray closer, the metal legs squealing faintly across the concrete floor. Rafe flinches at the sound, even before he sees what's on it. His eyes dart to the array of instruments—forceps, bone shears, scalpels, clamps—all gleaming under the overhead light. Tools for precision. Tools for pain.

He knows exactly what they're for.

"What are you doing?" he rasps, voice cracked and raw from screaming.

I don't answer. I don't need to.

He tries to speak again, maybe to beg, maybe to lie, but I cut him off with steel between his teeth. His head jerks, body twisting in the restraints, but there's nowhere to go. I clamp down on one of his molars, feel the root shift under the pressure.

His breath hitches. His eyes go wide.

I twist.

There's a sickening crunch as the root cracks. A sudden pop as I rip the tooth free. Blood gushes from the socket, spilling down his chin in thick, metallic ropes. He screams—loud, high, animalistic.

I hold the tooth up in front of him, then let it fall to the floor with a small, satisfying clatter.

"That," I say quietly, "was for putting your hands on her."

He shakes his head, coughing, sputtering through the blood in his mouth. "I didn't want to hurt her," he chokes out. "I loved her."

My grip tightens on the next tool—a bolt cutter. The kind used for steel cables. The kind that cuts bone like it's nothing. His gaze flickers to the tool in my hand. His breathing quickens. "I didn't mean to hurt her," he repeats, a little more desperate now. "She just—she wouldn't listen."

He starts shaking his head again, but it's too late. I position the bolt cutters around his smallest finger. He tries to pull away. The chair rocks, the restraints creak, but I keep the grip steady.

"This is the part," I whisper, "where you start to understand what pain *really* feels like."

I squeeze.

There's a crunch—louder, wetter than the tooth. His finger severs cleanly, blood spraying as he shrieks. The digit hits the floor, rolls under the chair, forgotten.

He screams and sobs in the same breath, body shaking, sweat pouring down his face in rivulets.

"Still think she wanted you?" I ask, standing slowly. "Still think you were owed something?"

He doesn't respond. Just cries. Broken. Pathetic.

I grab the scalpel next. Make a clean, shallow cut along the curve of his jawline—not deep enough to kill, just enough to sting. Blood wells up along the line, thin and bright.

He whimpers, but I lean in close, press a gloved thumb to the open skin, and watch him squirm.

"She'll never think of you again," I murmur. "Not with fear. Not with rage. Not even with pity. You're just a bad memory she's going to erase."

I slam the scalpel into his thigh—deep, vicious. Bone stops it with a jarring resistance, and he howls, his body arching against the restraints.

The sound of it echoes through the room.

I let it.

Because this isn't interrogation anymore.

This is what happens when you bleed something I love.

Rafe's breath wheezes through cracked ribs, his body sagging in the chair, limp with pain and blood loss. He's a mess of torn skin, shattered fingers, pulp where his teeth used to be. And yet—

He smiles.

Crooked. Blood-soaked.

"I'll never stop," he rasps. "You know that, don't you?"

I pause, mid-motion, the scalpel still in my hand.

Rafe lifts his head. There's nothing left in his face but obsession. Not fear. Not shame. Just raw, unrelenting fixation.

"You think if you kill me, she's free?" he whispers. "She's not. I'm inside her now. The way she flinched. The way she screamed. That never leaves."

I stare at him.

"You put a bullet in my head, Rothwell, and I'll still be there. In her dreams. In her silence. In every room you try to make her feel safe in. I'll be there. Watching."

My grip tightens.

"And if by some miracle she *forgets* me," he goes on, smiling wider, "I'll haunt the next one. And the next. Every woman who looks like her. Every voice that sounds like hers. I will keep coming. I will keep making them remember."

He spits blood at my boots.

"I *am* the fear," he hisses. "You can't kill that."

I look at him for a long time. I nod. "You're right," I say quietly. "I can't kill fear."

I step behind him. "But I can kill you."

Before he can blink, I drive the scalpel into his ear. It punctures clean through the cartilage, into the soft cavity behind his temple. He jerks once—sharp and high—and goes still. Eyes wide, mouth slack, breath catching mid-sound.

I pull the scalpel out slowly, the steel wet and red, nerves and blood clinging to the blade in strings as it slips free.

Rafe's body is slumped in the chair, his head pitched at an ugly angle. Blood spills in thick, lazy arcs from the wound behind his ear, trailing down his jaw, soaking the collar of his shirt. His eyes are still open. Wide. Unblinking. Fixed on nothing. There's something obscene about it—like he's still trying to see her, even now.

Alessio's the first to speak.

"Well," he says, leaning slightly to study the body. "That was conclusive."

Massimo tilts his head, one gloved hand smoothing down his coat front like he's bored. "Always something poetic about the quiet ones. He talked himself into hell, and you carved him into silence."

Dante moves closer. He crouches beside Rafe's chair and rests his forearms on his knees.

"Eyes open," he murmurs. "That's rare."

"He looks surprised," Alessio adds, voice dry. "Like he really thought you wouldn't do it."

"He thought he was still important," I say, the words tasting like steel.

Massimo hums. "They all do. Obsession's a poor substitute for worth."

Alessio grins, tilting his head toward me. "I was almost hoping you'd lose control. Would've been fun to see what a Rothwell rampage looks like."

Massimo glances at the body again, finally, turns to me. "You ready to leave this behind?"

I stare at Rafe. His mouth is slack now. His face already graying. A shadow of everything he claimed to be.

"I already have."

Dante moves to the table, picks up the forceps with practiced care. "We'll handle the rest."

"Burn it," Alessio says. "No burial. No file. No name."

I nod once. I walk out with Dante at my side.

We don't speak as we slide into the car—engine already running, the interior heavy with the clean, synthetic scent of leather and blood that doesn't belong to either of us.

I stare through the windshield for a minute. Pull out my phone and dial.

Gareth picks up with heat already in his voice. "Rothwell. What the hell is going on?"

"Cal Ames sent you the file," I say. "Surveillance, tracking logs, intercepted comms—everything. You should have it by now."

"I'm looking at it," he mutters, keys clacking in the background. "Jesus Christ. Rafe Donnelly abducted your wife? Are you fucking kidding me?"

"I'm not."

He doesn't even try to hide the disbelief. "I mean—Rafe? Donnelly? Quiet-as-fuck Donnelly? The guy who still says 'yes, sir' in emails?"

"That's the one."

"I swear to God, you people are a soap opera wrapped in a crime syndicate," he mutters. "Where is he now?"

"Missing."

"Missing?" he barks. "Don't play games with me, Stellan."

"He's on the run," I clarify.

"You found him," Gareth says, voice rising. "You found him, and now he's conveniently gone?"

Dante glances over from the driver's seat. "He's not conveniently anything. He's what happens when you push your luck past the edge of reality."

Gareth's voice spikes. "Is that Dante? Dante *Valera*?"

"Pleasure," Dante says smoothly, like he's ordering champagne.

"Jesus fucking Christ, you brought in the Bianchis?"

"No," I say. "They offered."

"I'm going to need you to say, out loud, that Rafe Donnelly is alive," Gareth grits out.

"I'm going to need you to stop asking questions you don't want the answers to."

"Oh, I *want* them," he snaps. "Because I have to write this up, and I'd rather not play dumb in front of a federal panel."

Dante hums. "I suggest you develop a talent for omission."

"Stellan," Gareth growls. "Just tell me what the hell you did."

"I handled it."

"*Handled it?* That's not an answer."

"It's the one you're getting."

"You killed him, didn't you?" Gareth pushes. "You fucking killed him."

I don't blink. "He's on the run. That's what you're going to put in your report."

"You expect me to just accept that?" Gareth fires back.

"No," I say. "But you'll do it anyway."

There's a pause on his end—not silence, just heavy breathing and quiet rage.

"I swear to God, Rothwell, one of these days—"

"Close the case, Gareth."

I hang up before he can finish the threat.

Dante lets out a low laugh. "You're more fun than you used to be."

"He made her bleed," I say, leaning back against the seat. "There was no version of this where he walked away."

Dante nods once. "Good."

There's only one place left to go.

Back to her.

Back to the woman picking up the pieces of what he tried to destroy.

Back to the life we're going to build from what's left.

One piece at a time.

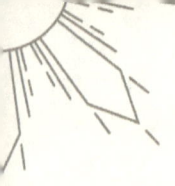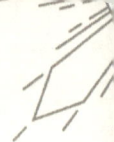

CHAPTER
TWENTY-FIVE

Talia

I got out of the hospital a few days ago.

After weeks of surgeries, stitches, blood, and too many people telling me I was lucky to be alive.

I thought I wanted to come home.

Turns out I was wrong.

Here feels worse.

At least in the hospital, I was a project. Something broken that could be fixed. I had machines. Drugs. People poking at me like I was worth saving.

Here? There's nothing. Just me. And the silence. And the ache no one can touch.

The physical pain? Manageable. Pills take the edge off. This other thing? The thing clawing up my throat, curling in my gut? No one tells you how to survive that.

Jean keeps bringing me food I don't eat. Stellan hovers. Always hovering. I wish he'd stop. I wish he'd—

I don't know.

Everyone tries. Everyone talks like they're doing something good, but they're not saying the thing that matters. They're not saying he's dead. They're not saying I let it happen.

Because I did. I let Rafe win. I let him take my baby. I let him ruin me.

I can't even look at myself in the mirror.

And Stellan? He's still here. Sitting in that chair like he can fix me. Like he's waiting for me to remember how to be the version of myself he fell in love with.

I hate that he's here. I hate that I need him.

And I hate that part of me already knows I'll never be her again.

I fall asleep. I wake up. I do it again.

Most days, I don't remember how many times it's been. I avoid mirrors. Food. Conversations.

I pretend to listen when people talk around me, but their voices don't stick. They blur. Like background noise I can't turn off.

Erin's voice filters in sometimes.

"She's handling the press," Stellan tells someone—I think Erin, maybe Dawson. I don't look up. "She's buried them. The narrative is airtight. Victim. Survivor. No one's questioning her story."

Not mine. Her story.

Kate's name gets mentioned next. She's been promoted to VP.

"She's running everything," Erin says. "So Stellan can be here. For Talia."

For me.

Like I'm a project they have to babysit.

Jean tries the hardest. Cooking. Leaving plates by the bed. Saying nothing when they go untouched. I see the worry on her face. I ignore it.

They ask Stellan how I'm doing. Never me. Like I'm not in the room. Like I'm already a ghost.

"She's..." Stellan never finishes the sentence. Like if he says it out loud, it'll make it real.

He sits in the chair across the room most days. Like he's guarding a tomb.

I don't tell him to leave. But I wish I could.

I hear them. All of them. Talking over me. Around me.

And I keep waiting for them to stop.

But they don't.

And now—I can't take it.

I rip the blanket off, stumbling to my feet, legs barely working, but rage carries me.

"Stop talking about me like I'm not here!" I scream, voice cracking on the words. "You all want to act like I'm some fucking ghost? Fine. Here I am."

The room freezes, their pity thick enough to choke on.

I laugh. It sounds wrong in my throat. Broken. Wild. "I survived, right? That's what you all keep saying? I survived?" I claw at my chest like I could rip out the emptiness inside.

"Hunter rapes me and gets to walk away smiling. Rafe takes my baby. And what do I get? A medal? A goddamn sympathy promotion? My own family turned their backs on me because I embarrassed them on the fucking news—bloody, pathetic, a Cerny disgrace."

Their faces blur, but I don't stop.

"You want updates? Here's your fucking update—I can't eat. I can't sleep. I can't breathe without thinking about what he did to me. What I let him do."

Erin tries to speak. I cut her off with a snarl.

"Don't. Don't you dare give me your strong-woman speech. Don't you fucking dare."

I stagger, grip the wall, hate the way my body shakes. Hate it. Hate me.

"You all want me to heal? To move on?" I laugh again, high and ugly. "I can't even look at myself in the mirror without seeing what's left of me. I'm empty. I'm fucking empty."

I slam my fists into my own stomach, as if I can feel him there. Gone.

"I failed him. I failed our baby. And all of you are standing around pretending you can clean this up with press releases and house-hunting."

I collapse, sobbing so hard it feels like I might choke on it.

"I don't want a house. I don't want a future. I don't want any of this."

They hover. No one moves. No one breathes.

"Just leave me the fuck alone," I sob, curling in on myself, shaking, breaking into pieces that can't be put back together.

"Leave," Stellan says, voice flat, cold, like steel scraping against stone.

They do. Of course they do. They always listen to him.

The door shuts and suddenly it's just him and me and this crushing, suffocating silence that feels heavier than all their words, and I hate it because now there's no one left to hide behind, no one left to pretend this isn't happening, just him and the wreck I've become, and I know he sees it, I know he sees all of me, and I hate him for it.

I expect him to say something. To fix it. To tell me to pull myself together or get over it or fight harder like everyone else always expects me to do.

But he doesn't.

He sits on the fucking floor like we're equals, like I'm not feral and broken and covered in self-loathing, and he just lets me sit there, lets me fall apart without trying to make it neat or palatable or pretty, and I hate that more than anything, because it makes me want to lean on him when I know I shouldn't.

And I cry like something dying, until there's nothing left in me but hollow space and an ache so deep I don't even know where it begins or ends, and when the sobs finally stop, I expect the speech to come. I brace for it. I want to scream at him to get it over with.

But what comes out of him is worse.

"I can't fix this," he says, voice low, ragged, like it's taking pieces of him to even say it, and the way he says it—like a fact, not a comfort—makes my throat close up all over again.

"But I can give you something," he adds, and I almost laugh, because what could he possibly give me now that would make any of this less of the nightmare it is?

He gives me a stack of papers. It looks like listings.

"I've been looking at houses," he says, like it's normal, like he's not sitting on the floor with me while I unravel. "Not Rothwell. Not anyone's but yours. I found a few. Places I thought you might not hate."

That's what gets me. Not love. Not home. Just places I might not hate. Like he knows I can't see that far ahead yet. Like he knows I'm still stuck in this dark place where everything feels like a punishment.

"I don't want to choose for you," he says. "You get to decide if any of them feel like something we can build from."

Build from.

Like I'm not already ashes.

"I can't give you back what he took," his voice cracks now, and I hate how much that sound wrecks me, because it's not fair, it's not fair that he still loves me, that he still sees me when I can't even look at myself, and I hate that he's still fighting for us when I don't even know if there's an us left.

But I don't let go of the papers.

I don't throw them.

I should.

But I don't.

I hate him for giving me something I might want.

I let him pull me off the floor. Because I'm too fucking tired to keep sinking.

"I took care of Hunter," Stellan says.

The name alone makes my skin crawl. It shouldn't still have that power. But it does.

"What?" My voice cracks. I hate that it cracks.

"He's in prison," Stellan says quietly.

I blink at him, disbelief curdling in my stomach. "You're serious."

He nods once. The ground tilts under me.

"How? How is he in prison? He—he gets away with everything."

"Not this time." His voice sharpens. "I made sure of it."

I shake my head, my chest tight. "But how?"

Stellan exhales slowly, like every word tastes like steel. "It wasn't just you, Finch. There were others. Too many."

My stomach twists.

"Over the last ten years, I tracked over twenty women who crossed his path. Staff. Escorts. Club employees. Girls he met through partners. Most of them barely legal when he found them. Some didn't even have contracts—they were off-books hires. Disposable."

He pauses, jaw tight.

"One of them was eighteen. A club attendant. That was last week." His voice drops lower. "That's the one that broke it wide open."

The air turns to ice in my lungs.

"She came forward," he says. "She wasn't the only one. Once I found her, I found the others. Some were paid off years ago. Others disappeared. He thought they were buried. I unburied them."

I clutch the fabric of my pants, my nails biting through the cloth.

"The club covered for him?" I rasp.

"They enabled him," he says darkly. "They built entire cover protocols around him. Footage erased. Statements rewritten. Medical records paid for. They moved his victims like inventory."

My pulse pounds in my throat.

"And the ADA?"

"She was bought years ago. Quiet money through private accounts. I traced every payment." His mouth hardens. "She didn't just lose her job. She's under federal investigation."

My voice is hoarse. "The DA—?"

"Controlled," he says simply. "I gave him the choice: cooperate, or burn with the rest of them."

"And his family?"

He leans in, voice quieter but deadlier. "Destroyed. His father's empire collapsed in a week. Every corporate tie severed. Board seats dissolved. Investigations everywhere. Every deal they ever made is being dissected right now. They'll lose everything before the year is out."

I laugh, but it's a strangled, cracked sound.

"You really did it," I whisper, almost like I can't believe it.

Because it doesn't feel like a win. It doesn't feel like justice. It feels... empty.

Hunter's in prison. His family's ruined. His world turned to ash. And yet... I still feel like I'm drowning. Still feel like I'm the one locked behind bars in a body that won't let me forget what he did.

What I lost. What's still rotting inside me, no matter how many files Stellan puts in my hands or how many men he eliminates.

I thought knowing he couldn't hurt anyone else would make it easier to breathe. It doesn't. Like now that the fight is over, there's nothing left to do but sit in the wreckage and try to remember how to live again.

That's the part that scares me most.

Because what if I can't? What if I never find my way out of this?

I don't know how to fix this. Maybe I never will. Maybe that was never the point.

But I can start. Small. Carefully. Like someone learning how to breathe after too long underwater.

Let Jean make me coffee and stop pretending I can't taste it. Pick up the phone when Erin calls, even if I have nothing to say. Sit in those rooms with women like me, who survived things that left them hollow and haunted, and let their voices fill the spaces where mine won't yet.

Walk into the therapist's office. Say the words that scrape my throat raw.

I lost my son. I lost pieces of myself I might never find again.

But I'm still here.

Stand in the house we buy. Pick the paint anyway. Plant something in the dirt, even if it never grows, because at least it's something.

Let myself imagine rooms filled with something other than ghosts. Let myself love Stellan in the messy, fractured way I know how. Let him love me back, even on the days I don't feel worth it.

Stop punishing myself for surviving. Believe that moving forward doesn't mean forgetting. It just means breathing through the ache.

I press my forehead to his, our hands tangled, futures messy and broken and still ours.

"We can't undo the scars," I whisper, softer now, truer. "But here... we can build something new. Together."

And this time, I let myself believe it.

Not because it's easy. But because I want to.

CHAPTER TWENTY-SIX

Stellan

T alia's healing. I can see it. Feel it in the way she moves. The way she laughs. The way she smiles. It's not perfect. But it's real.

She's back at work now. Four months since she came home from the hospital. I asked if she wanted to wait longer. Find something else. Stay home, if that's what she needed.

She refused.

Of course, she did.

I always knew they loved her, but seeing it—seeing the entire company show up for her, welcoming her back like she's family—that was something else. Something I think she needed more than she realized.

We'd been looking at houses.

Every place we walked through was more of the same—steel, glass, more square footage than soul. They were the kinds of homes people like us were supposed to want. The kinds you showed off, not lived in.

Every time, Talia stood a little stiffer. She'd walk the pristine halls, touch the cold marble countertops, and I could see the decision settling in her eyes long before the realtor stopped talking. It wasn't right. None of them were.

I tried to tell her we could wait. That we didn't need to force it. She wouldn't hear it. Told me maybe we'd been looking in the wrong places. Maybe we weren't meant to look at all.

Suddenly, it happened.

We took a wrong turn. Ended up in a part of Vegas people forgot once the towers went up. The streets were wide, lined with old palms and big brick houses that belonged to a different era. The kind of neighborhood built when Vegas was still trying to figure out what it wanted to be. Before everything turned glass and steel.

That's where we found it.

Two stories. Red brick. Southern-style, the kind with thick columns out front and a porch that wrapped halfway around the side. The kind of house that didn't need to be loud to make a statement. The shutters were faded. The fence had rust creeping up its posts. But the house? It stood like it didn't give a damn who was looking.

No signs in the yard. Just a weathered metal plaque on the gate with a realtor's name and a number I could barely read.

Talia got out before I cut the engine. She walked up the drive, eyes on the house like it was daring her to see it for what it was. She didn't ask me to follow. I did anyway.

We stepped inside and the place swallowed us whole.

High ceilings. Wide hallways. A kitchen that stretched bigger than some of the suites at the ONYX. Living room the size of a ballroom, fireplaces in every room like it got cold here. The bathrooms were oversized, the bedrooms bigger than most Vegas condos.

Everything was original. Solid. Untouched.

But it was old. The kind of old that came with creaking floors, wallpaper peeling at the edges, tile that would crack if you looked at it wrong. The air smelled like cedar and dust. Like no one had opened the windows in years.

But it had bones.

Good ones.

Talia walked through it like she was memorizing the space. She touched the worn banister, the chipped molding. She looked at the way the light hit the scuffed hardwood floors, the way the kitchen stretched open like it was waiting for noise, for people, for life.

She turned and looked at me. The smile. Her smile is back. The glitter in her eyes. Happiness. Pure happiness.

We bought it that day. Cash. No questions.

It finally feels like we have something that is ours.

We're moving in today.

The driveway's packed. Too many cars. Boxes everywhere. And people. Not strangers. Ours.

Kate's already in the kitchen, opening cabinets, moving things around like she's been here for years. Like this house has always been theirs. Erin's taken over the dining room, stacking plates and glasses like she's planning a party we never asked for. Beckett and Dawson are arguing over the couch—Beckett swearing it won't fit, Dawson betting him a hundred it will—while Frankie leans against the wall, beer in hand, calling them both idiots.

Talia's in the middle of it, laughing at something Kate says, her face lit up in a way I haven't seen in months.

It hits me.

This is what family looks like.

Jean showed up, too. I hadn't expected her today. Just walked in with enough food to fill the kitchen twice over, like she knew we'd need it.

Frankie catches me watching and grins. "Don't look so damn serious, Rothwell. You invited us, remember?"

I smile. For once, it comes easy. "Yeah, but I didn't expect all this."

"What? Friends? Food? People making your house feel like a home?" She smirks, nudging Talia, who's laughing beside me now.

Talia leans into my side, her hand slipping into mine. "He's still adjusting," she teases.

Kate pops her head out from the kitchen. "Honestly, I'm just here for the champagne. The rest of you can fight over who gets to hang curtains."

"Like hell," Erin says from the dining room. "I already claimed the master bath as mine for the night."

Everyone laughs, including me and Talia.

Beckett drops onto the couch with a groan, Dawson flopping down beside him. "Hell, Stellan. You might actually be human after all."

"Don't let that get around," I say, grinning.

"This is nice," Talia says quietly, looking at the mess of boxes, and the people filling every room. "It feels... right."

"It is," I say.

The afternoon slips into evening, the rooms filling with half-unpacked boxes and the smell of pizza that's been sitting out too long.

"The pizza's cold," Kate says, dropping the packing tape onto the counter like she's done for the day. "If I see another box, I'm reporting you to HR."

Talia laughs, brushing her hair off her forehead. "I'll add it to the agenda."

Beckett stretches out on the living room floor, arms behind his head. "I vote we make Rothwell finish the rest himself."

"You can try," I say, raising an eyebrow.

Dawson catches his keys midair. "We'll get out of your way. Let you two break the place in."

"Dawson," Frankie groans, rolling her eyes. "You're disgusting."

"Realistic," he fires back, grinning at Talia.

"You're all awful," Talia says, laughing now.

One by one, they start leaving. The goodbyes stretch, soft promises to come back soon. They'll show up when they feel like it.

Jean is the last to go. She steps close to Talia, resting her hand on her cheek, brushing a strand of hair back like she would do if she was her own child.

"We're home," she says quietly.

"Yeah," I reply, softer now. "We are."

The house is quiet. Our friends are gone. It's just us.

I watch her. The way her fingers trail along the kitchen counter. The way her breath slows like she's finally letting herself feel it.

"You okay?" I ask.

She nods. "Yeah. I think... yeah."

But when she turns toward me, there's more in her eyes. Something that doesn't need words.

She steps in close, her hand sliding to the back of my neck. She kisses me. No hesitation. No asking.

Her mouth is soft, sure, tasting like everything we've been holding back. I don't rush her. I let her set the pace, let her show me she's ready.

When she finally pulls back, she's breathing hard. "Take me upstairs."

I carry her, her arms loose around my neck, head resting against me. The bedroom is mostly empty. Just a mattress on the floor, no sheets yet, the walls bare, the windows still without curtains.

She looks around, lips curving into a small, tired smile. "Real fancy, Rothwell."

"Only the best," I say, setting her down gently.

She runs her hand over the mattress, raising an eyebrow. "You really know how to spoil a girl."

I kneel beside her, brushing her hair back. "Give me a few weeks. I'll get you a bed frame."

She leans in, her smile soft now. "I don't need one. This is enough."

I stroke her jaw, tilting her face up to me. "You deserve more."

"Don't tell me what I deserve, Rothwell." She smirks, but it's softer now. "This... you... is more."

She pulls me down, her lips brushing mine—slow, sure, no rush. Her hands slide into my hair, grounding herself in me, pulling me closer.

We kiss like we have all night. We do.

I lift her carefully, carrying her to the mattress on the floor. She doesn't tease me this time. She just curls her fingers into my shirt, holding on like she doesn't want space between us. When I lay her down, she glances around the empty room, bare walls, half-unpacked boxes.

"Very romantic," she says, dry but smiling.

I grin. "Only the best."

"We're such a cliché," she whispers, but there's no bite.

"Guess I can live with that," I murmur, kissing her again.

She tugs my shirt over my head, fingers dragging across the scars, the old breaks. She doesn't flinch. Never did. Her hands are soft, reverent, like she's reminding me I'm still whole.

"I missed you," she breathes.

"I've been right here."

"Not like this."

I swallow hard, pressing my forehead to hers. "No. Not like this."

Her fingers slip under my waistband, slow, patient. She takes her time, and I let her. I let her lead, show me she's ready. When she undresses me, it's not rushed. She looks at me like I'm hers, and somewhere deep down, I know that's what I've always been.

"I want you to touch me like I'm not broken," she says softly.

"You're not," I say, brushing her hair back. "You're the strongest person I've ever known."

She kisses me, her breath shaky. "Show me."

I do. I touch her slow, like she's more than what happened to her—because she is. I kiss every inch of her skin, listening to the sounds she makes, the way her body arches into mine, the way her breath catches when I whisper how beautiful she is.

When I slide inside her, it's not about possession or control. It's about coming home.

She holds my face, her legs wrapping around me, pulling me closer, deeper, her eyes on mine like she needs to see me, needs to know I'm here.

"I love you," she whispers, her voice breaking.

"I love you, Finch," I say, kissing her hard. "Always."

She moves with me, slow, aching, like she's letting herself feel everything for the first time in too long. Every sigh, every soft gasp is a promise between us. No walls. No pretending.

Her hands slide up my back, her nails digging in just enough to anchor me to her. "Don't let go," she whispers.

"Never," I say, my voice rough now. "I'm yours, Talia."

Tears slip down her cheeks, but she's smiling when she falls apart beneath me, pulling me over the edge with her.

We lie tangled after, the house silent around us, our breathing the only sound. She strokes my back, slow and steady, tracing patterns into my skin.

"This is the life I want," she says quietly. "You. Me. This house."

"It's yours," I tell her. "All of it."

She presses her forehead to mine. "We can make it ours."

"We already have," I say.

She laughs softly, her breath warm against my mouth. "You're getting soft on me, Rothwell."

I smile, brushing her hair back. "Yeah. You did that to me."

She falls asleep soon after. Her hand still curled against my chest like she doesn't trust the world not to take me if she lets go.

But the world's not getting near us. Not anymore.

I used to love quiet, being alone. Being around others and having them in my personal space used to make me restless.

Now? It feels right.

She's here. We're here.

I let myself hold her tighter. For the first time, I don't feel like I'm waiting for something to break.

It's not perfect. But it's ours. And it's fucking enough.

Epilogue

DANTE

I arrive at Rothwell's new house. His wife is having a housewarming party and I'm invited.

Not like I would ever consider this a party, but I couldn't say no. Rothwell and I have become friends since she was kidnapped.

I hate law enforcement. I hate when they're corrupt even more. I thoroughly enjoyed watching him kill the detective.

Now he is working with the Bianchis. They are long time friends. Hell, I'm the godfather of Massimo's son, Alessio. Massimo helped raise me.

But I wasn't expecting Talia Rothwell to come up with better plans than Stellan ever could. She never judges. She's smart. She is the perfect person to work with.

Which is why I'm even at this stupid party.

I walk in the house and see everything going on. My phone buzzes and I see it's Lucrezia Verraldi, general manager of my club. She's texting me.

Lucrezia: Hey, boss. We've got a problem. I know you're at the Rothwell housewarming, but I need you to call me. Now.

She picks up instantly. "Finally."

"What is it?"

"Anonymous report came in through the club's incident channel," she says. "Very formal. Very detailed. Too detailed."

"Detailed how?"

"They claim they were assaulted. In the private lounge. They named the bouncer—Marco. Described the layout, time, music, what he said, what he did. They said no one helped. That the staff looked away."

"And?"

"I checked the footage, Dante," she says. "Marco wasn't even there that night. He called out sick. That lounge was empty. But the report describes it like they filmed it themselves."

I go quiet.

"That's not all," she adds. "Another one came in. Different night. Different story. Same rhythm. This time they say one of the cocktail servers drugged them. Slipped something in their champagne. Called it a setup."

"Same server?"

"Nope. Different girl. But again—she wasn't even on shift."

"Who's coordinating this?" I ask.

"I don't know," Lucrezia says. "But they're not coming quiet. They're going public. Police reports, social media threads, 'anonymous sources' talking to the press."

"They named the club?" I ask.

"They named the club, the floor, the table, the music," she says. "They didn't name *you*—but Dante, come on. You *are* the club. They don't have to say your name to stain it."

"And the police?"

"Already opened a case," she says. "Vice and Special Victims are sniffing around. Two officers showed up this afternoon asking questions about employee records, camera placement, security protocols. They weren't browsing. They had targets."

"Are they asking about me?"

"Not yet," she says. "But you know how this goes. You're not a man, you're a myth. If they can crack the image, they don't need facts. Just fire."

I run a hand down my face.

"They're not asking for hush money?" I ask.

"No," she says. "They don't want a payout. They want destruction. This is orchestrated. Precise. Every accusation is built to break the reputation, not the man."

"They're the same thing," I say coldly.

"Dante..." she starts. "Maybe Rothwell can fix this. You pay him enough to."

"This isn't a scandal," I cut in. "They're not trying to take me down—they're trying to salt the fucking earth."

I hang up, pissed as fuck.

This has officially gotten out of hand.

I need to fix it—and fast.

I look up from my phone and they're already there. Stellan. And Talia.

Of course.

"That looked intense," Talia says, like she didn't just watch me wage emotional war on a touchscreen.

"Just another Saturday night," I mutter, slipping the phone back into my pocket.

"You want help?" she asks, folding her arms. "You need something stronger than PR. What you've got is rot. Deep, curated, intentional."

I arch a brow. "You offering a cleanse?"

"I'm offering a cure," she says as she glances at Stellan. "Maybe he needs a bride."

I snort. "I don't need an escort."

"You think that's what I was?" she fires back, a smile curling around the corners of her lips. "I wasn't here to look pretty on Rothwell's arm. I was trained. Conditioned. I was a tactical solution wearing lipstick."

"She's not wrong," Stellan says, deadpan. He reaches into his pocket and hands me a black business card.

Shadow Services.

I flip it over.

There's a number. No name. No logo. Just a phone number. Vegas area code.

I arch a brow. "What am I supposed to do with this? Order a cleanup crew?"

"You need help," Talia says, unfazed. "The kind that doesn't file quarterly reports. Just call."

I stare at the card for another second and sigh as I dial.

It rings once.

"Shadow Services," a voice answers. Cool. Professional. "This is Nyra."

"I was told to call," I say, clipped. I do not want a bride.

"One moment," she replies. "Transferring you to Director Noirel."

The name stops me cold. *Mirelle Noirel?* The philanthropist? Society luncheons, foundation galas, women's education funds. She's the polished face of virtue in a city built on vice.

And apparently, she's also the one who picks up when things get dark.

"This is Mirelle Noirel," she says, her voice smooth as polished glass—and just as capable of cutting straight through me.

I don't hesitate.

"My name is Dante Valera," I say, voice steel. "I need a bride."

"You'll need to be prepared to pay," she replies, like this is a transaction, not a lifeline.

"How much?" I ask, already knowing it won't be cheap.

"Ten million," she says, like it's nothing more than ordering champagne.

"Deal," I say, without a pause. Because I can't afford to be hesitant about anything anymore.

"We'll be in contact," she says, and the line goes dead like a door slamming shut behind me.

This is insane. Completely fucking insane.

I look up, and they're still standing there.

Talia's watching me like she's already seen the ending and finds it amusing.

"Welcome to the family," she says.

LFN

Talia Cerny,

You are hereby invited to a Preliminary
Consultation at La Fondation Noirel

Date: Wednesday, June 12
Time: 9:00 AM
Location: 23rd Floor
La Fondation Noirel, Las Vegas

Further details will be provided upon arrival.
Discretion is required. Consent is assumed.

No confirmation is necessary.

We look forward to your presence.

Mirelle Noirel

Bonus Scene

TALIA

I 'm not planning plan to write anything. I don't even mean to sit down.

It's late and I've been pacing for over an hour, like that'll shake something loose from my chest. It doesn't. The feeling's still there, dense and hot and terrifying. I try breathing exercises. I scan reports I've already memorized. I make tea and don't touch it.

None of it works.

Because I can't stop thinking about the way he looked at me today. Like I wasn't a job or a mission or some obligation handed to him in a velvet box. Like I was just me. And somehow, that was enough.

I sit down because I can't not.

I grab a sheet of paper and the pen I rarely use. I just start to write.

Stellan,

I don't know why I'm doing this. I'm not going to give it to you. You're never going to see it. But tonight something in me cracked, and this is the only way I know how to keep it from eating me alive.

I love you.

I don't know when it started. Maybe it was so slow that I didn't feel the fall until I'd already hit the ground. Or maybe it happened all at once, and I just pretended not to notice. Either way, it's here. And it's real. And I hate how much it terrifies me.

You were never supposed to matter like this. You weren't supposed to get under my skin, into my thoughts, into my chest. But you did. Not by trying. Not by breaking through my walls. You didn't need to. You just sat beside them until I started pulling bricks down on my own.

I don't know how to do this. I don't know how to feel this without falling apart. You make me forget the part of me that was trained to hold everything back. You make me forget how to be careful.

I love the way you make space without even thinking about it. The way you ask if I'm tired in that low voice, like you'll take over if I need to rest. The way you make companionship feel like something I could rest inside.

I've spent so long surviving by pretending—by controlling everything I feel so no one else can use it against me—and then you come along and made me want things I can't even say out loud.

You make me feel like I'm worth something when I'm not performing. And that... that's the most dangerous thing anyone's ever done to me.

I won't tell you this. I'll keep doing the job. I'll keep pretending I don't look for you when you leave the room, that I don't listen harder when you speak, that I don't ache when you ignore me because I know that means something in you is hurting. I'll keep being what I'm supposed to be, because that's what I was made for.

But this—this one page—is mine. And in this moment, I'm not the assignment. I'm just a woman who loves you. God, I love you.

And you'll never read this. But I needed to say it somewhere, just once.

—Talia

I don't reread it. I don't need to.

I sit there for a minute, maybe two, just staring at the page like it might undo me. And then I tear it in half. Then again. And again. Until it's unreadable. Until it's gone.

The pieces go into the trash, one at a time.

That's what this was always going to be—something I felt, something I meant, something I could never keep.

Now it's gone. Which means I can be fine again.

Which means I can be who they expect me to be.

Which means I can stop loving him.

Eventually.

Intake File: Cerny, Talia

Document Type: Internal Use Only

Clearance Level: Tier 3 – Behavioral Oversight Only

Prepared By: Anselma Roche, The Arrangement's Archivist

File Reference ID: CND-TC-042

Authority Oversight Panel

Mirelle Noirel, Director

Renata Charbonneau, Site Director, Western Division

Anselma Roche, Archivist, Behavioral Operations

Juno Merrix, Behavioral Surveillance & Systems Intel

Hallie Whitlock, Chief Legal Counselor

Brenna Kerrigan, Security Chief

Iris Rennick, Field Liaison

Candidate Profile

Name: Talia Cerny
Status: Approved for Induction
Designation (Projected): Shadow Bride – Strategic Infiltration
Projected Placement Tier: 1 / High Visibility / Legal & Media Containment
Projected Initiation Date: Pending clearance

Preliminary Assessment

Psych Profile: High emotional intelligence, elevated reactivity in prolonged interpersonal exposure. History of strong adaptive coping mechanisms, with intermittent resistance to top-down authority.

Trauma Index: Complex Loss (unresolved), Disrupted Family Attachments, Prior Institutional Review (sealed).

Control Markers: Prefers structure but rejects micromanagement. Tends toward over-functioning when emotionally compromised.

Projected Emotional Risk: Elevated

Evaluator Note (A. Roche): Subject presents as both asset and liability. Bond formation is probable under the correct conditions. Emotional entanglement should be anticipated—not avoided.

Prospective Placement Compatibility

Recommended Placement Partner: Stellan Rothwell (Subject R-ST-003)

Compatibility Index: 87%

Rationale: Subject exhibits traits that correlate with Rothwell's behavioral blind spots: empathy → trust, loyalty → access.

Projected Arc: Initial emotional detachment → Targeted erosion of boundaries → Trust via trauma response.

Override Note: "This match is not designed for sustainability. It is designed for transformation."

Conditioned Behavioral Guidance (Pre-Induction Notes)

- Discourage personal disclosure.

- Reinforce professional role over identity.

- Establish physical and emotional restraint as positive traits.

- Prepare subject for moral ambiguity.

Surveillance Flags (Initial)

- Subject may seek emotional grounding early.

- Likely to substitute connection for strategy if not properly contained.

- Observation protocols to begin immediately post-induction.

Candidate Status: Approved

Subject Cerny meets psychological and behavioral thresholds for Tier 1 integration. Awaiting final placement recommendation based on operational need and skill match. Early observations suggest high utility in emotional containment and moral flexibility. Recommend placement with high-resistance partner for maximum behavioral yield.

SARA MCCLAFLIN

Candidate File: Rothwell, Stellan

Subject Profile

Name: Stellan Rothwell

Status: Approved – Strategic Containment Candidate

Designation: Groom Placement – Legal/Corporate Stabilization Asset

Placement Tier: 1 / High Visibility

Projected Initiation Date: Pending match confirmation

Risk Index

Emotional Accessibility: Critically Low
Influence Radius: High (Corporate + Social Tier Penetration)
Containment Resistance: Severe
Volatility Risk: Elevated
Public Leverage Sensitivity: High

Behavioral Summary

- Strategic withholding is his default.

- Exhibits extreme control over personal narrative.

- Unlikely to show open aggression unless cornered—emotional retaliation preferred.

- Most dangerous when underestimated.

- Motivated by autonomy, not connection. Trust is transactional.

- **Surveillance Note (R. Charbonneau):** "He does not lash out. He *withdraws powerfully.* When pushed, he doesn't break—he isolates."

Placement Recommendation

Recommended Match: Talia Cerny (Subject CND-TC-042)
- Compatibility Index: 87%

- Projected Emotional Outcome: Disruption → Challenge → Mutual Reinforcement

- Strategic Objective: Stabilize Rothwell's narrative while studying long-term containment response to genuine intimacy

Override Note: "She is not designed to save him. She is designed to make him *see what he's protecting*."

Placement Risks

- May manipulate emotional dynamic to invert control.

- If emotionally activated, may reverse target psychology (Bride destabilization risk).

- Public narrative collapse possible if emotional bond perceived as genuine.

Groom Status: Approved

Subject Requires Monitored Emotional Entrance

Subject Rothwell is not expected to trust the process. He is expected to engage with it long enough to lose something meaningful. That is when observation begins.

Acknowledgments

To my ARC readers, beta team, and street team: Thank you for being absolute rockstars. You read early. You caught mistakes. You yelled (appropriately) at the characters when they made terrible decisions. You kept me sane when I was second-guessing everything. You believed in this story before it was fully ready, and I couldn't have done this without you.

To my team: Thank you for working tirelessly behind the scenes to bring this book to life. From edits to cover design to marketing and everything in between, you made sure I stayed (semi) organized and the story actually made it to readers. This would be a disaster without you.

And to every reader who picked up this book: Thank you for being here and for giving these characters a chance. I hope you loved Talia and Stellan as much as I loved writing them.

Up Next

Sexy as Sin: Vegas (The Shadow Brides Series, Book 1.5)

Frankie & Beckett are about to break every rule.
A fiery bartender. A privileged heir. One hotel caught in the crossfire.
Whiskey, wildflowers, and way too much temptation collide in a combustible mix that's anything but business as usual.
WELCOME TO SEXY AS SIN: LAS VEGAS, where ambition and passion always burn bright!
Coming November 1, 2025

The Devil's Bargain Series

Gilded Lies *(Book Two – Greed)*

He doesn't want a soulmate.

She already belongs to someone else.

But Greed doesn't care what's forbidden.

It only wants what it was never meant to touch.

Coming August 21, 2025

About The Author

Deliciously Dark, Beautifully Twisted

Sara McClaflin writes dark romance with feelings, flaws, and just the right amount of emotional damage. Her stories are character-driven, morally gray, and often ask one very important question: what if love was a little dangerous—and we liked it that way? After years of reading and reviewing books with too much angst, she finally started writing her own.

She lives on the West Coast with her husband, their chaotic dog, and more book boyfriends than she's willing to admit. Her TBR pile is a cry for help, her playlists are 80% heartbreak, and she's always chasing the next character who'll ruin her in the best way.

Newsletter Sign Up: https://subscribepage.io/saras-ne wsletter

amazon.com/stores/Sara-McClaflin/author/B0CR8VHBHJ?ref=ap _rdr&isDramIntegrated=true&shoppingPortalEnabled=true&ccs_i d=1fcaa1c2-62ac-4142-ab01-dce9c490e471

bookbub.com/profile/sara-mcclaflin

goodreads.com/author/show/47632250.Sara_McClaflin

instagram.com/authorsaramcclaflin/

facebook.com/profile.php?id=61551822185090&notif_id=174422 8205391402&notif_t=page_user_activity&ref=notif#

tiktok.com/@sara.mcclaflin

Also By

The Devil's Bargain

The Devil's Canvas

The Huntington Brothers Series

Destined for Love

Tangled Hearts

Promises to Keep

Standalone Novels

The Keeper's Secret

Love on the Edge

Anthologies

Head in the Clouds: A Romantic Comedy Anthology

Desperate: A Deadly Thriller Anthology

Did you love *Veil of Fire*?

If you enjoyed the story, I would be so grateful if you took a moment to leave a quick review. Thank you for reading, for your support, and for spending time with these characters. I can't wait for you to see what happens next!